THE BYRNE BROTHERS

# RUTHLESS
## Salvation

Cover Model: Vinicious J
Photographer: Wander Aguiar
Edited by Editing4Indies

❀ Created with Vellum

# RUTHLESS SALVATION

JILL RAMSOWER

## Before you Begin

*I wanted to give one final caution that this book touches on matters of domestic violence (not between the main characters), as well as pregnancy, loss, and infertility. If you are particularly sensitive to any of these topics, this might not be the book for you.*

# CHAPTER 1

*Stormy*

*Present*

EVERY HANDSHAKE WAS A GAME OF RUSSIAN ROULETTE. WHEN I told people I worked in a strip club, they always asked how I could stand to be around all the creepers who flocked to those places.

My response? At least that lot didn't pretend to be anything but what they were.

What scared me more than anything were the chameleons—people adept at camouflage. Nothing was more terrifying than a handsome, well-mannered psychopath.

I'd learned the hard way that you never knew what lurked beneath the surface of a pretty face. That charming man at the coffee shop who struck up a conversation could be the bullet that got you.

Every day, we spun the chamber, went out into the world, and pulled the trigger.

A chat with your Uber driver.

Ordering lunch in a small café.

Picking up dry cleaning.

Every interaction bore the potential to be catastrophic.

Thankfully, the barrel was usually empty because most people, no matter how seemingly odd, were harmless. If that weren't the case, we'd all be agoraphobics hiding in our homes. Instead, we greeted new acquaintances with a smile and hope in our hearts—even those of us who'd played the game and lost.

No point in living if I was going to live in constant fear.

And besides, what were the chances a girl would get thrown together with two psychos in one lifetime? Surely, fate wouldn't be so cruel.

That wasn't to say I was naive. I liked to hope for the best but plan for the worst. And I also liked to surround myself with people who didn't hide behind false pretenses.

Cue the strip club.

Most of our customers were ordinary folks who wanted to unwind. The troublemakers were easy to spot and generally harmless. If I'd been a dancer, I might not feel the same, but I was a server and had relatively few altercations that I couldn't handle.

Despite being a strip club, Moxy had become my home away from home. It was the perfect balance of nice enough to keep out the seediest parts of society but not upscale enough to draw in the repulsive sort who hid their malignant souls behind fancy clothes and flashy cars.

So I might have been a tinge jaded.

I generally enjoyed being at work, and I even liked my boss—possibly a touch more than I should have. Technically, I had two bosses, both devastatingly handsome with eyes so deep blue, they should have been illegal. A warm blue that reminded me of the beach and sunscreen and coolers packed with snacks. But what appealed to me most was the gruffness of their beauty. These guys were shady AF but weren't the clean-shaven, suit-wearing type who cloaked themselves in an air of refinement. These Irishmen were salt of the earth and didn't give a crap what anyone thought of them. Unapologetically transparent in their nature.

In my book, that type of honesty outweighed a manufactured facade every day of the week.

Keir Byrne was cool in an unnerving way that made a person wonder if he felt emotion at all. His younger cousin Torin might come off as similar because they were both relatively reserved, but Torin was nothing like Keir. Where Keir's impassivity came from genuine stoicism, I sensed that Tor's detachment was owed to a great deal of effort. He worked hard to keep the world at a distance, which fascinated me.

News flash.

Torin Byrne was the last man on this planet I should have found interesting. And yet...

My eyes drifted to where he sat with Keir and one other cousin, a woman named Shae who came by on occasion. All three seemed to be in good spirits as an expensive bottle of whiskey passed between them. That alone was enough to stir my curiosity. Neither of my bosses was the celebratory type.

They'd had a family meeting at the bar two days ago. It had been very hush-hush, so I knew something was happening.

Whatever it was must have turned out well. The three talked with ease, and I wasn't above listening in on their conversation as I moved closer to enter orders into the main computer.

"Flynn got better than he deserved. Better than he would have if I'd gotten ahold of him first." Torin's casual comment roused my curiosity, but I knew better than to ask. Men like the Byrnes preferred to keep to themselves. They wouldn't have said something in this setting had it been confidential, but that didn't mean they welcomed questions.

"Well, at least you were there," Shae shot at him. "Some of us got left off the phone tree and never got the call. As if I can't outshoot and outfight every one of you."

"You were busy with something else, and you know it."

"Not *that* busy," she grumbled.

Keir smirked as our eyes met. He gave me a nod. "Evening, Stormy."

"Hey, Keir. You all having a good night?"

"Trying to. This one's got her panties in a wad, and you know how fun this ray of sunshine is." He motioned to Torin, then winked at me.

Keir freaking Byrne *winked* at me while teasing his cousin. I burst into a peel of laughter.

These three had definitely been at it for a while.

Torin grumbled, casting a scathing glare at Keir.

"Hey now," I chided playfully. "It's my job to give him a hard time. Don't be moving in on my turf."

"Knowing this surly bastard, there's plenty of opportunity to go around."

My gaze locked briefly with Torin's smoldering blue stare. The alcohol must have interfered with his intentions because the irritation I expected to find looked more like ravenous hunger. So much so that it sent a cascade of electric tingles down my spine. I drove the man crazy with my teasing. If he had any idea his intended glare had come off heated rather than glacial, he'd have been mortified.

"You're probably right," I murmured distractedly while lifting the full drink tray onto my right palm. It was time for a quick escape. "You three enjoy." I shot a quick smile to Shae and fled back toward the middle of the club.

*What the hell was that?*

Tor had never once looked at me like that. I'd have remembered because the single stare made me feel like he'd stripped me naked and was seconds from devouring me.

It had to have been the alcohol, right? Eyes hooded from intoxication could easily be confused with lust. And if the alcohol *had* made him horny, that didn't necessarily have anything to do with *me*. I was probably just the first non-family female to have approached since they opened the whiskey.

That needed to be the case because Torin showing me interest, while shamefully tempting, was problematic in more ways than I could count. As much as my brain wanted to fixate on the situation, the club was too busy. I had a rowdy bachelor party occupying one of my booths that had been waiting for their drinks and were not shy about advertising that fact. I'd clocked two potential creeps in their group the minute they walked in, and both were waving their arms at me.

I hurried over and unloaded my tray with their next round. They'd been generous with tips for me and the dancers, so I did my best to ignore their more obnoxious elements.

"You gents all good for the moment?" I asked after I'd handed out the last drink.

"I suppose for the moment..." The young guy sitting at the end of the booth spoke up right before placing a resounding slap on my ass.

Bingo.

Creep.

His buddies responded with wide eyes and an uproar of laughter. Only one had the decency to look embarrassed.

I didn't give him the gasp of shock and laughter he likely anticipated. It wasn't the first time or even the twenty-first time a man had tried to take liberties with me. Instead, I gave him a look I liked to call the Smiling Assassin—a bright Southern grin with daggers in my eyes.

"Now, now, *Chad*. You don't want to ruin your friend's fun by getting all six of you kicked out, do you? And you certainly wouldn't want everyone to know you're too green behind the ears to know the rules at a place like this. You don't touch the girls—any of us—unless given express permission. Understood?" That last word packed a condescending punch, accented by a single brow raise.

He lifted his hands in a plea of innocence. "Just having a little fun."

"Well, if you try to have any more fun, it'll be Blaze's turn to have a little fun with you."

His gaze followed mine to the mountain of muscle standing against the wall near the stage.

I rapped my knuckles on the table. "You boys enjoy. I'll be back to check on you in a few."

You didn't have to work at a place like this for long to learn who the problematic customers were. Chad and his buddies weren't even close. Now that I'd set them straight, they'd fall into line twittering the rest of the night about how they almost got thrown out of a strip club.

After checking on two other groups, I noted we were running low on cocktail napkins behind the bar, so I slipped away to the storeroom in the back. While scanning the shelves, I felt someone join me in the small room.

Torin.

Why did he always look so damn imposing in small spaces? His dominating presence filled up what little space his physical body left unoccupied until hardly any oxygen remained in the room.

"Hey," I said on a shaky breath. "Everything okay?"

"That's what I wanted to ask you. That guy put his hands on you?" he asked in a low, even tone.

Had he asked me this sort of thing a week ago—or even earlier tonight—I would have assumed he was just protecting his employee. But now, after that look he'd given me, questions surfaced. Was he being more protective of me than the other girls? Had this sort of thing been happening without me realizing? And why the heck did the prospect stir up a swarm of butterflies in my tummy rather than unease?

Sure, he was beyond beautiful. He had a way of lighting my insides on fire with a few simple words ... and zero intent. No matter how hard I racked my brain, I couldn't come up with a time he'd ever shown the slightest interest in me. Not even the hint of a flirtation since the day I started. If anything, I would have said I irritated the tar out of him.

Early on, I convinced myself it was best this way because the last thing I needed was to get involved with a man like him. Or any man, for that matter. Besides, he was my *boss*. That was the biggest no-no in the book. I loved working at

Moxy and didn't want to jeopardize that by making things awkward.

So why did the world seem to tilt on its axis when he was near?

*Because he looks out for you, even if only out of a sense of duty, and there was a time when you were desperate for that sort of security.*

True, but if he hadn't been motivated in a professional capacity, did that change things? Shouldn't that douse the flames he ignited in me? I wasn't sure how I should feel, so I did what I'd been doing for the last six months since starting at Moxy and pretended to be unaffected.

"You don't have to make a scene," I told him. "No reason to scare people off just for an entitled punk."

"I'm well aware I don't *have* to do anything, and I'm pretty sure that's not what I asked." He took a slow, measured step forward, the intensity in the room flaring. "Did he put his hands on you?" Each word was controlled and concise yet brimming with chaos.

What the heck was going on?

I'd never seen Torin act so riled up. He was perpetually indifferent, at least on the surface. Even when he manhandled unruly customers, nothing ever seemed to test his tightly held control. He was so self-possessed and impassive that I'd even questioned whether my theory about an emotional undertow had been accurate. So what had changed? Or had this side of him always lurked in the shadows?

"Just once," I answered quietly. "But Blaze is keeping an eye on him."

"You talked to Blaze about it?"

"Yeah, I gave him a heads-up, just in case."

I'd swear lightning flashed in his stormy eyes. Maybe I imagined it, but I definitely saw the flexing strain of his jaw muscles as he clenched his teeth. "Next time, you come directly to me."

"I didn't think there was any need to bother you and Keir."

"How about you let me be the judge of that, yeah?"

I nodded, too dumbstruck for words.

"Words, Stormy. I need to hear them."

"Yes. Next time, I'll tell you."

He grunted. "Now, you need something in here?"

"Oh ... um, yeah." I shook free of my daze and spun toward the shelves. "I was grabbing more napkins. There they are." I spotted the blue and white box on the top shelf and quickly turned over a bucket at my feet to use as a step.

"I can get it—" He reached up for the box at the exact moment I stepped on the bucket.

"No, I can—"

We collided, knocking me off balance with a squeal. Torin's arms clamped around my middle, pulling me back into him before I crashed to the ground.

"Fuck's sake, woman," he grumbled, setting my feet back on the floor.

Then we stood there, his arms still firmly around me, my back to his chest, neither of us so much as breathing. Time itself stood still, save for the pulsing music filtering through the walls.

I'd known my body was a traitor, responding to men I had no business wanting, so it shouldn't have come as a surprise when I instinctively relaxed into his rock-hard body like honey on a hot biscuit.

I'd never been so close to him before.

If the feel of his strength around me hadn't been intoxicating on its own, his smoky sandalwood scent was more than enough to muddle my thoughts.

I was a glutton for the worst sort of punishment.

I took in a gasping breath and spun away from him as though I'd surfaced after being caught beneath a wicked undertow.

Torin kept his eyes averted, grabbing the box and handing it to me. "You need something, ask." He'd regained every ounce of his composure, speaking with perfectly crafted indifference before leaving the room in his usual unhurried gait.

Meanwhile, little bits of my brain were short-circuiting with puffs of smoke and sparks.

That couldn't have been a figment of my imagination. But what exactly was *that*? Why did he care if I alerted him or Blaze? Why did his hands linger on my body after stopping my fall? Where had all this come from, and what on earth was I supposed to do about it?

I was so damn glad we were busy because otherwise, I would have spent every minute of my shift overthinking our exchange. However, when Moxy closed for the night, my worries returned, and for good reason.

Torin's change in behavior would have been confusing but not disconcerting if it weren't for the fact he'd been following me home after work every night for the past month.

The sweet old man who ran a flower shop on the corner had let me see his security camera feed to verify my suspicions when I first noticed I had a shadow. I was shocked when I saw who it was. Then I started to freak out until I remembered an incident where a man had gotten handsy with me at the club. Tor had kicked the guy to the curb and likely followed me home to ensure I was safe. That was when I first noticed the feeling of being watched.

The series of events had made sense. I assumed that when he saw how close I lived, he decided it was easier to walk the couple of blocks than to deal with the fallout of an employee being attacked. After all, he'd never shown any interest in me whatsoever. In fact, it made more sense that he'd rather follow me than make a big deal out of escorting me.

My panic subsided at the time, though I still put careful consideration into looking for a new job and even moving, but with each day that passed, his actions seemed more and more benign. And in a messed-up way, I kind of appreciated knowing he was there. It had been an awfully long time since I had someone watching out for me.

But now I had to ask myself where was the line between watching out for someone and stalking? Because he was out there. I felt his eyes on me from where he lurked in the shadows.

My steps carried me home faster than normal. I made it to the front of my building without incident, my relief doubling when I saw the security keypad had finally been replaced. I'd been hassling the super about it for a week. The buttons on the last one had been going out for ages. A few nights ago, I'd almost given up getting the darn thing to unlock. At times like that, it was an odd sort of reassurance, knowing I wasn't alone.

I walked up the stairs to my third-floor apartment and debated whether I'd misjudged Torin entirely. I'd been confident he wasn't a threat. But maybe that had been my hormones talking. Was it even possible to have a stalker if you were attracted to the man in question?

*Good Lord, Stormy. You are a hot mess express.*

Didn't I know it?

"How was your day, Blue Bell?" I scooped up my precious kitty and ran my thumb up and down the bridge of his nose while he purred. Nose rubs were his favorite. "Anything exciting happen today?"

He chirped at me. That was part of why he made such a great companion. He was a surprisingly good conversationalist for a cat.

"Is that so? *Two* birds on the fire escape? I hope you didn't scare them away."

*Meow.*

"Good. My day was somewhat eventful as well." I walked over to the drapes and pulled them almost all the way shut. I stared at the gap, a gnawing sense of guilt clawing at me.

I'd been leaving them cracked every night since I realized Torin was following me. It was stupid and reckless. I had no good explanation as to why I was repeatedly going against my better judgment.

People off the street couldn't see much from down there, even if they wanted to, but that was irrelevant. I shouldn't have wanted anyone looking in at me.

Not with my past.

The feeling was too good to push away when I thought Torin was looking out for me. I didn't want to sever that connection. But if Torin's motives weren't purely protective —if he wanted … *more* from me—I should have instantly yanked the curtains closed. The thought of a man as dangerous as him having any interest in me at all should have repulsed me.

So why couldn't I force my hand to slide the fabric those few inches farther?

"Blue Bell, what's wrong with me?" I kissed my sweet kitty on his forehead and sat cross-legged on the sofa.

No matter how irrational my reluctance, I still couldn't do it. I couldn't cut myself off from the fantasy of a ruthless protector keeping me safe. From the feeling of comfort I got when simply thinking about Torin. He'd looked out for me and the other girls at work, and somehow, my brain had latched onto the association.

Shouldn't my feelings change after learning he might actually be stalking me?

*Hells bells.*

The answer was unsettling, not because of my extreme fear but the opposite. A surge of exhilaration tingled in my palms and down the back of my legs.

"This is bad, Blue. This is so, *so* bad." I shouldn't have responded this way. It wasn't normal.

*You think after everything you've been through that you're normal?*

True. Despite my best efforts, my past had changed me. I was proud of the woman I'd become. She was savvy and resilient and maintained compassion that could easily have been lost. She'd survived remarkably well despite the past, but sometimes crazy left a stain that could never be bleached out.

It had apparently left its mark on me, inside and out.

# CHAPTER 2

*Stormy*

*The Past: Six Years Earlier*

I CLAMPED MY LIPS SHUT TO KEEP FROM THROWING UP. THE airplane I was in was making a sketchy touchdown, but that wasn't the reason my nerves were acting up. I was more concerned with what I'd find once I stepped off the plane.

Honey would have said nerves were good and kept a person grounded. I adored my grandmother, and most of her advice was spot-on, but I wasn't sure I agreed on this one matter.

*Agree or not, there's no escaping it now.*

I swallowed down another surge of nausea.

I knew this wouldn't be easy for so many reasons, but I'd

made the decision to try, so I wasn't going to chicken out. Who cared that I hadn't stepped so much as a foot beyond the Georgia state line since first arriving when I was a year old? Did it matter whether my first solo trip was one thousand or ten thousand miles away?

*Somewhere English-speaking would have been nice.*

Okay, yeah. That was true. But this wasn't just any destination. I had arrived in one of the coldest, most inhospitable places on earth. My birthplace of Moscow, Russia.

This was a trip into my past, an exploration of the culture I was born into, and a chance to meet my birth mother. I knew that part was a long shot, but my chances were zero if I never tried.

Honey acted like she was going to have a seizure when I told her my plans.

"Sweet child, I know your heart is hurting, but this just ain't right. You don't know a single soul over there, not to mention the language or anything else about the place." She began to fan herself. "Good grief, I need a nip. You've got my insides twisted up somethin' fierce." She pulled out a bottle of peach schnapps secreted away at the bottom of her china cabinet and poured a healthy dab into a porcelain teacup.

She'd sipped from that same set of floral finery my whole life. I only discovered once I was older that the contents weren't always tea. The cherished china had been passed down from her grandmother. It should have gone to my mother next, then to me. Instead, it would be skipping a generation when I took possession.

"I know there are no guarantees, but I have to try. And yes, I fully understand that even if I found my birth mother, she won't magically fix things." Nothing could ever fill the gaping hole in my heart gouged out by the unexpected loss of my parents. "No one could ever take their place, but that doesn't mean I'm not interested in learning more about my roots."

"Your roots is here, under these oak trees, draped in moss and swaying in that warm ocean breeze. You're no more rooted in that giant iceberg than Miss Scarlet over there." We both looked at her small white poodle napping in a patch of sunlight on one of Honey's cozy armchairs.

People always thought Miss Scarlet was named for the epic character Scarlett O'Hara in *Gone with the Wind*. The assumption made sense unless you knew about Honey's obsession with the game Clue. Her previous canine companion had been Professor Plum—the Professor for short.

Miss Scarlet refused to step outside when the weather dropped below fifty degrees. I couldn't help but smile at the thought of her layered in doggy sweaters and yipping angrily in the Russian cold. She would have been furious.

When I turned back to Honey, my eyes softened. She was the only family I had left in the world, and I adored everything about her, even her penchant for worrying over nothing.

I closed the distance between us and took her wrinkled, knobby hands in mine. "It's only a couple of weeks, Honey. I'll be back fussin' at you to lock your door at night like always." I fought back a quiver in my chin as my emotions threatened to overcome me. "This is something I have to do, and I sure don't want to argue with you before I go."

She pulled me into a bear hug stronger than should have been possible for an eighty-year-old. "You always been stubborn as the day is long."

I huffed a laugh as we pulled apart.

Honey nodded. "I suppose I should get cookin'. I'm not sending you off without plenty of snacks and a full belly."

"With all the sweaters I'll need, there won't be much extra room in my bag," I warned her.

"Nonsense. There's always room for a box of praline cookies."

Mmm, praline. They were my favorite. I supposed it wouldn't hurt to let the old woman win at least one battle.

I grinned. "I'll grab the pecans."

That was a week and nearly ten thousand miles ago.

*You can do this, Stormy girl. You can do anything you set your mind to.* My father's voice filtered into my head. He always called me his stormy girl because it was storming the night they found out the adoption had been approved.

My chest tightened, but I didn't allow the emotion to take hold. I couldn't. It was too crippling. The three of us had been a team—we used to do everything together. Rather than scheming about going to college out of state, I'd been the kid who put a strict hundred-mile radius cap on schools I'd consider. Mama said I needed to go outside of Savannah to be more independent. I never understood why I couldn't do that from across town and still have Taco Tuesdays with them.

Sure, I'd been spoiled as an only child, but in the very best way. My parents had been understanding yet firm and unconditional in their love for me. Life without them felt meaningless. Colorless and cruel. I'd spent two months clutching at the hole in my chest, wondering if I'd ever be able to breathe again.

When the third month rolled around, the idea of this trip had taken root, and I saw the tiniest hint of a silver lining.

The grief was still present, but it was manageable. I still had moments when I felt like nothing but a puddle of sorrow. I didn't have time for that right now. I needed to be clear-headed and confident to navigate this foreign landscape. And if I was honest, having a reason to force away the grief was a significant part of why I'd decided to launch into this journey. I could have waited—I could have planned and taken my time—but I preferred to have the distraction. And boy, had it worked like a charm.

Between planning and packing and the actual journey, I'd hardly had room for thoughts about my parents. Navigating my way to the hotel was no different. Three exhausting hours after landing in Moscow, I fell back onto the bed in my hotel room and thanked the good Lord that I'd made it.

I felt like I'd been awake for days. It was only four o'clock local time, but I didn't care. My burning eyes demanded it was time to sleep. I didn't even change out of the leggings I'd worn on the trip before crawling under the covers and passing out. My search would begin tomorrow, but for now, peaceful oblivion.

♦

I'D NEVER GIVEN much thought to the Russian language until I was surrounded by it. Compared to the gentle embrace of the Southern drawl, everyone here sounded remarkably hostile. They even looked a little scary.

Then again, maybe that was simply the way city people looked and sounded. How was I to know? I'd spent most of my life in the suburbs of Savannah. Now, if I had to live in this ungodly cold all the time, I'd probably be cranky, so I couldn't blame them. Not even halfway into October, and even the sun struggled to permeate the thickly blanketed clouds and bone-chilling cold. I shuddered to think what February might bring to a place like this.

Despite the inhospitable environment, I managed to arrive at the location I'd obsessed over for weeks—the address for the orphanage I'd been left at as a baby. I'd found the adoption papers when going through Mama's and Daddy's things about a month after the accident. They'd always been up front about the fact I was adopted. They were such amazing parents, I'd never felt much need to dwell on my origins. Not that I hadn't thought about my Russian heritage. I'd spent loads of time wondering about my past, but I hadn't felt compelled to actually seek out any answers.

That all changed when my world cratered in around me. My parents were my world. Without them, I was adrift in a meaningless void. Hunting down my birth family gave me a distraction and a purpose. It gave me hope that the endless gnawing grief that weighed each of my steps might one day be manageable.

At first, I'd only pulled up the address on Google Maps to look at the building and see if it still existed. It was only curiosity, I'd told myself. Once I laid eyes on the image of the large brick building, it was impossible not to wonder what more I could find out from the people inside.

The story I'd told myself growing up was that my struggling mother had dropped me off in hopes of a better life. That she was kind and selfless for making such a sacrifice, and even more importantly, she was out there somewhere thinking of me.

It was a romantic perspective, and I was okay with that. Why let yourself think the worst when you can choose to believe the best? According to my imaginings, I could possibly have a whole other family out there waiting for me to return. I'd never had any brothers or sisters. I hadn't thought I'd wanted any until I truly entertained the possibility of their existence.

Once the questions buzzed in my head, they were worse than flies at a cookout. I'd had to at least try to find some answers. If my search led to a dead end, then so be it. At least I'd know I tried.

The first thing I did was place a phone call to the number listed online. I couldn't understand the recorded message that played on the other end, but the angry tone that pulsed in the background gave me the impression that the number was no longer in service. Not to be deterred, I emailed the facility. No response. Had the email been sent to junk? Had they been unwilling to do a quick translation or find someone who could read English? Was the email sitting in someone's inbox who no longer worked for the agency? I had no way to know what had happened, but I continued my efforts.

I called three other orphanages I found listed online. All three were answered ... by someone who didn't speak English. After several pointless back-and-forth exchanges, the calls each ended in futility.

The one avenue in which I found some success was via an email direct to the Ministry of Labor and Social Protection. I was told in no uncertain terms that I had a better chance of dying from heatstroke in Siberia than I did of getting information unless I presented original documents to them, live and in living color. And even then, I might need a miracle.

I decided to take the leap. My alternative was to remain mired in grief, and that was losing its appeal. My shoulders ached from the weight of my sorrow. I was ready to shed that burdensome cloak and rediscover the many reasons life was worth living.

The exhausting emotional journey had led me to this moment, standing out front of that brick building I'd first googled. I should have known something was wrong when the phone number didn't work. In my haste for an escape, I'd clung to optimism. I'd assured myself that the number had been misprinted or changed. But now, an unexpected wariness anchored my feet to the concrete sidewalk.

The building before me looked as abandoned as the children who'd once called it home. I could tell it was the building shown on the satellite imagery, but the harshness of many unforgiving years had passed. It hadn't occurred to me that the grainy photo had been outdated. Even more disconcerting was the absence of the orphanage sign affixed to the dirty brick facade. If it weren't for someone moving about inside, I would have assumed the building was soon to be condemned.

Several window panes were cracked, a film of dirt made it hard to see any details within, and a section of gutter along the roofline hung from the building haphazardly. Compared to the well-kept storefronts on either side of it, the crumbling building looked forgotten. The desolation must have been contagious because I could feel it settle heavily on my shoulders.

*This isn't the end. Maybe whoever's inside knows what happened to the orphanage.*

Even if it was closed, the records had to have been stored somewhere. Surely, even in Russia, records of such importance were archived in more than one location. I hadn't come all this way to quit now. Maybe whoever was inside could direct me to a central office or the orphanage's new location. It certainly wouldn't hurt to ask.

I sucked up my courage and approached the front door. Lifting my fist, I paused to assure myself the area was adequately populated to limit my chances of being outright murdered, then I knocked and waited.

No answer.

I was certain I'd seen at least one person moving about inside, so I checked the handle. Unlocked. I hesitantly pushed the door open enough to poke my head inside. "Hello? Is anyone here?"

Again, no reply.

My view into a front sitting area to the right of the entry piqued my curiosity. The dusty lounge contained furniture from an era long forgotten, along with peeling wallpaper draped with cobwebs. The scuffed wood floors were likely original to the building, but they'd been decent enough quality to have survived the years intact.

I ventured a hesitant step inside when I saw what looked like a group photo of past residents hung on the wall. Wondering how long ago the portrait had been taken, I was two steps inside before my gaze drifted left to where a circle of four men stood watching me.

I gasped, my hand flying to my chest. "Good *grief*, you 'bout scared me to death. I didn't realize … I called out, but no one answered, and the door was unlocked. I hope I'm not intruding." I suddenly realized I was rambling, and judging by the incredulous looks on their faces, they didn't understand a word I said.

Once I took a second to truly see who was before me, my discomfort intensified. These guys looked meaner than a bunch of junkyard dogs, scarred and sneering with tattoos dotting what little skin I could see beneath their bulky winter layers.

That was when it hit me that I was trespassing.

I had barged in on some sort of meeting, and these guys weren't the type to care about my sob story. At least, that was the case for three of them. The fourth man stood apart from the others in every way. His tailored wool coat fit his shoulders perfectly and hung to his knees, an expensive suit peeking out from beneath. He was clean-shaven with a curious glint shining from the most striking eyes I'd ever seen—so pale blue they reminded me of the hydrangeas Honey grew in her garden.

This man wasn't a thug. He was sophisticated. Imperial. He radiated importance in a way that made it hard not to stare.

I focused my attention on him, hoping he was as genteel as advertised, and flashed my best pageant grin. "I'm so sorry to interrupt. Do you by chance speak English? I don't speak a word of Russian."

One of the brutes grumbled something, but the blue-eyed Adonis cut him short with a smooth motion from one hand. Our gazes remained locked on one another. When his lips quirked upward in the corners and amusement shone bright in his cerulean eyes, I felt like the sun had seared a path through the heavy Moscow cloud cover and bathed me in its radiant glow. Warmth tinged my cheeks and pooled in my belly.

"How could such beauty and charm ever be an interruption?" His deep voice was comforting, despite the coarse undertones of his Russian accent. He extracted himself from behind the others and closed the gap between us with a few unhurried steps. "Please, what can I do to help you?"

My thoughts up and abandoned me. His proximity sucked the air from the room, leaving my head spinning, and my brain a vacuous bubble.

*Come on, Stormy girl. Get yourself together.*

"Yes, umm... thank you. I was looking for the orphanage that used to be here."

"Ah, yes. I believe you are right. There was an orphanage here years ago."

"I don't suppose you know anything about what happened to it?"

"I do not, but I am sure we can find out."

My eyes widened as he placed a hand at the small of my back and directed me toward the door. "How long can we expect to have the pleasure of your presence here in the city?"

Had I stumbled onto the set of a live-action Disney movie? All the telltale signs were present. Young woman, totally out of her element, rescued by the devastatingly handsome prince. Was I currently sidestepping the fact that he was buddied up to three classically villainous thugs? It sure looked that way.

I peered up at him, winded by the brilliance of his answering grin.

Yeah. I was totally ignoring the goons. They might have been part of a hired construction crew for all I knew.

"A couple of weeks. I just arrived yesterday."

"That is wonderful news." He grinned.

"Is it?" A coy smile teased my lips.

"Absolutely. That will give us time to acquire the

information you seek, and in the meantime, I can show you around the city."

I stilled. "I couldn't possibly ask you to do that. I'm sure you're a busy man."

His hand raised to trail his thumb tenderly along my jaw. "I have never come across such an enchanting creature as you. I would never forgive myself if I didn't spend every moment available to me by your side."

Sweet mother-of-pearl.

I couldn't move a muscle. Not even to blink.

Who was this enigmatic man? He was incredible—too good to be true—yet my ravaged heart wanted nothing more than to surrender itself to the comforting reassurance he offered. Having the help of a local would be an enormous relief. He could be the difference between success or returning home in defeat. Who was I to look a gift horse in the mouth?

"What did you have in mind?" I asked breathily.

We stepped through the door onto the landing outside.

"My driver is over there." He pointed across the street. "We could start with a little drive to orient you before stopping for lunch. I know the perfect place in the heart of the city where you can get the best stroganoff. Others may claim to have the best, but there is no comparison."

I studied the black SUV with heavily tinted windows. I might have been struggling with my grief, but I wasn't completely out of my mind. "I was taught not to get in cars with strangers," I said with a grin, hoping not to offend him. "Would you be open to meeting up somewhere?"

He bowed his head. "Of course—and that is very wise of you. An admirable quality."

"Paranoia?" I teased.

"Caution. I would not be the man I am today if I had not cultivated a healthy sense of self-preservation. Will you at least allow me to walk you back to your hotel and offer you my number? You can call me if you would like to meet for dinner, perhaps."

I beamed up at him with relief and barely repressed excitement. "I don't suppose I could say no to such a thoughtful offer."

"Wonderful! However, there is one thing I will need from you first."

My smile faltered. "What's that?"

"A name. That way, we will no longer be strangers to one another."

My teeth grazed my bottom lip to keep from grinning. "Alina. Alina Shelton."

He took my hand in his and raised my knuckles to his lips. "Alina—that is a beautiful Russian name." He raised a brow.

"I started off at the orphanage here but was adopted by my wonderful American parents when I was a baby. They loved my given name, so they kept it."

"Respect for your origins. I like them already."

"They were amazing parents." I was unable to keep the sadness from creeping into my words.

"Were?" he asked softly.

"Yes, that's actually why I'm here. They passed away a few months back, and I decided it was time to explore where I came from."

"Sladkaya angel, I'm so sorry for your loss."

I didn't understand his first words and didn't want our conversation to turn morose, so I waved him off. "I'm sure they'd be pleased to know I came, and I'm excited to see what

I can learn." I peered back at the old building. "Though, I had expected to find the orphanage still operational."

"Not to worry." He gave the building a dismissive wave. "We will locate whatever information you seek."

"Well then, that only leaves one thing," I said, fighting back a grin.

"And that is?"

"I still don't know *your* name."

His eyes glinted with delight as though he'd been waiting for me to ask. "Damyon Karpova, at your service." He bowed, this time from the waist, his arm sweeping wide with the gesture.

My heart fluttered her thick lashes, then melted into a gooey puddle deep in my belly. I'd come to Russia for answers, but I had a feeling this trip would uncover much more than I ever could have expected.

# CHAPTER 3

*Torin*

*Present*

DIDN'T SHE REALIZE ANY SICK FUCK OFF THE STREET COULD have been watching her? I'd been following Stormy home after work for weeks, and every time it pissed me off when she didn't close her fucking drapes all the way. She was so damn naive. Every time she opened her mouth, it was obvious she thought the world was made of bubblegum and rainbows. It was unnatural.

I told myself that was the reason I was there night after night—morbid curiosity. I was fascinated the same way other people couldn't look away from the scene of a disaster.

I needed to put an end to it, no matter the reason.

A hundred different women had come and gone during my years working at the club. I'd never paid any mind to them, and she shouldn't have been any different. Blond hair and common brown eyes. Soft, feminine features with legs that went on for miles. She was attractive, but I could have been describing half the girls who have worked at Moxy.

The thing about Stormy that sank its claws into me was an intangible quality, making it harder to shake. Like the woman had spun some fucking Southern voodoo spell over me. I hadn't acted this recklessly since I was sixteen years old.

That thought was the reminder I needed to push away from the cold brick wall and get the fuck out of there. I was playing a dangerous game. I'd chided myself all night about the scene in the supply closet. I kept telling myself to keep my distance, but goddamn if she didn't rile me. I didn't trust her to ask for help when she needed it, and that pissed me off. She was so fucking optimistic and polite that she tried to handle everything on her own. I'd seen it happen time and again, which was the other reason I kept such a close eye on her. If she had any street smarts at all, I wouldn't have to.

*You're one dumb fuck if you think that would stop you.*

I kicked an empty bottle left on the sidewalk, shattering the glass and the calm night air. When I reached the club, one of the dancers was out front scowling at her phone. Her light jacket did nothing to compensate for the tiny outfit she wore underneath. I wasn't sure why she was still here, nor did I care. I gave her a curt nod and walked to my bike parked on the sidewalk.

"Hey, Tor!" She flashed an exaggerated smile. "I was hoping you'd turn up. My ride bailed on me, and if you couldn't tell, I'm not exactly dressed to walk home. Could you give me a lift?"

"No."

"It's only a couple of miles," she continued to plead.

"Don't care. I don't do rides." That was one of the reasons I loved my bike. A minor reason, but still a factor. People were less apt to ask for a ride, though it happened on occasion.

"That's some shit karma you're stirring up, you know that?" she shot back at me. "No one's gonna wanna help you out when you need a hand if you don't do the same."

"There's no guarantee they would even if I did."

"Chances are better."

I straddled my Ducati and brought her to life before looking back at the girl. "No, they're not. People will fuck you over every chance they get. You're old enough to know that by now." Exactly the sentiment I should have directed at Storm. It came so easily to me where anyone else was concerned. Why the fuck was she any different?

I let the bike kick forward, the sound almost drowning out the angry *asshole* she called at my back. I smirked, not that she saw it. I was halfway down the block in a matter of seconds.

◊

"Any word on that crazy Russian motherfucker?" Bishop held up padded hands for my cousin Conner to work combinations. Bishop worked for the family and was Conner's best friend, but he wasn't a blood relation. He and Shae were my most frequent training partners.

Today, Conner and Bishop were doing drills while Shae

and I sparred. I liked working with her because she kept me on my toes with her jiujitsu moves. She'd achieved such a high skill level that it almost made up for our size difference. Almost.

We were taking a breather for the moment while the other two continued training.

Conner took several measured strikes before answering. "Nothing since he sliced Flynn open from ear to ear."

"Wish we knew what that bastard was up to." Bishop's words were breathy as he steadied himself to absorb Conner's strikes.

"Talked to Oran yesterday." Conner continued. "He said some of the men Damyon had with him were on loan from Boris."

"The fuck are those two doing working together?" Shae interjected.

Boris "Biba" Mikhailov was in command of the largest Russian outfit in New York, and those guys didn't play nice with one another. I couldn't imagine a situation where he'd be willing to hand over some of his men to an outsider.

"Don't know," Conner said between jabs, "but the Italians have Russian connections. I'm gonna give them a call today and see what I can find out."

"They willing to give you information like that?" I chimed in. Conner may have had Italian genetics that had gained him a Mafia wife, but I couldn't imagine the Genoveses truly considered him one of their own. We would never hand over sensitive information to someone in his position, and it would be stupid to think otherwise on their end.

"Don't know unless we ask," Conner rightfully pointed out. "Boris isn't the type to share power, and he doesn't scare easily. I'd say he got something out of the arrangement. I'd also say it lends me to believe Damyon was telling the truth when he said he had no interest in this city. Boris wouldn't help anyone he thought was going to become his rival."

"True," I agreed. "Then what the fuck is he doing here?"

"No goddamn clue." He struck with two right jabs, then a quick left cross straight into a right uppercut before dropping his arms and stepping back, chest heaving.

"Break's over," Shae announced. "You can't afford to be lazy with a fight next week."

Conner nodded, sweat dripping from his brow. "You ready?"

"Are you kidding?" Bishop grinned. "That angry bastard's always ready for a fight."

Shae slid her mouth guard into place with a wicked glint in her eyes. I matched her ready stance and tried to draw my focus back to sparring.

Three seconds later, she'd somehow climbed me like a fucking tree, wrapped her thighs around my head, and sent me crashing backward to the padded floor of the ring. Damn woman knocked the wind right out of me. I coaxed air back into my lungs while she loomed over me, a devilish grin appearing as she removed her mouth guard.

"Ready to *lose*," she goaded me.

"Fuck you, Shae," I wheezed back at her, pissed that I sounded so damn pathetic. Never would have happened if thoughts of Storm and that damn Russian hadn't distracted me.

Once I got back to my feet, we started another round, and this time, Shae got as good as she gave. I forced myself through a punishing workout to drive out thoughts of Stormy. No matter how hard I tried to focus on family business and questions surrounding the Russian, my thoughts always drifted back to guileless brown eyes and a charming Southern twang.

Something about her had sprouted an insidious infection in my brain—a diseased addiction that I couldn't shake. I hated feeling out of control. And where Storm was concerned, I was in the passenger seat with my fixation behind the wheel. I had to find a way to get out of that damn car because its trajectory ended in a fiery ball of flames.

# CHAPTER 4

*Stormy*

*Present*

A FAMILIAR KNOCK ON MY DOOR BROUGHT A HUGE GRIN TO MY face. I used to spend my days off alone, but since moving to New York, my life had grown remarkably fuller.

I opened the door to find Micky chatting with Luke, our mutual friend who lived across the hall from me. "Hey, you two! Y'all grab coffee without me?" I looked at the steaming cup in Luke's hand, my brows arched high in mock offense.

"My budget's too tight this week for coffee," Micky grumbled. "We just happened to have good timing."

I eyed them playfully. "I suppose I'll let you off the hook ... this time."

"Off the hook! We didn't do anything," Micky teased back.

"Besides," Luke added, "looks like you two are the ones leaving a guy out. You have something fun planned today?"

"Hardly," Micky grumbled. "My roommate has a *friend* over, and I need to study."

"She's going to hang here while I hit the laundromat," I explained.

Luke's smile morphed to a cartoonish grimace. "Yikes, that sounds like more fun than I can handle."

"Oh, hey!" another familiar voice called out, this one far less welcome. "I'm glad I caught you."

The three of us looked over to where Ralph, the building superintendent, exited the stairwell onto our floor. He looked genuinely excited to see us, which was disconcerting. Ralph usually did his best to avoid all contact with residents. Jerk.

At a hair over five feet, he was several inches shorter than me, which gave me a perfect view of the black spray paint he used to cover the bald patch on the top of his head. It was that, or he had a gangrenous skin condition—either way, it was bad news.

"I wanted to check and make sure you guys saw the new panel downstairs. It was installed yesterday."

"Yeah, actually, I did. It worked like a charm, thanks." I tried to sound genuine because I did appreciate being able to get into the building, but his odd behavior was throwing me.

"Good, good. Sorry it took so long …" His eyes darted from one of us to the other. "You know, always a lot to juggle in these places."

"Yeahhh, um. Thanks." Okay, this was getting seriously weird.

Luke cut in, joining the circle of awkward. "We definitely appreciate it, Ralph. Now, if you'll excuse us, we were just headed inside." He placed a hand at my lower back.

Grateful for the rescue, I shot a hurried wave at Ralph, then jumped back into my apartment, my two friends close on my heel.

"You three have a great day," Ralph called in his comically heavy Brooklyn accent.

The second the door clicked shut, we burst into a fit of silent giggles, each doubled over with our hands plastered over our mouths.

"What the hell was that?" Luke asked when we regained our composure. "Last time I asked him to get the hallway light bulb replaced, he griped at me for ten minutes about the entitlement of today's youth—or yute as he calls them."

"Maybe he found Jesus?" Micky suggested, leading to another round of snickers.

"I don't care if he started worshipping the seven circles of hell if it means he'll actually start doing stuff around here," Luke grumbled.

"I'll believe it when I see it," I said, shaking my head. "A leopard doesn't change his spots."

Micky shot me a look of incredulity. "Girl, you are the most cynical optimist I've ever met."

I shrugged. "Life is better when you have a good attitude and focus on the positive. That doesn't mean I can't smell bull crap when it's at my feet. I just choose to smile as I walk past it."

"Amen to that," Luke said with a grin. "All right, I'll let you ladies get to your books and laundry. Come get me if you want to grab food later."

"Will do!" we chimed in unison.

Micky and I chatted for a bit about work and the upcoming test she had to take. Hanging out with her always felt so comfortable. I realized as we were talking that I felt more at home here than I had since my parents were alive. It was such a relief to finally allow myself to get close to the people around me.

When I'd moved from Chicago six months earlier, I'd told myself if I made the move to New York, I could settle in permanently. No more moving. It had taken everything I had to leave Chicago, but knowing it would be my last move had given me the incentive I'd needed. I'd let myself stay there a full year—twice as long as I'd stayed anywhere else in the past five years—but I forced myself to start over one last time. I'd known from the beginning that I couldn't live my life on the run forever. That sort of lifestyle had already taken a toll on me. I was ready for a home and friends and maybe even … a relationship.

The prospect filled me with excitement and dread.

I assured myself that this time I'd find a kind, affectionate man and take things slowly. Someone who was gentle and understanding. Someone the exact opposite of Torin Byrne. He'd gone from brooding to unpredictable—both were potential red flags. I knew better than anyone not to romanticize a dangerous man.

So why on earth did I still find him so alluring?

Did it matter why? He was simply not an option. If I was going to stay in Manhattan, I needed to set boundaries with him so I wouldn't be forced to leave my home yet again. I had to convince Torin that he needed to let go of whatever interest he might have in me.

An idea started to form.

One of the few things a man like him respected was the

territory of another man. Maybe having a boyfriend in the picture was all I needed to defuse the situation, even if that other man was a smokescreen. At the very least, it would help me diagnose how serious the issue was.

A cautious hopefulness filled me with energy. I had a plan, and that gave me a sense of control over this otherwise uncertain situation.

"I better get to the laundromat before all the machines are taken." Sundays were always busy, but also, I wanted to find out if my plan was feasible.

"Yeah, and I should get to studying. Text me, though, if you need me to pop in and watch your stuff while you take a break."

"I will, thanks!" I pulled the canvas bag from my laundry basket and situated the strap over my shoulder. "Good luck studying." I grinned at Micky's grimace, letting myself into the hallway. Instead of heading for the stairs, however, I knocked on Luke's door.

He answered, a grin lighting his face. "That was quick. You need something?" Luke was such a great guy. I'd had plenty of crappy neighbors, so I knew how lucky I was to live across from him. He was also more than a little handsome.

"Just a quick question. Mind if I come in?"

"Of course not, come on in." He stepped aside to give me and my bag room. "What's up?"

"I have a favor to ask, and it's a big one, so I understand if you're not up for it."

"Now you've piqued my curiosity." He studied me with amusement.

"How would you feel about coming to the club when I get off work tomorrow and walking back home with me?" I shot him an apologetic grimace, knowing an outing at four o'clock in the morning for someone who worked regular daytime hours was a big ask.

Luke's good humor evaporated, his features taking on a sharper edge. "You feeling unsafe at night?"

"No, not exactly. It's kind of hard to explain. My boss worries about me, and I want to show him that he doesn't need to. It's a little deceptive, but I think he'll stop worrying if he thinks I have a boyfriend." Was that insensitive of me? I suddenly realized I hadn't taken Luke's feelings into account. Pretending to be my boyfriend was an entirely different ask than walking me home.

Luke wasn't merely a good guy with a pretty face. He was also smart. His gaze narrowed to skeptical slits. "What do you mean he *worries* about you?"

"I know it sounds sketchy, but it's not." I infused my stare with earnest sincerity—a trait I'd perfected in high school when I'd needed to fudge the truth to my parents. "He's talking about cutting my hours back so I don't have to walk home quite so late, but I need those hours. Some of the best money gets spent in those early morning hours."

Why didn't I tell Luke the truth?

Because he'd worry, and because sharing my problems with him made things complicated. When a person opens themselves up like that, they leave themselves vulnerable. I preferred to handle things on my own. My way.

If the situation changed, I could always come clean later when I truly needed help, but I wasn't to that point yet.

He didn't look totally convinced but didn't push the matter. "Yeah, I'm happy to help. You know I'm here for you anytime."

I beamed up at him. "Thanks, sugar." I gave him a grateful

hug. "'Kay, this thing's getting heavy. I'll shoot you a text later."

"Happy sorting."

I rolled my eyes playfully. "Don't remind me."

Operation: Anti-stalker engaged.

I didn't know what Torin had going on in that head of his, but I would not under any circumstances repeat my past mistakes. I would rather send a clear message from the beginning than risk entangling myself with another dangerous man.

# CHAPTER 5
*Stormy*

*Past*

LIFE WAS A PENDULUM. SOMETIMES IT SWUNG LOW AND SLOW with little consequence, and at other times, its momentum gathered so much force that the jarring swings were unavoidable.

In two short weeks, I swung from some of the darkest, most desperate days of my life to a new stratosphere of existence where every day was filled with more joy than I could comprehend. Maybe the despair itself had made my new circumstances shine so brilliantly. Daylight could be blinding when emerging from the dark. Maybe God knew I'd been through hell and felt I deserved a break. Or maybe

Damyon was simply so incredible that euphoric happiness was an unavoidable consequence of being with him.

Whatever the explanation, I had the most incredible two weeks of my life and never wanted them to end.

I checked out my red satin dress in the gilded full-length hotel mirror. I'd always felt somewhat lanky at five foot seven, most of that height consisting of pasty-white legs—my fair complexion never tanned well—but in the dress Damyon had bought me for our night out, I felt like a movie star.

The fancy hotel room only encouraged the fantasy. After spending a week with him, Damyon had insisted on getting me out of the dingy hotel I'd booked and putting me up in a suite at what had to be the nicest hotel in Moscow. I had tried to refuse, but the man was more stubborn than a mule and richer than God.

Yeah, you heard me right.

Damyon was rich. Not wealthy. Not well-off. The man was filthy stinking rich and generous beyond my imagination. Between the shower of gifts and his unwavering devotion to making me happy, I felt like I was living a fairy tale.

But like all good things, our time together had an expiration. My departure loomed like a storm cloud building on the horizon. One more day, and I would be returning to Georgia. We'd only known each other such a short time, but the thought of suffering another loss so soon after my parents' deaths made the prospect of leaving him feel even more crippling than it would have otherwise. And I wasn't the only one struggling. A hurried pressure to stop the clock buzzed in the air around us a little louder each day. Damyon's stares lingered longer, and he'd begun to fidget when the days grew dark.

He'd taken me out on several incredible dinner dates, but tonight felt different. The weight of my impending departure added a bittersweet poignancy like the approaching climax to a spectacular movie. You didn't want it to end but couldn't wait to see what happened next, thrill and longing inextricably bound together.

If my parents' unexpected passing had taught me anything, it was to appreciate every moment I was given. Find the silver linings and never lose focus of what was most important to me. Life was too dang short for anything less.

My time with Damyon was too precious to give over a single moment to dread. I would focus on the gift I'd been given and appreciate every second we were together.

I smiled at my reflection to reinforce the sentiment when a knock sounded on the door to my suite. Hurrying to greet my date, I swung open the door only to discover the hotel concierge standing on the other side.

"Oh! Hello." My words felt bumbling since he'd caught me completely off guard. Not only was it not who I'd expected but he also carried champagne and strawberries on a silver platter. "Are those for me?"

"Pardon the interruption, madam." He bowed his head. "These were sent over for you along with a note." He lowered the tray so I could see the ivory envelope with my name scribed on the front.

I reached for the note, then opened the door to allow the man inside. "You can set it anywhere, thank you."

I broke open the seal and raced through Damyon's words, fearing he was canceling our date. But I shouldn't have worried. He was too sweet for that.

. . .

*MOY ANGEL, I am running a half hour late. Please forgive me and enjoy these while you wait. D*

WARMTH FLOODED my cheeks as a smile spread across my face. He'd given me so much of his time over the past two weeks, despite the vast real estate development enterprise he ran. The fact that he wasn't late more often was a testament to his attentiveness and dedication. The least I could do was be flexible in return.

A clanking sound seized me from my thoughts. The bubbling champagne flute had tipped over when the man had tried to set down the tray on a small table, sending the pink liquid spilling onto the carpet below.

He shot me a horrified look, eyes round with fear. "How foolish of me. I cannot apologize enough. Please, please let me fix this." His hurried and frantic words matched his actions when he raced to fetch a towel from the bathroom.

"It's no big deal, really. Accidents happen."

On his hands and knees, he attacked the spill with vigor. "You must forgive me. Please, I will bring another glass. There is no need to tell him what has happened. I beg of you."

I could hardly comprehend his response. Why was this man freaking out? Damyon could be intense, but he wasn't a monster. "It's fine. Please, don't worry." I placed my hand on his back, hoping to calm him.

He sat back on his haunches, eyes peering up at me pleadingly. He eventually nodded somewhat defeatedly and stood. "I bring another and replace the towel." He exited the room in reverse, bowing repeatedly on his way.

It had to be one of the strangest encounters of my life. I

wasn't sure I'd ever truly understand the Russian culture. The people here surprised me at every turn.

Shrugging, I sampled the strawberries while I waited for the champagne. The man must have run the entire way back to the kitchen because he returned within minutes. I took the glass from the tray this time, hoping to avoid another scene. He apologized yet again before leaving me to savor the drink. It was the perfect complement to the sweet fruit. Damyon's gesture had been incredibly thoughtful, and I let him know the moment he arrived a half hour later.

"It was the least I could do, Sladkaya angel. I hated to keep you waiting." He pressed a kiss to my lips, then drew away from me to allow his gaze to take a languid trip down my body. "You are exquisite, Alina. Totally and completely breathtaking."

"And you are awfully good with words." My blushing cheeks had to be as red as my satin dress. How did he always know the perfect thing to say? I'd met Southern charmers before, but Damyon was in a league of his own.

"With you, it is easy. I have never met a woman who captures me the way you do." He brought my hand to his mouth and placed an ardent kiss on my knuckles. "Now, let us leave for dinner before I devour you instead."

*Please, God.* Yes.

The words never made it past my suddenly parched throat, but I felt them down to my weeping core. I wanted this man so desperately. My body ached for him. However, I'd been raised with traditional Southern values, so I never raced into a physical relationship. I wasn't a virgin or anything, but I preferred to form an emotional connection before I was intimate with a man.

We'd talked about everything under the sun. Spent

sunsets and sunrises together. Laughed together, and once, when I saw a painting in a museum that my mother had a print of in her bedroom, he held me while I cried.

*Connection signed, sealed, and delivered.*

My heart waved the green flag with enough force to knock my entire body off balance. I was practically giddy with the revelation. Wanting to ensure the night was perfect, I allowed Damyon to help me into my coat and take me to dinner.

He escorted me to a lovely French restaurant, which was empty save for a small number of staff who greeted us both like royalty. I smiled and saved my questions until we were seated.

"I don't understand. Why is no one else here?"

"Because I reserved the whole restaurant for us. That way, I can have you all to myself. No distractions." He poured us each a glass of wine from the uncorked bottle waiting at our table.

"That's very sweet of you but unnecessary," I said softly, a smidge overwhelmed by his grand gestures. "I hope you know that all I really want is to spend time with you."

His hand covered mine, drawing my gaze back to his. "Moy angel, I have never wanted anything more in my life than I want you. To be with you and call you mine." He paused with something more like poignancy than uncertainty. He wanted to emphasize the importance of whatever he was about to say next, and I waited with bated breath. "Tell me you will stay here in Moscow with me. Tell me you will not leave."

"You ... you want me to stay?" I asked in a whisper, too hopeful to believe my own ears. I'd imagined this exact scenario but hardly expected it to happen. These things didn't happen in real life, did they?

There were reasons for the stereotype of men avoiding commitment and being slow to admit their feelings. That sort of man was more common than not, but Damyon was an exception to the rule. He was refreshingly transparent with his desire for me. He could be doting and affectionate without losing an ounce of the masculine prowess that radiated off him. I would have been crazy to let him slip through my fingers.

"This is all awfully fast. Are you sure you want this?" I couldn't help but give him one more chance to reconsider.

He leaned closer, eyes as pale as the winter sky, holding my gaze unflinchingly. "I have never been more sure of anything in my life." Concise and unequivocal. Damyon wanted me to stay in Russia with him.

A cocktail of elation and relief filtered into my bloodstream.

Logic dictated this important decision was worthy of careful consideration, but logic and reason were rooted in reality, which had been rather harsh to me of late. This entire trip was about self-discovery and healing my soul. Who was to say this wasn't the exact path I was meant to take? If my heart pleaded with me to say yes, wouldn't it be counterproductive to refuse?

The only problem was Honey.

My friends had all left home for college, and without my parents to help me, I'd had to withdraw from the school I'd planned to attend. If I was honest, I didn't have a job waiting for me or pets or anything. The only true downside was how badly my heart would hurt to be so far from Honey. Knowing her, however, she'd insist I follow my heart. I had no doubt on that matter. Honey was a sucker for a good love story, and she only ever wanted me to be happy.

"I heard back from the minister of family affairs." Damyon's statement brought my thoughts to a sputtering halt.

My racing heart slammed against my ribs. "You did?"

He nodded. "We do not have your file yet, but they have located the records from that facility. He expects to have the file for us next week. Stay, Alina. You do not have to decide to stay forever but stay for now. We can have a little more time together, and you can learn about your past."

He made a good point. Extending my trip didn't mean I could never go home. I had dual citizenship, so I could come and go as I pleased.

Maybe I'd been overthinking everything. All of it.

I peered across the candlelit table and offered a soft smile. "I suppose a couple more weeks couldn't hurt."

If I wasn't sure of my decision already, Damyon's answering grin sealed my fate. "This is truly worthy of a celebration."

I had to fight back the toothy grin of a kid at Christmas. "Under one condition, though." I forced as much authority into my words as possible.

His body stiffened with resolute intent before he motioned for me to continue.

"I have to find someplace else to stay. I'm not comfortable letting you pay for that hotel for another two weeks." I held up my hand surreptitiously and lowered my gaze. "No arguing. My conscience won't allow it."

When my words weren't met with opposition, I peered up at him hesitantly. Damyon wore a triumphant smirk, his eyes almost silver in the dim lighting.

"Agreed, no more hotel."

My eyes narrowed. "That was too easy. What's the catch?" I adored the man, but he was used to getting his way. He had relented too easily, and I needed to know why.

Damyon leaned forward, his hand reaching for mine across the small table. "I was thinking that if you agreed to stay longer, you might consider staying at my place. You could be my guest." He let the offer soak in like the warm glow of the flickering candle between us.

"You want me to stay with you?" I hadn't even been to his house.

"Come home with me after dinner. Let me show you around, and then you can decide." He lifted my hand and brought it to his lips for a delicate kiss.

"Okay," I breathed.

He swept us both to our feet and planted a kiss on my lips and a promise in my heart. "You were made for me, Sladkaya angel, and tonight, I will prove it."

Damyon was a man of his word. He spent the entire night worshipping my body until I couldn't fathom parting from him. His devotion made me feel whole again, and I never wanted to lose that feeling.

# CHAPTER 6
*Torin*

*Present*

"CAN'T BELIEVE WE NEVER THOUGHT ABOUT THIS TYPE OF place before. It's fucking perfect." Keir surveyed the work we'd done to prepare for this week's fight. The abandoned building had needed adjustments, but nothing drastic.

"No shit." I tugged at one of the ropes, testing its tension. "And considering how many old roller rinks went under since the eighties, we'd have our pick of locations to add to the rotation."

"I'd planned to come watch you tonight, but I won't make it. I'm not ready to leave Rowan alone after the week she's had."

I waved away his concern. "Nah, man. She's definitely more important. How's her mom doing?" I never thought Keir would be one to get married, but over the span of a month, the guy had fallen hard. I'd never seen him so close to losing it as when his wife was attacked only a few days ago. Her mom had been shot in the ordeal.

"She's good. Still in the hospital, but they should release her soon."

"Glad to hear it. That guy was a real piece of shit. How long did he last?" I'd helped Keir take custody of his wife's attacker, but he hadn't let me participate in the punishment. He'd insisted on handling that part himself.

"He's still breathing, technically."

"No shit?"

Keir's gaze cut to mine, an eerie mix of placid malice. The man was a fuckin' legend. As a kid, I'd wanted nothing more than to be like my older cousins. The fact that they trusted me to be a part of the family business was an honor I would take to the grave.

"You know," Keir mused, "Oran is looking into that family and their businesses."

"Is he?" I granted, not totally surprised. "Maybe he can dig up something on the Russian while he's at it. I don't like the way things ended with him."

"I saw him one time outside of a fight night."

My back and shoulders clenched tight as though bracing for a hit. "You fucking serious?"

"I think it was a coincidence. Who knows? But it's good to stay on guard just in case."

"Planned to anyway." I wanted to ask why the fuck he hadn't told us that already but thought better of it. "Any word from Conner about him?"

"Let's find out." Keir took out his phone and placed the call on speaker.

"You got some kind of psychic ability or something?" Conner answered.

"What's that supposed to mean?"

"I'm here with the Genoveses. I figured you'd want to know what they had to say. They've got a friend named Michael Garin, one of Boris's crew."

"I'm not on speaker, am I?" Keir asked.

"No, though it sounds like I am," Conner said in a jabbing tone.

"Tor is with me. Wanted him to hear."

"Hey, man," I called to Conner.

"That works. No need to repeat myself."

Keir brought the talk back to the subject. "They trust this guy Michael?"

"Yeah, it's a long story, but he's got ties to the family. According to Boris, Damyon runs half of Moscow."

Keir's visible agitation mirrored my own. "What the hell is he doing here, then?" We knew the Russian was bad news but never expected him to have quite so much power.

"Not sure," Conner continued. "But having Moscow owe Boris a favor was too good an opportunity to pass up. No chance of them colluding, though. These guys don't trust one another even a little."

"Guess that's good to hear," Keir said, tension still tightening his voice. "Thanks for checking on that."

"No problem. Michael says he'll let us know if he hears anything else."

"Pass along our appreciation." In our world, a phrase like that was as good as gold. Michael had done us a solid, and we'd return the favor, should he ask. I hoped the Genoveses weren't leading us astray.

"Will do."

The call clicked dead.

Keir slid his phone in his pocket, a hint of a frown tugging at his lips. "I suppose if Boris isn't worried, we shouldn't be either, but I'd much rather find out that asshole is on his way back to Russia where he belongs."

"My sentiments exactly. Until that's the case, I say we stay on high alert."

"Agreed."

We wrapped up our business at the rink, then went our separate ways. Preparations for fight night kept me preoccupied most of the day, and since it was Sunday, I didn't have to go by Moxy.

The next day, I got up early enough for one last gym session before resting for Wednesday's fight. Early as in noon. Overseeing the club kept my schedule opposite most folks. I preferred it that way. It gave me an excuse to be antisocial.

After my workout, I strengthened my resolve to ignore Stormy Lawson. She was scheduled to work, and I wanted to show up mentally prepared. I had to stop thinking about her and following her like a goddamn puppy. It didn't matter what customers said to her or what idiotic danger she put herself in. It wasn't my responsibility. *She* wasn't my responsibility.

I absolutely, without exception, could not give in to the temptation to engage with her because I had no self-control where she was concerned, and that simply wasn't an option. Maintaining control in all aspects of my life was paramount. Without discipline and predictability, chaos ensued. Neither she nor anyone else outside of my family was worth that sort of risk.

♦

I was remarkably successful at avoiding Stormy the first half of the night. No eye contact. No greetings. No interaction whatsoever.

I started to believe I had day one in the bag when a swell of cheers snagged my attention, and I looked at the main stage. Micky had started her set, but instead of dancing, she pointed into the crowd, motioning for someone to join her.

"This is your song, baby. Come show me what you've got," she called over the music.

What the fuck was she doing? She knew as well as the rest of us that it caused chaos when clientele ended up on the stage. My irritation ignited into fury when I saw Storm waltz up the steps into the limelight.

Motherfucking no.

The beat dropped to a pulsing grind, and both women began to move in unison. Every muscle in my body instantly coiled and was ready to lash out.

*So if you fucking want me,*
*Don't fucking leave me.*

Micky raised her arms, and Storm drew slowly down into a squat as though worshipping the dancer's body. The wide stance of her legs and her tiny shorts gave way too good a view of her ass. Something I could have enjoyed had thirty other jerkoffs not been storing the image for their own fucking spank banks.

Fuck this, and fuck my resolution. I could only take so much.

Surging through the crowd, I forced my way to the front of the stage. "Get the fuck down from there," I roared over the music.

The women paused to look at me while every man in the vicinity booed.

My scathing stare bore into innocent brown eyes. "Down. *Now.*" Confident my message had been received, I made my way over to the stairs.

Stormy shrugged to the crowd, blowing them kisses, and skittered off the stage. Micky picked up her routine flawlessly. Her graceful, erotic movements had the crowd subdued in no time, leaving me free to return to work.

See, I could interact without losing my head completely. It *was* possible.

Or it would have been if things had ended there. Unfortunately, Storm had other ideas.

The carefree smile she'd worn seconds ago disappeared as she charged up to me. "What in the *hell*, Torin? What was that all about?"

Shit. I hadn't exactly thought this through. Tonight wasn't the first time a server ended up on stage, and I'd never had a problem with it before. Customers were never allowed because that led to chaos, but the crowd usually loved when one of the bar girls took a spin on the pole. Anything that made the customers happy was generally a good thing. So what was my excuse?

"Don't need men thinking you're on the menu." That was the best she was getting. It wasn't my job to explain myself to her or anyone else.

"I'd say I'm on the menu if I wanna be," she shot back, hands locked on her hips.

That Southern sass might as well have been a red flag in

this bull's face. I leaned in close, bringing my face inches from hers, relishing the way her eyes grew wide at the possessive gleam in mine.

"The only man who gets a taste of you inside my club is *me*. So unless you're lookin' to ride my cock, this discussion's over." I pulled back, my gaze detouring to her parted lips for the briefest second before I walked away.

Fucking Christ.

One night. I'd tried to control myself for one goddamn night, and I hadn't just failed. I'd done a one-eighty all the way to crazy town instead.

I spent the next two hours in my office, waiting for closing time. I had to clear my head, and I didn't feel like dealing with Jolly when he called me out on my behavior.

Once I knew he'd left and the last customers would be filing out, I slunk back downstairs and sat by the front door. I kept my stare glued to my phone to ensure no one tried to talk to me. For everyone's sake.

I did finally look up when someone entered rather than exited. A young guy who looked too sober and well-kept to wander in at this hour.

"We're shutting down. You'll have to come back tomorrow."

The guy lifted his chin in acknowledgment. "Just here for Storm." His eyes cut away dismissively, but I was now fully alert.

Who the fuck was this asshole?

Storm came bounding toward us before I could ask the guy his name. "Hey, Luke. I'm all set." She wrapped her arm around his, offering up a devoted grin as he escorted her outside.

My phone was in pieces before I realized what I'd done.

*Fucking hell.*

I surged to my feet, then froze with my eyes on the door.

I wanted to follow them. I wanted to follow them so fucking bad it physically pained me to remain in place, but that was exactly why I had to stay put. I had to get control of myself. I didn't want to want her. I especially didn't want to let outsiders into my sphere of control. Bad things happened when our lives were left to the whims of others. The only way to combat that was to keep a strict distance between me and anyone who didn't carry the Byrne name.

No one else could be trusted.

That creed had served me well for a solid decade, but every time I turned around, *she* was there, immune to my efforts like fucking Teflon.

I stared at the glossy black door, then down at my broken phone, before launching the damn thing at the wall across from me. The device crashed into a large beveled mirror, which shattered into thousands of pieces, scattering loudly on the ground below.

Fuck. Me.

# CHAPTER 7

*Stormy*

*Present*

I WAS SO ANXIOUS ABOUT SEEING TORIN THE NEXT DAY THAT I almost didn't notice the mirror missing from the entry. It had hung next to the bathroom hallway near the club entrance in such a way that it reflected light deep into the club when anyone opened the door before the sun had set. Today, the only thing shining in the light was a thin layer of dust shaped in a perfect rectangle where the mirror used to hang.

"What happened there?" I asked Jolly over the music that was already playing.

He sat at the bar, scrolling on his phone, never looking away as he answered. "Cleaning crew."

"Good grief, what'd they do—clean the thing with a brick?" Our mirrors survived nightly encounters with rowdy drunks. I wasn't sure how the cleaning crew had managed to break the thing.

Jolly only grunted.

"You know what, Jolly? I've worked here six months now, and I'm beginning to think your nickname wasn't an ode to your sparkling disposition."

That earned me a side-eye glare.

I beamed at him. "Go ahead, tell me how you got the name. I want to hear the story."

He took a weary breath and leaned back in his chair. "Since I know you won't leave me alone until I tell you, I got the nickname when I was workin' at a juvenile detention center."

"You worked with troubled youth?"

"Not sure I'd put it that way. I was a juvenile corrections officer. That's where I first met Torin."

Did I hear him correctly? He met Torin at a juvie center? I turned my head so my right ear was closer to him. "Did you say you met Torin in a detention center?"

He looked at me like I was dense. "That's what I said, wasn't it?"

"The hearing in my left ear isn't great. I thought maybe I'd misheard you. I didn't realize you two had known each other that long." I had so many questions, but I didn't want to pry.

Jolly chose to ignore my casual probe into Torin's and his past. He leaned back, resting his arm on the back of his chair to get a better view of me. "You're a bit young for hearing loss."

"Bad ear infection as a kid." It was my turn to be evasive. "You gonna tell me any more about that detention center?"

"Nothin' much to tell." He shot me a challenging look and turned back to his phone.

Message received. If I wanted to know more about Torin in juvie, I would have to ask the man himself. That wasn't happening anytime soon, especially after our exchange.

*The only man who gets a taste of you inside my club is me. So unless you're lookin' to ride my cock, this discussion's over.*

I'd played those words over in my mind hundreds of times, searing them into my brain. They were crass and harsh and shockingly unexpected, but they'd also made me so wet that I'd had to clean myself up in the bathroom minutes later. The entire situation baffled me.

"Always a pleasure chatting with ya, Jolly." I patted him on the back and continued to the girls' locker room. Micky was already seated at a vanity in her bra and underwear, but she was staring at her phone instead of getting ready.

"Hey, Mick. How's it going?"

"Oh my God. Tell me you have tomorrow off."

"I have tomorrow off."

She lifted wide eyes to face me. "Wait, are you just saying that because I told you to say it?"

I laughed and rolled my eyes. "No, Micky. I really have tomorrow off."

"Hell to the yeah. You're going out with me."

"Is that so?"

"Yes. It's fight night, and I've wanted to go to one since Blaze told me about them. Torin has a match, and I would *kill* to see him in the ring. Something tells me he'll be incredible." She bit her lip in a way that made me unexpectedly stabby. I decided not to examine the odd reaction.

"I'm not sure that's my scene." I'd never understood how people could enjoy watching two men beat one another to a bloody pulp.

Micky was on her feet, hands on my shoulders like a coach pep-talking her star player to bring home the win. "*Please*, Storm. I don't want to go alone, and I really, *really* want to go."

"Aren't those fights illegal?" I couldn't risk getting arrested, and it was just as important that Torin not think I'd gone to watch him fight, though I had to admit to having a degree of curiosity.

Her head cocked impatiently to the side. "From what I hear, there are *tons* of people. And they have these things down to a science; there's hardly any risk of it being busted."

"Tons of people?" It was the wrong thing to say. I realized my mistake the second the words were out, and Micky's lips spread in a giddy grin.

"*Yes!*" She threw her arms around me. "You won't regret it. We'll have so much fun watching all those rippling muscles."

I hadn't technically agreed, but I couldn't seem to refute her either. She was so dang excited, and her mention of rippling muscles had conjured a mental image of Torin that made my throat suddenly dry. Surely, if there would be loads of people, he wouldn't notice us in the crowd. I could assuage my curiosity and indulge my friend. It felt so good to have friends again that I wanted to do what I could to keep them.

"Alright, alright. You can figure out the plan and text me. I need to set up the bar before Jolly comes looking for me."

"Shit, yeah. I don't even have my eyelashes on, and I need

to make some cash so I can put money on the fights tomorrow. It's way more fun when you have a little stake in the game." She gave me a wink, then turned back to her mirror, a grin still lighting her face.

I got to work without any run-ins with Torin. A small part of me had worried how he might react to seeing Luke, but when he stopped by the club briefly, he never even looked my way. As far as I could tell, my ploy had paid off. There were no awkward interactions, and I didn't detect a shadow tailing me on my way home.

The successful turn of events reassured me that a night at the fights wouldn't be an issue. My daddy used to watch pay-per-view fights. I was never a fan of the violence, but I could endure one night for a friend.

♦

"I DIDN'T KNOW you were into wigs!" Micky trailed her fingers through the long auburn strands of hair draped over my shoulder.

"I'm not really." What I was into was not being seen by my stalker boss. "I just have a couple for fun."

"I've thought about it, but those things are pricey. Maybe when I'm out of school and not watching every dime."

"Like the dimes you plan on gambling tonight?" I razzed her with a playful quirk of my eyebrow.

She reflected my attitude right back at me with an epic side-eye. "We all gotta have our priorities."

We both stared at one another for a pregnant second before bursting into laughter.

Thirty minutes and three subway stations later, we walked up to a crumbling old building with a faded sign reading Electric Avenue Skating Rink. The entire neighborhood looked forgotten in time. It was the perfect place for a pop-up fight night.

We filtered inside the front entrance past a pair of scowling thugs. Each person to enter was then patted down for weapons in what used to be the rink lobby. The wood paneling original to the 1970s was still present, though warped in areas. The floor was checkerboard with what was probably asbestos tiles, and the speckled drop ceiling was missing in sections. Otherwise, the place wasn't in terrible shape. Brightly colored prints still hung in their frames, and ornamental light fixtures that reminded me of the old *Jetsons* cartoon hung overhead.

However, the vibe was different once we entered the main part of the building. The rink had been gutted. The room retained almost nothing related to its original purpose save for a giant disco ball hanging from the ceiling. An elevated boxing ring had been set up directly underneath it in the middle of the room, and several hundred people were packed in around the ring or standing in lines at the row of booths housing bookies along one wall.

The air was thick with moisture and anticipation. And sound. So much noise that pressure built in my ears. An announcer commentated from a microphone but was still hard to hear over the cacophony of shouting and music.

The energy was overwhelming.

My heart thundered in my chest as I watched a fight already underway. I knew from seeing bits of pro fights with my dad that a series of smaller fights took place leading up to the main event. I had no idea where Torin might fit in that line-up. For all I knew, his match could have already ended.

The possibility brought on a wave of unexpected

disappointment. I shoved the emotion into a cute little Mason jar and vacuum sealed that sucker shut. I had no business wanting to see Torin in a fight or any other capacity aside from a paycheck.

*That's why you're wearing this ridiculous wig, remember? No entanglements with dangerous men.*

Adequately chastened, I stood dutifully in line with Micky. As soon as she placed her bets, we squeezed our way through the crowd of bodies.

Micky said something over her shoulder, but I couldn't make it out. Between the hearing trouble I had in my left ear and the ruckus everywhere, it was all a blur of sound.

"What?" I tugged on her shirt to get her attention.

"Let's get a little closer," Micky said even louder.

"You sure? It might be better to stick near the back." That would make it easier to cut and run. I had put the suggestion out there, knowing it was in vain.

"Are you kidding? We didn't come all this way to stand at the back! I want to see the testosterone dripping off them."

I'd figured as much.

She finally settled on a spot about halfway to the ring. We watched three fights over the next two hours. I was relieved to see that illegal fights didn't necessarily mean gruesome. The same rules professionals followed seemed to apply, and the referee didn't tolerate any abusive behavior. I'd been a tad worried it would be some sort of fight-to-the-death Mad Max style.

While that particular fear subsided, my anxiety over watching Torin fight magnified by the minute. It was one thing to be a spectator when two strangers pummeled one another. Watching someone I knew possibly get knocked unconscious sounded more and more horrifying. I wanted boundaries between us—I didn't want the man dead.

And to make matters worse, the crowd was swimming in alcohol. The lack of a concession stand hadn't stopped anyone from drinking. Even Micky had pulled out a jewel-studded flask at the start of the second fight. Booze-laden breath was all around me. Everyone had steadily grown louder and more animated. By the time Torin "the Streak" Byrne was announced, my chest felt tight with the threat of a full-out panic attack.

The crowd came alive as Torin and his opponent, Joe "Razor" Roman, each walked to the ring. Cheers. Angry slurs. Fists waving in the air for any number of reasons. Micky ate it up. She bounced on her toes and added her voice to the mix while I stood stock-still, my heart wedging itself between my ribs.

Terror, fascination, and a heady dose of lust combined in a cocktail of emotions that spiked my bloodstream until the room around me spun.

I'd never seen Torin without a shirt. His muscled body was perfection, but anyone passing him on the street could tell that much. What had me speechless was the jagged expanse of a lightning bolt tattooed across his back. I'd expected the tattoos on his arms to continue onto the rest of his body, but that wasn't the case. The single piece of artwork on pristine skin reminded me of a Grecian statue marbled with a catastrophic crack.

"I knew he'd be hot, but sweet *Jesus*," Micky hollered next to my ear. "You okay? You look a little funny."

"Yeah," I answered distractedly. I couldn't tear my eyes away from the sight of Torin as he loosened up, his tightly coiled muscles visible even to those of us thirty feet away. "The intensity's just ... a lot, you know?"

"I feel you. It's got me so fuckin' horny."

I turned to gape at her, but she was already hollering something about "rip his fucking arms off."

What had I been thinking when I agreed to this? Coming here was such an epic mistake.

I wanted out, but we were walled in by bodies all around us. I scrunched my eyes shut and prayed it would be over quickly, then panicked that I hadn't specified a winner, so I repeated the prayer with a caveat that Torin would win.

*What if he doesn't win? What if I have to stand here and watch him get pounded round after round?*

My stomach dipped and rolled like a tiny rowboat braving an ocean storm.

A single ping of the bell pierced the air.

My eyelids wrenched open.

The two men circled each other the same as each pair of fighters before, but their predatorial movements stirred nausea in my belly this time. Torin's opponent was similar in height, but his shoulders and arms were more solid with mass and muscle. He was covered in tattoos, his head shaved clean to the scalp, and he stared down Torin with a palpable hatred.

Torin bobbed lightly closer, coaxing out a swing from Razor. The two measured up one another with a few easy jabs. I started to feel a tiny tendril of relief before Torin took a solid uppercut to the gut followed by a mean right hook. He stumbled to the ring as the referee stepped between them.

Each time Razor's fists made contact with Torin, tiny snippets of memory assaulted me. Furious blue eyes. White-knuckled fists. Fear. So much crippling fear.

I closed my eyes and begged the contents of my stomach to stay put.

For three rounds, the two went at one another, the crowd growing more feral by the minute. I wondered if their rabid cries had consumed all the oxygen in the room because I swore it was getting harder and harder to breathe.

Despite the heated bodies around me, my hands were cool and clammy. And had the room gone quieter, or was that a ringing in my ears?

I desperately needed to get a grip.

*Focus on Tor. He's okay. He's alive. He'll be okay.*

I stared at where he sat in his corner as though that link between us would somehow keep us both safe. I stared with such intensity, I could almost feel myself touching him. Maybe I had, in a telepathic sense.

I didn't know how else to explain the way Tor's gaze lifted from the ground and collided directly with mine. He hadn't scanned the crowd or been lost in a daze. His piercing eyes shot with intention straight to mine and locked on me with the precision of a sniper scoping his target.

The wig had been pointless.

He knew exactly who I was.

Fury darkened his face as he shot to his feet just as the bell rang.

# CHAPTER 8

*Torin*

*Present*

I COULDN'T BELIEVE MY EYES.

Stormy was there at the fight. And that look on her face? I'd never fucking scratch it from my memory. The desperation and torment. It transformed me from man into pure primal instinct, and that instinct demanded I get to her. The fight didn't matter. The bets and spectators and obligations—none of it mattered. None of it even registered. There was only Storm and her need for help.

The bell rang as I lurched to my feet, and Razor made the mistake of coming at me. He got in one hit while my focus was divided. That was it. A strike to the jaw that didn't even register.

The beast raging inside me wasn't about to let this motherfucker stand in my way. I attacked with savage, merciless blows one after the other, never giving him the opportunity to defend or counter.

When he crumpled to the ground, the referee came at me as though expecting to have to restrain me, but I wasn't interested in spending a second longer than necessary in that ring. I only had one thing on my mind.

Jumping from the platform, I charged into the crowd that was now going ballistic. The unexpected assault had riled them to a frenzied state, making it harder to form a path through the chaos. Some wanted to congratulate me. Others were spitting angry.

I didn't give a fuck about any of them.

Ripping off my gloves and discarding them to the ground, I shoved people out of my way until she was finally within reach. The only way to get her out safely was with her in my arms, so I scooped into my arms in one swift motion and continued my momentum toward the exit. The crowd thinned toward the perimeter. Increasing my pace, I tore past everyone I knew and didn't stop until Storm and I were safely in the locker room. Alone.

I set her on her feet and slammed the door shut behind us. Only then was I able to gain some semblance of control over my ragged breathing and racing heart. I didn't take too long, though, because I needed to know what was wrong.

Turning to face her, I placed my hands on either side of her face, angling her eyes up to meet mine. My hands reeked in their sweat-soaked wraps, but I didn't care. All that mattered was making sure Storm was okay.

"Did something happen? Did someone hurt you?"

She shook her head in tiny, uncertain movements. "I'm okay." Her voice was so goddamn small that it wasn't even her—not the Stormy I knew. What the hell had happened to upset her so deeply? If she wasn't hurt, then what?

I swiped the wig off her head and tossed it aside. She tugged a cap off her head and let her golden hair fall to her shoulders. A twinge of pain stabbed deep in my chest. She was so fucking beautiful—an angel.

*My angel.*

"The fuck are you doin' here, Storm?" My words came off harsh. I'd already been on edge, but those two words still echoed in my mind, stirring up my anger. I had no business thinking of her as mine.

*If not yours, then whose?*

My chest clenched tighter at the mental image of her leaving the club with that man. Someone as vivacious as Storm would end up with a ring on her finger sooner rather than later. Was I ready to accept that?

"Micky. She wanted to come."

I'd been so preoccupied that I hadn't even seen Micky.

Storm continued. "We were going to see you fight, but ... I couldn't ... the others were different. I couldn't stand..." Her now glassy eyes cut to my busted cheekbone, then drifted to each bruise and scrape like she was cataloging my injuries. Was she reassuring herself I was alright?

*Fucking Christ, this woman.*

This was bad. I was too on edge, and she was too fragile. We were going to do something we'd regret.

I needed to walk away, but there was no chance in hell. I needed to feel her. Taste her. Reassure myself she was whole and healthy and mine.

Fuck.

I needed to *own* her.

Maybe once I had her, the obsession would ease. So much of this was probably my own damn fault for telling myself she was forbidden. If that was the case, maybe I could free myself with one quick fuck. I'd see that she wasn't anything special and move the fuck on.

My dick was already solid stone, ready and impatient. He didn't care what rationalization I used, so long as it got him buried where he wanted to be.

Storm bit down on her lip then peered up at me through her forest of black lashes.

The air around us shifted as the last tether of my self-control unraveled.

I walked her backward, ripping off my wraps to free my hands. I didn't want anything getting in the way of my ability to touch her. To feel her body shiver and shudder beneath me. With her back against the cold metal lockers, she was mine for the taking until the door opened behind us.

My eyes stayed glued to hers. "Get the fuck out," I barked.

"Everything okay in here?" Bishop. Annoying fucker.

"We're good, so long as you disappear," I growled back.

The door clicked shut, and I knew he'd gotten the message. He wouldn't allow any more interruptions.

I guided her jacket over her shoulders and let it fall to the floor. Finally breaking our stare, I slowly lowered my gaze to where her chest heaved beneath a thin cotton shirt. A moth drawn to the flame, my hand rose to cup her breast. It was involuntary. As necessary as breathing.

My eyes clenched shut as I relished the feel of her warm body in my grasp. How many fucking times had I imagined this moment?

Stormy gasped at my initial touch but didn't stop me. In fact, her chest swelled on a heavy breath, pressing herself harder against my palm.

"I don't understand. I thought you didn't..." She paused, as if reluctant to continue her thought.

I stilled, wanting to know what she was thinking. "Didn't what?"

"Didn't want anything to do with me. You act like I'm a pain in your ass."

"You *are* a pain in my ass." My voice was as ragged and unforgiving as my need to possess her. "Doesn't mean I don't want to bury my cock deep inside you."

Her eyes widened a fraction, the pupils dilating. She liked it when I talked dirty. Jesus, she couldn't be any more perfect.

"Pants. Off."

She started to obey, getting so far as to lower the zipper, then paused. Her brows drew together. "I need to know why, Torin."

"Why I want to fuck you?"

"Why you came for me." Vulnerability softened her voice and stiffened my cock.

The answer was simple. "Because you needed me."

I'd known that down to the marrow of my bones. She'd needed my help, and no force on earth could have stopped me after that.

I hooked my thumbs in her pants and tugged them down. She could tell me to stop, but I wasn't asking permission.

Thank Christ, she slid off her shoes. That was all the consent I needed.

I lifted her against me and relished the feel of her long legs circling my hips. With her back against the locker, and my eyes boring into hers, I freed my cock and found her entrance.

"Shit, Stormy. You're already drenched for me." I slid between her folds three times, slowly back and forth. Teasing her. Teasing myself. Testing my self-control and coating my cock in her juices. When I pressed inside her, she stiffened.

"Jesus *fuck*, you're tight." My eyes clenched shut at the feel of her pussy walls squeezing the head of my cock, sending shock waves of pleasure up my spine.

"It's been a while," she said on a shaky breath.

A while? Try years. I would have reveled in my discovery had all my concentration not been devoted to controlling myself. I was only halfway inside her and had to clamp down on my overpowering need to surge deeper until I was fully sheathed in her warmth. That sort of force would have ripped the woman in two. Instead, I slowly rocked my way past the gates of heaven.

Storm clung to my shoulders, her small gasps and moans teasing my ear and riling my cock to a point of excrucation. She was fucking perfection. If I'd known. *Jesus*, if I'd only known.

I would have done this sooner.

I never would have allowed myself to go this far.

Either. Both. I wasn't sure, but I knew one thing. There was no going back.

"I can't be gentle, Storm."

"Don't be." Her panted words were a checkered flag.

I gave myself over to my desire. To every fantasy she'd starred in and each tormented dream I'd been trapped in since the day she stumbled into my club. They all united in one perfect moment of savagery.

I fucked Stormy against the lockers, ramming my cock so

deep inside her that she'd feel me for days. She clutched my shoulders for dear life. Thrust after jackhammered thrust, we watched one another. She drank in my unguarded fascination, and I memorized the perfect way her lips parted in pleasure.

I didn't last long, nor did I care. She made me so fucking hard every damn day that I knew I'd be ready for a second round. Maybe even a third and fourth. I'd fuck her until my dick fell off if I could.

A sharp surge of tingles drew my balls up tight before white lightning exploded through my veins. My back curved with release, my body's last ditch effort to reach as far inside her as possible.

I lay my forehead on her shoulder while I recovered. I'd never been so damn dizzy after sex.

*You fucked her within an inch of your life. Both your lives.*

And I'd do it again in a heartbeat.

Speaking of … I lowered us to the ground and lay Storm on her back. She watched me with a glint of curiosity. When she recognized my intent as I brought my face to her spread thighs, she tried to sit upright.

"But your cum…" she protested warily.

"Is exactly where it should be," I assured her firmly. And the fucked-up thing was, I meant it. I hadn't used a condom, and I couldn't bring myself to care—about tasting myself on her or the possibility of pregnancy.

I'd never pulled that shit in my life—not even at my drunkest—but Storm was different. Always had been and always would be.

"We aren't leaving here until those thighs try to squeeze the life from me." I pressed her legs apart and circled her opening with my tongue before licking up to her clit. The taste was intoxicating, if only because she tasted like *mine*.

I pulled down the cups of her bra and teased her nipples into puckered pebbles with my fingers, wishing my mouth could be in two places at once. I wanted to run my lips over every damn inch of her. Lick the salt from every one of her delicious curves.

If one person could be made for another, then I had no doubt Storm was made just for me. Everything about her was so fucking perfect. She captivated each of my senses until nothing else existed but her. And judging by the arousal dripping from her pussy, her body was responding to mine in a similar fashion.

She was already primed from riding my cock, her body desperate for release. I pumped my fingers deep inside her while I flicked my tongue over her swollen clit. Her knees spread wider, a silent plea for more. She was so fucking responsive. I loved the feel of her hand clenched in my hair and the occasional sting of pain. All of it drove me onward in a desperate pursuit to see her come undone.

When her legs began to pulse and jerk, I knew she was on the cusp. I kept my fingers inside her and circled that internal bundle of nerves relentlessly.

"Oh God. *Yesss.*" Her body arched up off the concrete as it exploded with release, making me wish I could see the curve of her spine from behind. I wanted to see her come in every way possible, in every position and from every angle. I wanted more of her in any way I could get it. My brain violently rejected the possibility that I might never touch her again.

Consumed with a desire for more, I slowly eased my

touch and allowed her to recover, but only because I needed her ready for more. I'd never been a patient man, however.

As soon as I kicked off my shorts, I scooped Stormy into my arms and took her over to the ancient Formica vanity.

"Hands on the counter," I instructed after I'd set her on the ground facing a dusty mirror.

"Again?" Her wide eyes stared at me in the mirror.

"This time, we come together."

Her head made small jerking movements back and forth. "I can't. I haven't ever…"

"Haven't what?"

"Come … during penetration."

I leaned in so that my lips were close to her ear, my cock teasing her backside. "There's no rules here, Stormy. I want back inside you. I want to watch your fuck-me lips part as I push inside you. If that heavenly pink pussy of yours wants to feel how painfully hard you make me, lay those palms on the counter and let me make you feel good."

Hesitantly, she leaned forward. It was the most beautiful goddamn sight I'd ever seen. Ass pressed out, round and curvy and begging for attention. My hand absently caressed her smooth skin. The thought of my handprint marking her was an impulse I couldn't resist. A resounding slap pierced the air as my palm made contact with her right ass cheek.

A tendril of worry surfaced that I might have hurt her, only to have it vanquished with intense satisfaction when she arched even further and produced a guttural moan.

"*Fuck*, you'd look incredible with my cum shot across your back." I soothed the heated skin with a caress. "Do you touch yourself when you're alone?"

"Yes."

"Show me." I adored the way she immediately obeyed except that she dropped her gaze to the sink. "Eyes on me."

As soon as her eyes met mine, I surged inside her. She felt so damn good that my hands clamped down on her hips with a bruising grip. I breathed deeply, in then out, trying to maintain control of myself and not fuck her like a goddamn animal.

When I started to move inside her, Storm's lips parted, and her hand picked up speed. She wasn't just following instructions; she was feeling it. Lost in the moment with me.

*Fuck it. Restraint is overrated.*

I lay my hand flat on her upper back and bent her farther forward. "You drive me out of my goddamn mind." My ragged words were the only warning she had before I pounded into her, pistoning relentlessly in pursuit of my sanity. As though somewhere deep inside her, I might find a cure for the madness that plagued me.

Stormy didn't just steady herself against my assault; she pressed back into my thrusts with all her might as though *she* were the one fucking *me*. She rode my cock, her eyes never leaving mine. The sight unraveled my DNA until I was nothing but the most primal of my basic instincts. My body clenched with preparedness to fight off rivals, and my lips parted with the release of a savage roar. As the possessive bellow rang in the air, Storm's inner muscles clamped like a fucking fist around my cock. She let out a wanton moan as her release overtook her. Wave after wave, her body seized and clenched, driving me over the cliff's edge with her.

Never in my life had I experienced anything more fundamentally raw.

I had to wrap Storm in my arms and hug her to me to keep her upright, her body trembling all over. Our chests heaved in tandem as we steadied ourselves and processed what had passed between us. Not that it could be fully processed or understood, the same way the indiscriminate chaos of a tornado struck with no explanation. This consuming chemistry rendered us powerless.

Once I regained a granule of sanity, I eased my grip on Storm and allowed her to face me. Her tangled, sweaty hair fell in thick waves next to her face. I swept it over her shoulder, bringing to my attention that her breasts were still exposed. Her lungs froze for a second as I swept a finger inside the cup of her bra and eased it up over her breast.

I saw her entire tattoo for the first time and realized it had been inked over a scar. Only the upper edge was normally visible, peeking out from her shirt. Three flowers in full bloom with a bee buzzing above them. I should have known it would be something simple yet feminine. That was so ... *her*. But the scar was a surprise. It looked like it might have been a burn, though the shaded ink made it hard to discern.

"What happened?" I started to trace the area, but Storm shifted away from me and righted her shirt.

"Car accident." She kept her eyes averted. I might have said it was the effects of the awkward aftermath of a first time, but something told me it was more. She didn't like to talk about the scar. Why? What had happened? I wanted to know. I wanted to know every goddamn thing about her.

I'd hoped beyond hope for both our sakes that tonight would rid her from my system. That I could let her be and not darken the glow that radiated off her, but fate had other plans. As we stood and prepared to go our separate ways, the gravitational pull I felt only intensified.

We were both in so much fucking trouble.

"Let me grab my stuff, and I'll take you home," I said gruffly.

"I can't. I came with Micky, and I don't want her to have to go home alone."

I wanted to delay our separation as long as possible, and I sure as fuck wasn't letting her wander the streets with Micky in this shit part of the city. I opened the door and stuck my head into the hall while unwinding my wraps. Bishop stood at a healthy distance. Smart man.

"You seen a girl named Micky try to come back here?"

On cue, the slender woman herself stepped into view, arms crossed harshly over her chest, and a look of supreme accusation hardening her feminine features. "You gonna let me have my girl back?"

"No." I returned my attention to Bishop. "Find someone to take Micky home."

"Tha *fuck?*" Her voice followed me back into the room.

"All taken care of." I slid on a shirt and pants from my duffel, then threw the rest of my crap in the bag. "Come on." I took her hand in mine and led her from the room.

"Storm, honey. You okay?" Micky called from where Bishop kept her at bay.

"It's all good, Mick. Promise." Stormy shot over her shoulder. "I'll talk to you tomorrow, okay?"

I kept us moving, not interested in Micky's reply.

I'd owned motorcycles my entire adult life and had never felt the need to own a helmet until now. I was equally torn between having Storm unprotected on my bike and sending her home with someone else. It may have been selfish, but I trusted my skills on a bike more than turning her over to some other asshole. Tomorrow, I'd buy a goddamn helmet.

"You ever been on a bike?"

"I've been on a Harley, but nothing like this. Is there even room for me?"

It was technically outfitted to carry a passenger, though not comfortably. And not that I let anyone on the back of my bike. No rides outside of family or emergencies.

Until now.

That was going to be my new goddamn mantra.

Storm was shredding every ounce of structure I'd painstakingly crafted in my life. All in a matter of days.

*You could end it. Walk away and let life fall back into its routine.*

Fuck that.

I threw my leg over the bike and positioned my duffel across my chest. "Step here on this peg and hold my shoulders." Once she was seated, I revved the motor to life. Storm wound her arms around my middle, overcoming her hesitancy, and *Christ* did it feel good.

"It's 55<sup>th</sup> and Michigan," she called over the rumbling pipes.

Hell, I'd almost forgotten to ask. That would have been an interesting conversation when I pulled up at her building. I chided myself to get my head out of my ass.

The drive was just long enough for reality to set in. I'd fucked Stormy. The woman I'd been borderline obsessed with for months. My employee.

I couldn't even imagine how complicated this could get.

I couldn't bring myself to regret being with her, but I knew it had been a mistake. Who knew what expectations she'd have now? No matter what they were, I was bound to disappoint. My issues had issues. She'd never understand, nor would I expect her to without a glimpse into my past that she was never going to get. That was exactly why I'd always insisted I was better off alone. My fixation on Storm shouldn't change that fact.

When we arrived, I steeled myself for her to linger at the bike or ask me upstairs. It would have played out like that with most women, but Storm wasn't most women. I should have known that by now.

I'd barely stopped the bike when she hopped off, murmured thanks for the ride, and disappeared inside. I should have been relieved.

Spoiler alert.

I wasn't. Not even a little.

# CHAPTER 9
*Stormy*

*Past*

WHERE THE HECK HAD MY PHONE GONE? I'D LOOKED everywhere. And since we hadn't gone out much in the two months since I'd moved in with Damyon, I was sure it had to be in the house.

I got off my knees from where I'd been searching under the bed again and made my way to Damyon's office. We'd settled into a new normal. A two-week extension had morphed into four, then a decision to leave my return open-ended. I was glad I'd stayed, but I was starting to get a little homesick, especially now that winter had set in.

"Hey, sugar. Have you seen my phone lying around

anywhere?"

He took a second to respond, his eyes locked on the computer screen. "No, I haven't," he murmured distractedly.

"I've looked everywhere and can't figure out what happened to the darn thing."

He finally looked at me, a touch of annoyance lining his face. I'd noticed the change in the past weeks and was pretty sure it was work, though I couldn't help but worry that I was the source of his irritation. Without any friends or a job here in Moscow, I had no social outlet besides him. He tried to balance it all but was so busy all the time.

"We'll go in the morning and get you a new one, angel. For now, I have work to do."

Disappointment formed my lips into a frown, but I nodded and slipped away, not wanting to bother him further. A new phone was great, except I didn't know anyone's phone number. How was I supposed to get all my old data? I didn't think they had the same cellular carriers here in Moscow.

I was already isolated from my old life. Losing my phone felt like a door slamming shut behind me, the lock falling into place. My life in Georgia would never be the same after my parents died, but that didn't mean I wanted to turn my back on the place forever.

*Don't overreact. People lose their phones all the time.*

I stood in the living room and closed my eyes, trying to calm myself. I could always use email to contact people and help collect numbers. My recent photos would be gone, but I'd put all my voice messages and photos of Mama and Daddy on the cloud after the funeral. I'd almost deleted a message from Mama one day and panicked. I didn't want to lose any more of them than I already had.

Thinking about it helped loosen the knot forming in my

stomach. Just to be sure, though, I continued my search, certain the dang thing was bound to reappear.

Two days later, I still hadn't found my phone or gotten a new one. I tried to be patient, but it was a losing battle. After my morning swim in the large indoor pool, I showered and wound my way down to Damyon's office to bring up the matter again.

I didn't realize he had company until I'd swept into the room through the open door. I froze at the sight of the two men sipping vodka on either side of Damyon's grand wooden desk.

"I'm so sorry. I didn't mean to interrupt."

The unfamiliar man grinned, flashing a gold tooth before muttering something in Russian to Damyon. With one look and a couple of unintelligible words, he'd managed to make me feel dirty inside and out. I didn't need to understand Russian to know his words had been crass.

Damyon swirled the clear liquid in his glass, his arctic eyes looking positively glacial. "Nyet." He spoke to his guest, but his eyes remained glued to me. "I'm busy right now," he said, finally addressing me.

"Yes, of course. Sorry again." I excused myself awkwardly and hurried from the room a little hurt at the way he'd handled the situation. He'd dismissed me as though I were one of the staff. I wasn't expecting him to make a scene or even introduce me, but I didn't want to be coolly brushed-off either.

I went to the library where I spent most of my time and stared out the window to the unforgiving cold clutching the arid landscape around us. I hugged myself as a chill crept beneath my skin. Or maybe that was uncertainty icing my veins.

Everything about coming here had felt like a dream when I first moved in, but each day, I felt increasingly lonely. Damyon worked a lot. I knew someone as wealthy as him would have little spare time, but I just hadn't realized how little. I wasn't sure I was interested in wealth if it meant loneliness—especially when I lived so far from everything and everyone I'd ever known. I wasn't sure what to do about the situation. I could tell Damyon that I'd started feeling lonely or bring up me possibly going on a visit back home, but I hated to put more on his plate when he was already so stressed.

I never heard him come up behind me, giving me even more of a shock when his hand clamped tight around my upper arm and yanked me around to face him.

"What the *fuck* did you think you were doing?" His eyes spit furious blue flames.

"*What?*" I gasped, stunned at his sudden attack.

"Do you have any idea how dangerous it is to flaunt yourself in front of a man like that? How could you be so fucking stupid?"

"Damyon, you're hurting me," I whimpered. I'd have purple lines where his fingers had been, though his bruising grip was nothing compared to the lashing I felt from his words.

He dropped his gaze, then yanked his hand away and paced toward the middle of the room. He ran a hand through his hair and took several deep breaths. When he turned back, he was calmer but still eerily cold.

Tears burned the backs of my eyes.

Why had he been so harsh? The door had been open. How was I supposed to know it was dangerous to go in? Thoughts swirled in my head, but seeing how close his temper was to the surface, I kept my lips sealed tightly shut.

"I am so sorry, Alina." Wariness drew his brows together.

I'd learned in our time together that Damyon was twelve years older than me, putting him at thirty-two. It was a gap that had hardly felt noticeable ... until now. I felt like a child being lectured by my angry father.

"You know I worry about you. If something happened to you because of me..." He didn't continue as though the thought was too much to bear. Instead, he cupped my face in his warm hands. "I would never forgive myself."

I nodded, emotion clogging my throat.

"I have been neglecting you," he continued. "Come, let us get you a phone and get out of this house, da? A few hours out in that miserable cold will make us both happy to be back here again."

I gave him a shaky smile. "That sounds good."

We took a step toward the door when he stilled. *"Der'mo.* I cannot believe that I forgot." He gave me a half grin. "Yesterday, I got word from my contact in the Ministry of Labor and Social Protection. He found your file. Would you like to know your birth mother's name?"

I couldn't believe what I was hearing. I'd almost given up hope after so many weeks had passed without any luck. A cocktail of potent emotions flooded my system until I didn't know what to feel. "You have a name?" The question sounded almost as fragile as I felt.

Damyon wiped the tear that plunged over my lashes. "I do, and if she is still alive, I vow that I will find her for you."

I threw my arms around his middle, so grateful I had him in my life. What was one little outburst of temper when he tried so hard in every other way to make me happy?

# CHAPTER 10
*Stormy*

*Present*

MEMORIES OF THE PAST HIJACKED MY BRAIN AS I CLUNG TO Torin on the back of his bike. I tried to fight them off, but a slideshow of images flashed one after the other in a vicious cycle. By the time we arrived at my building, I was submerged in a vat of sticky, putrid self-doubt.

I'd had mind-blowing sex with Torin Byrne. Irish mobster. Boxer. Possible stalker. And my boss.

My *boss.*

*Good Lord, Stormy. Will you ever freaking learn?*

I gave Blue Bell a few quick rubs before going straight to the shower. I wanted to wash it all away—the memories and uncertainty—everything about the past. And the present, too. I wanted to rid myself of the desire that still thrummed in my veins. Of the feel of Torin's body on mine, making my heart sing.

They said hindsight was twenty-twenty, but with each minute that passed, I was more confused than ever. Sex with Torin was incredible. I'd never been so swept away by a man's touch in my life. It was also a gargantuan mistake. That should have been clear to me now that I was free from the overwhelming lust that clouded my brain when he was near. So why couldn't I summon any regret?

*Because you needed me.*

When he'd said those words, my heart had come undone. Logic evaporated. Because I *had* needed him. Desperately. I'd needed him not to be hurt, and I'd needed out of that crowd. Without a word from me, he'd known. He'd come to my rescue with ruthless ferocity. Why was that a bad thing?

I knew why. Red flags might start out smaller than those cute little drink umbrellas, but before long, that same red fabric was long enough to braid into a red rope that would cinch tight around your neck.

He was dangerous if only because he made me reckless. I'd let the man come inside me not once but *twice*, and I'd never said a word. I could have. I considered it. But if I was being brutally honest, I had wanted to feel him inside me without anything between us. Pregnancy wasn't an issue, but who knew what diseases I could contract.

Stupid. *Stupid, stupid, stupid.*

I hadn't confronted him about following me. I'd even given him directions to my place to avoid suspicion. Hell, I'd been leaving my curtains cracked in an open invitation to watch me. I hadn't fully appreciated his motives at the time, but the fact that I'd ignored the obvious danger was problem enough.

I couldn't seem to make good decisions where he was concerned, and I knew what that meant. If I couldn't stay away from him, I would have to force the issue and leave. There was only one thing more repulsive than the thought of moving again, and that was reliving my past. I refused to fall victim to another abusive man.

I wasn't certain that Torin would hurt me, but I couldn't guarantee that he was safe either. He was a fighter and a gangster. The odds were stacked against him, which meant the risk was too great. I couldn't allow myself to be blinded to the dangers. Not again.

# CHAPTER 11

*Torin*

*Present*

THERE WAS NOTHING MORE MADDENINGLY FUTILE THAN trying to guess what a person was thinking. I was one to know. I'd spent the last twelve hours trying to do just that and was no better off than when I'd started.

Something had changed for Stormy between getting on the back of my bike and arriving at her apartment. I wanted to know what that was. More than anything, I wanted to know that she didn't regret letting me fuck her.

Was it a mistake? Hell yeah, it was. Should never have happened.

Did I want her to regret it? Fuck, no.

Three issues stood out in my mind as the most likely sources of conflict for her. First, she was seeing someone and felt bad about being unfaithful. If that was the case, she'd get over it. I certainly had no remorse about interfering and would go so far as to say I hoped he never touched her again.

That left two somewhat more complicated circumstances: the fact that I was her boss, and the fact that I hadn't used a condom. Both were perfectly sound reasons to worry. As for her job, I could reassure her with a few quick words that nothing had to change. I wasn't going to fire her or treat her differently because we'd had sex.

The condom was a little trickier. I was clean, so that shouldn't have worried her, but I wasn't sure what to do about the possibility of pregnancy. Hell, I wasn't even sure how I felt about it. I'd never had a particular desire for kids. It was too hard to imagine me settling down with anyone to even entertain the possibility. Yet now that I was forced to imagine the scenario, it didn't sound so bad. A new life that would bind us together forever? I found that disturbingly reassuring.

I hadn't decided on a course of action by the time the club opened, but it turned out that I didn't need one. Stormy wouldn't even make eye contact with me.

After an hour, I forced myself to go over. "Can I talk to you for a second?" I wished it wasn't necessary, but I didn't see any other way to deflate the awkward tension poisoning the air around us.

"Actually, Jolly needed my help with the girls." She flashes a smile, her eyes grazing mine for the briefest of seconds. "I better get back there."

I let her walk away despite the growing irritation clawing under my skin. The fact that I was so bothered by her behavior added frustration to my billowing storm cloud of a mood. I'd told myself we'd be better off apart. She was saving me the trouble of raising a barrier between us, so why did that piss me off so much?

I let the thought simmer and fester for an hour before I intentionally crossed paths with her in the bathroom hallway. Things were picking up for the night. If I was going to talk with her, now was the time.

"Step outside with me. We need to talk." I cranked up my authoritarian tone so she'd be more likely to listen.

"Women's toilet is clogged." She gave a remorseful smile. "It'll have to wait." She tried to push past me. I shot out my arm and barred her exit.

"Outside. *Now*."

Her shoulders sagged, and she gave me a jerky nod as though finally accepting the inevitable. I slowly lowered my arm, noting my body's reluctance to pull away. She was so damn close, yet so totally unreachable. I wanted to wrap her in my arms and refuse to let go until she quit pushing me away.

We stepped into the cool evening air out front of the club. I led us off to the side away from customers trickling in.

Once we couldn't be overheard, I took a deep breath and blurted, "I wanted you to know I'm clean."

*Smooth, motherfucker. Real smooth.*

I swiped a hand through my unruly hair. "And I don't know what to say about the other ... if you were on the pill or not ... but I can go grab Plan B if you need it. Or not. I didn't mean to push you to ... *Fuck*." Words spilled past my lips without tact or intent. I hadn't known what to say, so it had all come out wrong.

Storm sighed, a shadow marring her usual cheer.

"Pregnancy isn't an issue, Torin. And I'm clean, too." She offered me a thin smile that grated on my last nerve. "So it sounds like neither of us has anything to worry about." She rocked back on her heels, then turned and slipped back inside.

I made no move to stop her. I couldn't. I was too busy keeping my short fuse from detonating. What the fuck was that? Did she just give me the brush-off?

*Take it for the gift that it is, dickhead.*

Shit.

Why the hell was this such a problem? Ever since losing my faith in human decency during my year away in juvie, I preferred to keep people at a distance. I should have been relieved that Storm had no expectations of me. It should have been my get-out-of-jail-free card, but instead, her casual indifference toward me felt more like salt rubbed into an open wound.

Frustration and anger blistered beneath my skin.

Without any other outlet, I kicked a rock at a parked car, then went back into the club just long enough to grab my jacket and keys. I had to get the hell out of there.

◊

I SPENT an hour at the gym burning off steam, then went into the office above the club to do paperwork. Neither activity gave me the relief I'd hoped for.

When closing time came around, I found myself ducking out of the club minutes after Storm and skulking behind her in the shadows. I had desperately hoped that fucking her would put an end to this damn obsession, but how could I let her go when something was so obviously wrong?

*Like that's the only reason, you sick fuck.*

I needed to know she made it home safely. I wanted to see for myself.

*You want to be near her.*

What I wanted was to silence that damn harpy in my mind. I already carried enough shame with me, no reason to pile on more.

Storm went inside, and as usual, I waited to see the lights go on in her third-floor apartment. My angle from the street gave me barely enough visibility to see into her place from a distance.

Now came the hardest part. Forcing myself to leave.

It was a nightly battle I didn't always win. But tonight, she gave me no option. For the first time since I started this masochistic practice, Storm pulled her drapes all the way shut.

She'd always left a gap before. Always. Why not now? Could the change in her routine be a coincidence?

Did I suddenly put stock in the unrealistic existence of coincidences? No. I was way too fucking cynical for such whimsical beliefs. But that would mean she closed the drapes as an extension of that barrier between us. But that couldn't be right because it would have meant she'd known all along. She'd known I was watching her ... and she'd let me do it. And now ... she was putting an end to it.

Fuck no.

I didn't like where this was headed. In fact, I hated it. I hated the way she was withdrawing. I hated that some other man had walked her home two nights ago. I hated that something was so obviously upsetting her, and I was clueless as to what. I hadn't forced her to have sex at the fight. That was one thing I felt certain about. She had wanted me inside her as much as I'd wanted it—so what was the problem?

Was she sleeping with that other guy? Were they in a relationship?

It occurred to me that I could go up to her place and see if there were signs of someone else. Now, I was truly traipsing into stalker territory.

Did I care?

Not enough to stop myself.

I waited until the sun started to light the sky before letting myself in the building. I wanted to make sure she was sound asleep. One of the benefits of forcing her slimy superintendent to update the security panel was getting access to the code. Getting into her place wasn't a problem. I'd copied her key ages ago. I hadn't used it until now, but damn had it been tempting.

Fascination filled me as I took inventory of her personal space. The L-shaped studio allowed for the illusion of a bedroom, and the main living space centered around a tiny sofa, a two-seater dinette, and a small but modern corner kitchen. She had a good amount of stuff crammed into the apartment, but nothing of a personal nature. I didn't see one photograph or memento hung on the wall or displayed on the windowsill aside from an empty ceramic vase.

I peeked into the bathroom, unable to see much in the darkness except to confirm only one toothbrush lay by the sink. No beard-trimmer. No men's boxers lying about. Nothing to indicate anywhere that she had a man coming over with any regularity.

My relief was diminished by a gnawing sense of irregularity that I couldn't explain. Maybe I was projecting a sentimentality she didn't possess. Not every woman was a fan of photographs and momentos. Yet she seemed like the sort who would display memories to keep them close, even when limited on space.

That conundrum would have to go unanswered.

Unable to leave without seeing her, I rounded the corner and felt a piece of my soul sigh at the sight of her, like a weary traveler returning home. Something about her called to me on an elemental level. I'd spent my adult life always on edge, but with her around, I felt a foreign sense of peace.

It was no wonder I'd developed an addiction to her.

Even now, I craved the taste of her. If I didn't think she'd run from me, I'd wake her up with my tongue and remind her how good we were together. Not today. Not when she was already wary of me.

I took one last long look, then turned for the door. That was when I noticed the magnets on her fridge. She had those multicolored letters made for children to practice learning letters and words. She also had printed words on small strips of magnet—the sort used to make fridge poetry—but the thing that caught my eye was despite the chaos, I could make out my name right in the middle. The letters weren't placed together or even all right side up, but they were there. T.O.R.I.N.

Before I knew what I was doing, my finger gently guided them around until they were all straight. What were the chances those letters happened to be close to one another? Had she spelled my name on her fridge at some point?

Even if she hadn't, I liked knowing it was there now. That was why, despite my better judgment, I left them as they were before slipping out as quietly as I'd let myself in.

# CHAPTER 12

*Stormy*

*Present*

MAYBE IT WAS TIME TO TRY OUT THE MOUNTAINS OUT WEST. I'd seen beautiful photos of Montana in the summer. I hadn't ventured that far north because of the cold, but maybe it was time. Maybe leaving big cities behind was exactly what I needed.

If that was the case, why did I feel like crying?

Each website I visited displaying the amenities of a potential destination ratcheted the vise around my chest tighter and tighter until my heart was lodged in my throat. I didn't want to leave. No, it was worse than that. The thought of leaving scratched open the scabs littering the surface of my heart.

I had friends for the first time in years. I had an apartment I loved, and a job I enjoyed when my boss wasn't making me feel a hurricane of emotions. How was I supposed to leave Micky and disappear without a word? I'd been so cautious in the past not to let myself get close to people for that reason. Leaving would have been so much harder.

This time was supposed to have been different.

I was supposed to be free to establish roots, but that had all fallen apart. Not only was I contemplating leaving but it would be ten times worse than any move I'd made before. I couldn't leave a trail. I would have to keep Micky in the dark. How insufferably cruel for both of us. I'd miss her down to my toes, and she'd probably call the National Guard when I turned up missing.

I closed my laptop, needing a break. My poor ravaged heart could only take so much. Getting the mail wasn't particularly enjoyable since it was only ever bills and junk, but it was a distraction I sorely needed, so I grabbed my keys and made for the elevator.

Lucky me, Ralph was in the lobby where the mailboxes were located. I kept my head down hoping to avoid him.

"Hey, Stormy. Long time no see!"

I grimaced. "Hey, Ralph. How's it going?"

"Good, good. I saw that friend of yours leaving this morning. Hope he saw the new security panel. No need for him to worry anymore." Ralph came closer, but I hardly noticed. I was too confused trying to figure out what he was talking about.

What friend had he seen leaving this morning? Did he mean Torin dropping me off out front?

"This morning? Or do you mean last night?"

"Nah, this morning. What was it … about six thirty, I think." He puffed out his chest. "Can't sleep the day away, lots to do around here."

That wasn't Torin. Then who?

An icy chill engulfed me. "What exactly did this friend look like?"

"Tall with curly brown hair. Blue eyes. Looked like he'd seen a fist or two recently." He leaned in conspiratorially. "Gotta say, not sure he's the sort you wanna hang around wit."

A whole new set of alarms sounded in my head. That *was* Torin. But what had he been doing at the building hours after he'd dropped me off?

"Just out of curiosity, was he in the building when you saw him?"

Ralph's eyes narrowed with the dawning suspicion that this man might not actually have been my friend. "Yeah, he was headed out the front door when I came down the stairs. I didn't want to call after him and wake anyone up."

What the heck was Torin doing in my building? How did he even get in?

"Wait, why were you wanting to know if he'd seen the panel?" I asked, trying to sound casual. "Did he talk to you about it?"

A fleeting sneer tugged at his upper lip. "Yeah, he has a real way with words, that one." Ralph's right hand clasped his left elbow as though implying Torin had gotten rough with him.

Holy crap! Had Torin threatened Ralph on my behalf?

Maybe it was a coincidence. Maybe he knew someone else in the building.

*Seriously, Storm? You think he's stalking two of you in the same building?*

"He's an intense kind of guy." I gave him an awkward smile. "I left the oven on, so I'd better get back upstairs." I hurriedly unlocked my mailbox, grabbed its contents, and waved my goodbye.

What the heck was I supposed to think about this new information? Every time I turned around, Torin was looking out for me—at the fight, with customers, and now with my super—but he did it in the most unconventional, overbearing sort of way. What if his protective gestures turned possessive? I knew all too well how these things could morph before your eyes.

I stood inside my apartment, the closed door at my back, and wondered why Torin had been in the building this morning. Why had he come back?

Sorting through the handful of envelopes, I found nothing that looked out of the ordinary. He hadn't dropped off a note in my box. Nothing had been slipped under the door, and the lock showed no signs of a break-in. What had he been up to?

Taking in a slow sweep of the room, I looked at my surroundings with fresh eyes. Could Torin have possibly been inside my apartment while I was sleeping? Nothing looked amiss. I took a slow sweep of my apartment, and that was when something caught my attention. I wasn't sure I'd have noticed if I hadn't been across the room. It was the sort of thing that was easier to see at a distance than up close.

Torin's name was spelled out on my fridge. It wasn't super obvious. The magnet letters weren't close together, but they were all right side up. I knew they hadn't been that way because I'd intentionally moved them before Micky's last visit. I'd had no desire to explain to her why I had our boss's name on my fridge.

This was no coincidence. He'd been here—in my personal space—while I'd been asleep and unprotected.

*Yeah, but did he do anything truly bad?*

If I could have slapped my inner optimist, I would have. Was I supposed to wait until he *did* do something unhinged before I cut ties? And had I totally forgotten the fact that he was my *boss*?

*Come on, Stormy. You're smarter than that.*

New York was a big city. What if I got a new job but moved so he couldn't find me? That way, I could keep my friends and still protect myself.

The idea had merit. After all, there was no reason to assume he'd try to track me down. A girl couldn't end up with two psychotic stalkers at once, right? What were the chances?

I wasn't interested in finding out.

The question was, did I relocate within Manhattan, or was it truly necessary to leave the state. My logical and emotional sides were at war over the answer.

I RODE my mental hamster wheel until I was dizzy and resorted to binge-watching reruns of *The Big Bang Theory*. The simplicity of the show was cathartic. By the time I had to show up at work, I'd summoned a cloak of cool resolve to keep myself safe by whatever means. End of story.

I was pleasant yet professional to Torin. I didn't want to

set him off before I'd had a chance to make my move, but I also wanted to ensure I didn't send mixed signals.

Judging by the glares coming from his direction, he sensed the change in me and wasn't thrilled about it. Halfway through the night, he tugged me into the supply closet and closed the door. He'd been so stealth in his actions that I never had a chance to protest.

"What's going on?" I stared at him with wide eyes, unsure if I should be worried.

Tor set his hands on his hips and studied me. "What's with the attitude?"

Something inside me snapped.

How dare he shoot accusations my way when he knew darn well what he'd been doing in his spare time? What gave men the right to think they could do whatever the heck they wanted without consequence?

I hadn't planned to confront him, but I wanted answers. I wanted him to explain himself. If I was going to call him out, best to do it in a place full of witnesses.

My eyes narrowed into angry slits. "You want to ask questions? How about this one—were you in my apartment building this morning?"

"Yes." No hesitation.

Was he not at all embarrassed to be caught in the act? Did he not see how inappropriate his behavior was?

Determined to get to the bottom of his intentions, I pushed further. "Did you break into my place?"

"No, I used the key," he offered evenly.

"Where did you get a key?"

"I copied the one in your purse."

My lips parted, then smacked together before any real words emerged. "My purse is always locked up when I'm here. How could you have possibly gotten my key to copy it?"

The look he shot me was mildly insulting.

My temper pricked with resentment. "Why would you do that? What did you think you'd achieve?"

Torin inched forward, his face growing unreadable. "Who was the guy who walked you home?"

Luke? Was Torin jealous?

I gritted my teeth. "A friend."

"Male *friends* don't show up to walk a woman home at four o'clock in the morning unless they expect something in return."

"Even if he did, it's none of your business." I pressed my finger into his chest, all sense of self-preservation smothered by righteous indignation.

Predatorial. That was the best word to describe the way he leaned in and towered over me. "The second I came inside this…" His hand firmly but gently cupped my sex. "It became my business."

The feel of his possessive touch heated me in places it shouldn't have. The blood in my veins coursed like raging rivers. Thoughts spun out of control.

*What about before? You were stalking me before I ever let you touch me.*

The words were on the tip of my tongue, trapped like flies on sticky paper. Why didn't I tell him that I knew what he'd been doing? Why didn't I push for more answers?

*Maybe you're scared he'll stop.*

That was absurd. Totally and utterly ridiculous. Of course, I wanted him to stop.

*Then say it. Tell him you know the truth.*

Silence.

The internal argument had only lasted a second, and what followed was the most telling length of silence I'd ever experienced.

I knew it. So did Torin.

He brought his hand up and cupped the back of my neck, bringing our foreheads together. And hells bells, I could smell myself on him. Through my panties and leggings, my arousal had clung to his hand. Our faces were too close. If I could smell it, then he could, too.

My eyes clenched shut with frustration.

"I'm going to ask again, Stormy. What's with the attitude?" This time, his words were a coaxing caress I could feel winding its way around my hardened heart.

"I need to set some boundaries," I whispered, eyes still shut.

Torin was quiet for so long, I gave in and peered up at him. The intensity in his turquoise irises stole my breath.

"Boundaries make me think you don't like what's happening between us." He brought his lips close to my ear, grazing his teeth over my lobe. "Makes me think you didn't enjoy what we did." He kissed my neck in languorous, unhurried reverence, his fist closing in my hair and angling my head for better access.

His touch was assertive yet devout. My breath shuddered, and my body arched into his, desperately needing more. No matter how soundly my mind believed Torin was bad for me, my body and heart disagreed. The conflict devolved into outright mutiny.

"Tell me you don't like what I'm doing. Tell me to stop." He breathed against my heated skin.

My shaking hand clasped his shirt in answer, pulling him closer.

I felt his lips pull apart in a smile. "That's my girl. You want this just as much as I do." His hand slipped effortlessly into the waist of my leggings. Not only did I not stop him but my eyes rolled back into my head as I spread my legs for him.

His touch unraveled me.

Maybe I'd simply gone too long without sex. I didn't have an explanation. I just knew I needed to feel him touching me more than I needed life itself.

In seconds, he stirred a storm of sensation, a tsunami of pleasure threatening my shores. Right before the wave could crest, he stilled.

"I can stop, Stormy. I can walk out of here and leave you alone. Is that what you want?"

I shook my head frantically, embarrassing myself with how quickly I'd abandoned my principles.

"Not enough, beautiful. I need words." He gave one lazy stroke over my clit. "Did you like it when I fucked you?"

Like it? I freaking loved it. His otherworldly touch was the only reason I couldn't think straight.

"Yes, I liked it. I wanted it," I conceded hoarsely.

"Mmm…" His masculine rumble purred across my skin, summoning an army of goose bumps. "Tell me to make you come. Make me believe you mean it."

"*Please*, Torin. I need it. Please, let me come." I didn't even recognize myself anymore. This Stormy wasn't the woman I knew. This was Torin's Storm, and she frightened me. She did exactly as she pleased; consequences be damned.

"Fuck, you're *perfect*." Torin's voice was pure reverence. "You're my little taste of heaven, and I'm going to make you come so hard you'll forget the word boundaries ever existed."

He was half right. He did make me come, and it was

spectacular. So exquisite that it took a half hour of waiting tables before I felt steady on my legs again. But I didn't forget about my need for boundaries. All he did was solidify in my mind that my heart was a damn fool.

I had zero control where he was concerned.

First thing the following morning, I started my job search. I would try to move within the city. If that didn't work, it would be time to disappear.

# CHAPTER 13

*Torin*

*Present*

I SHOULDN'T HAVE ADMITTED WHAT A CREEPER I'D BEEN, BUT damn did it feel good.

At first, I'd just wanted to see her set aside the constant sunshine and show me what lay underneath. That felt pretty fucking phenomenal, but I was surprised at how good it also felt to come clean about my true nature and not have her run screaming. Far from it. She possessed so much strength and tenacity—her courage was incredible. I was drawn to her warmth, but the fight inside her captured my respect.

Storm didn't cower from me. I'd let her see more of me

than I'd shown anyone else, and she accepted me exactly as I was. Begged me to touch her.

*Please, Torin. I need it.*

When I heard those words, I felt like I'd won a fucking world title.

Except I hadn't won anything. She technically wasn't mine, and that fact chafed more and more each day. Everything about Storm was a slippery slope, and I inched nearer to the edge with each interaction. If I wasn't careful, I would lose myself and career to the bottom in a mindless plight to claim her.

I tried not to dwell on that eventuality. If I began to believe I had no control over the matter, I'd surrender myself to my cravings for her. That was dangerous for both of us.

Fortunately, her modicum of surrender had quelled my insistent thirst. For the moment. Enough to allow me to regain some semblance of rational thought. I was able to let her be even though I could tell she still wasn't her usual self. The rest of the night was uneventful—girls danced, horny men tossed money at them, and I stuck to the shadows as I watched the woman who was slowly driving me insane.

♦

I WAS WORKING on monthly numbers in my office with Keir the following day when Oran came by. While he had an office across from us, we usually worked opposite hours, so Keir and I didn't see him.

"Hey, what's up?" I asked, leaning back in my chair.

Oran sat in the vacant guest chair, elbows propped on his knees. "I want to look into what happened to Darina, the server who disappeared. I know Caitlin said the woman was dead, but I want to know exactly what happened. Thought if you had an employment file on her, it would give me somewhere to start."

"Yeah, let me see what we've got." I sifted through the filing cabinet behind me and extracted her folder. She hadn't worked for us long before she quit showing up without even asking for the week's worth of money she was owed. We found out later that Oran's psychotic wife Caitlin had gone after the poor woman, hoping to hurt Oran because she'd seen the two together. The whole situation was fucked. It was a good reminder of why I didn't like outsiders.

Oran looked at the admittedly thin file and grimaced. "That's it? No background check or anything?"

"We only do those for the dancers to make sure they're of age. If we did checks for every staff in and out of here, it'd be a full-time job."

He shot a disapproving look at Keir, who was totally unaffected. Those two had always had a strange dynamic. They were the same age, so they were close as kids, but vying for positions in the family business seemed to put distance between them. The great thing about family, though, was that no matter how pissed we got at one another, we were all still blood at the end of the day.

"There's nothing here that I can use except for an address. I suppose it's a start," Oran muttered.

Keir finally spoke up. "The other staff might know more. She was friendly with a few of the girls. And you had a couple of conversations with her, right?"

"Yeah." Oran frowned. "But I didn't pay as much attention as I should have." His voice was thick with guilt.

"Is this some form of punishment—you looking into her disappearance?" Keir asked, point blank. He never was one to bullshit. That was why I preferred working with him over any of the others.

"Caitlin said the girl was gone. Never said she was dead. I'd say I owe it to her to make sure there isn't anything I can do. My ex was a fucking coward and a liar. I wouldn't put it past her to have manipulated the truth."

Keir dipped his chin in a nod. "Fair enough. You need a hand, let us know."

Oran was most likely beating his head against a wall, but we all had our demons. Who was I to deny him his?

Oran tossed the folder back onto the desk when Keir's phone buzzed. He stared at the screen, eyes narrowing. "Better not be a damn spam call," he groused before accepting the call. "Yeah ... oh, yeah. Storm said I might get a call."

I was instantly on alert. Who the fuck would be calling Keir about Stormy and why?

"We haven't had any problems with her at all. In fact, I kind of hate to see her go."

The fuck? See her go?

Had she applied for a new job and listed Keir as a reference? Not fucking likely.

Before I had a chance to think, I snatched the phone from his hand.

"What my cousin here is too PC to say is that Storm has a little problem with sticky fingers. He doesn't want to get sued, but I'm not afraid to tell the truth. You're going to want to steer clear of this one." As I spoke, I could feel Oran and Keir staring at me like I'd lost my goddamn mind. News flash, I had.

"Oh, I see. That's disappointing to hear, but I appreciate your honesty."

"No problem. Good luck on your search." I hung up and held out the phone for Keir. He didn't move.

"You gonna tell us what the fuck that was all about?"

"Why didn't you tell me Storm was lookin' to leave?" I asked instead of explaining.

His gaze sharpened. "Why's it matter to you if she stays or goes?"

I'd wondered if word had gotten around about my actions at the fight. Bishop had a big mouth, so I assumed Conner had heard, but it looked like the news hadn't reached my other cousins.

"I thought she and I had worked out our differences. If she's looking to leave, she should have told me herself rather than go behind my back." I dropped his phone on the desk, sick of holding it like a fuckin' golden retriever.

"Your differences? Your foul attitude running off our employees? 'Cause you can't hardly find a girl as good as her."

*Fuck, don't I know it.*

Keir was really starting to piss me off.

"Last I checked, I don't have to explain myself to you." I stood with the intent to leave, but Keir did the same, bringing us toe-to-toe.

"You may not owe me an explanation, but you do have a duty to honor our family name. If you're mistreating a woman, we're going to have a real problem."

"I would think you'd know me better than that," I bit out through clenched teeth. How fucking dare he insinuate I'd hurt Storm or any other woman for that matter?

"No one in this family knows what goes on in that head of yours. Not since you spent that year away."

The blood boiling in my veins instantly cooled and coalesced like lava pouring into the sea. My entire body stiffened.

"We're family. That's all there is to know."

His shoulders visibly deflated as I pushed past him, done with the conversation.

EVERY FIBER in my being wanted to confront Storm the second I left that office. I wanted to so badly that it physically pained me not to, but whether he knew it or not, Keir's admonishment had hit home. I hadn't made things easy on Stormy. The least I could do was give myself time to cool off before talking to her.

It was her night off from work. I managed to control myself until the following day with the intent of talking to her when she got to work.

A good plan, except that I was blistering with frustration by the time she showed up for work the next day. I felt so fucking powerless, and I hated it.

I stationed myself by the front entrance so I could get to her before anyone else. I didn't want her coming up with any excuses to avoid me.

"Hey, Storm. Can we talk for a minute?" I asked with measured calm, motioning to the nearby bathroom hallway. It wasn't an ideal location for a conversation, but it gave us at least some semblance of privacy.

"Uh, yeah." The uncertainty in her voice sent a wave of

guilt crashing over me. I might have been a surly bastard, but the last thing I wanted was to make her scared of me.

I took a steadying breath, trying my damnedest to be gentle. "I thought we were working things out, you and me. I thought we had somewhat of an understanding after the other night, but then I learned you were looking to leave. Why would you do that?"

"Are you serious?" she hissed.

All of the shields I'd been forcing to the ground were instantly back up and armed. Didn't she realize how hard I was trying? Didn't she see the sincerity?

"Yeah, I am," I bit back at her.

"Torin, I know what you've been doing, and it's not okay. I thought you were just being overprotective at first, but now … I know it's more than that. And it's not healthy."

"Letting myself in your place? You're absolutely right, but I didn't lie about it, and I can swear I won't do it again."

"*No*, Torin." Her voice dropped to an angry whisper as though protecting my secret from eavesdroppers. "The *stalking*. You've been following me for weeks now."

"And you left your shades open on purpose," I shot back, growing more defensive.

Storm stiffened. "I didn't realize the extent of the problem at first. That's an extension of my own issues. What you did is still wrong. The stalking. Letting yourself in my home. How can I feel safe around someone who's doing those things?"

How could I ever convince her that a man as fucked up as me would never harm a hair on her head? It was impossible, which meant only one thing. I was going to lose her.

I felt myself dangling from a cliff, my fingers straining to cling to the tiniest twig, keeping me from careening to my death. My ears rang, and my heart thundered to exhaustion.

"Tell me one thing," I growled breathlessly. "Have I ever done a single thing to hurt you?"

Tears gave her wide brown eyes a glassy sheen before she whispered the most heartbreaking words I'd ever heard.

"Not yet."

# CHAPTER 14

*Stormy*

*Past*

*DON'T PANIC. IT HAS TO BE HERE.*

First my phone, now my passport. I couldn't figure it out. I'd left the stupid thing in my suitcase when I unpacked at Damyon's house, and now it was gone. I hadn't taken it anywhere—how could it possibly have disappeared?

Could the staff be stealing? Damyon was a stern boss. I couldn't imagine anyone in the house taking that sort of risk. But what other explanation was there?

Could Damyon have come across it and put it somewhere for safekeeping? It wasn't unreasonable to put something like that in a safe. Daddy used to do that. But why wouldn't he have mentioned it?

*You know why.*

My gaze drifted to mirror where I could see the still-healing cut on my lip. It had hardly been Damyon's fault. I'd known better than to give him sass when he was in a mood. Honey always said my mouth would get me into trouble one day.

God I missed her. She was probably worried sick about me. I'd texted her early on, but had yet to put her number in my new phone. I hadn't even told Damyon much about her. At the time, I wasn't sure why, but now ... I touched at my lip. Maybe somewhere deep down, I'd suspected.

*Too good to be true.*

Could Damyon have done something so premeditated as take my phone and passport so that I couldn't leave him? Sure, he had a temper, but stealing such personal items as a phone and passport seemed so much more sinister. So controlling and calculating.

He hadn't forbidden me from going out, so long as I took security with me, but that was for my safety. I'd always felt protected and cared for with Damyon, aside from the few hiccups we'd had. He gave me everything I wanted and spent as much time with me as he could. But I didn't know how else to reconcile what had happened to my missing items. Could I have so sorely misjudged him?

In the month since Damyon had bruised my arm, he'd only let his anger get the better of him two other times. Once, he tugged me by my wrist so hard I thought he'd dislocated my shoulder. I'd told myself he didn't recognize his strength. That he hadn't meant to hurt me. Then, a week ago, he'd struck me. I was so shocked that I'd been speechless. I couldn't imagine a situation where my father would have hit my mother. I couldn't fathom how it had happened, but Damyon was a passionate man in every regard, and I'd argued with him, knowing he'd had a rough day.

He'd been overcome with remorse as soon as it happened. He knew it was wrong. I didn't think he'd ever intentionally do something so hurtful.

The days that followed had been filled with every form of affection I could imagine until my heart was bursting. When I thought about how sweet he'd been, I was reassured that I'd overreacted about the passport. There had to be a reasonable explanation. All I had to do was ask. And if by chance his staff was responsible, Damyon needed to know.

"Hey, babe." I grinned, finding him sitting at the kitchen table reading the paper. "I was tidying up my side of the closet and realized I can't find my passport. I know I left it in my suitcase, but it's not in there now."

He stilled. "You were looking for your passport?"

"No, not at first. Just organizing my things. When I remembered it, I decided to check and make sure I remembered where I'd left it. I'm glad I did because the darn thing isn't there. You don't think one of the staff could have taken it, do you?"

"I don't because I put the passport in my safe a while back for that very reason."

*See, there you go. A reasonable explanation.*

"Oh, okay."

Yes, a totally acceptable explanation. He wanted to look out for me, so he searched my things without asking and locked my only means of identification in his safe.

Well, that didn't sound quite so benevolent. I hated to

look at things with a jaded eye. My old neighbor, Mr. Meyers, thought the worst of everyone he came across. He was a bitter, nasty old man. I didn't want to fall into that trap, but I couldn't shake the feeling that something was icky.

Damyon came over and placed a kiss on my forehead. "Don't be worried. If it makes you feel better, you keep it where you like." He took my hand and led me to his office where he opened the safe and handed over my passport with a soft smile. "Better?"

I smiled sheepishly. "Yeah, I guess so. It made me a little anxious to think that if something happened to you, I couldn't get to it."

His brows lifted with amusement. "And what, little angel, do you think is going to happen to me?"

"Hopefully nothing, but I've seen the scarry men you work with."

His head tipped back on a laugh. "Nyet, that is just how it is to be Russian. We all look a little scarry."

I traced his bottom lip with my thumb. "Not scary, beautiful. I could hardly believe my eyes the first time I saw you."

His arms were instantly around me. "And you were the vision of an angel—my own little piece of heaven. It was impossible not to want you. How could a man lay eyes on God's most perfect creation and not go mad with need?"

God, he could make me blush. "Now you're being silly."

"Nyet." He sobered, eyes piercing me through. "You are the air I breathe. I would do anything to keep you at my side."

"Just be you," I whispered. "That's all I want. You and me together."

# CHAPTER 15
*Torin*

*Present*

NOT YET.

I felt those two words like a fist straight to my solar plexus. I'd been so winded that I hadn't tried to stop her from walking away. She genuinely expected me to hurt her in one way or another.

*Can you blame her, dickhead? Look at you. Think about the message you've been sending.*

Being the man I'd been had always served me well. It kept people at a distance, just as I preferred. But I didn't want Storm to keep her distance. I needed her to know she could trust me.

I was an avid believer that actions speak louder than words. I'd always told myself so long as my actions remained true to who I was, a grizzly exterior wasn't an issue. But I'd kept the good actions a secret, like getting her building superintendent to do his job and adding extra money to her paycheck and keeping overzealous customers at bay. She couldn't use them as part of her measure if she never knew that side of me.

In a way, I knew that I'd sabotaged myself on purpose. I hadn't wanted her to know the little things I'd done to make her life easier because it felt like admitting to weakness. I would expect someone in her position to question my intentions. However, Stormy wasn't like everyone else. She was always so damn optimistic and gave everyone the benefit of the doubt. Why, if I hadn't actually done anything to harm her, was she so convinced it was inevitable?

I knew what cynical looked like—I was a goddamn expert —but that was because I had firsthand experience with the ugliest parts of human nature. Could that be true of her as well?

Her freakishly cheery disposition made it hard to reconcile. When human depravity touched a person's life, it marked them. Tainted the soul.

Storm was too goddamn perfect to be hiding that sort of corruption. Wasn't she?

My thoughts consumed me throughout the night. I couldn't be sure about Storm's past, but I decided the one thing I could do was try to make her understand that she had nothing to fear from me. In the end, if she decided she wanted nothing to do with me, so be it. I could take rejection. What I couldn't stand was knowing I'd frightened her. That had never been my intention.

I would find a way to prove she could trust me.

*And what about you? Are you willing to trust* her?

That was another matter entirely.

*If you think that's true, you're a goddamn moron. How do you expect her to trust if you aren't willing to do the same?*

My palms tingled with a layer of sweat.

Was I actually considering this—letting someone in? How could I not? The thought of allowing Storm to walk away without attempting to change her mind felt like an epic failure. Worse, it reeked of cowardice.

I was no fucking coward.

I stewed in my thoughts and fears for the remaining hour until close. Each minute drew out into eternity until the last of the customers left.

My gut churned. My head pounded.

A small voice in the back of my head begged me to reconsider, but I ignored that little bitch and stood my ground. When Storm came to the front to leave for the night, I met her at the door.

"Can I give you a ride home tonight?"

I wasn't sure what she heard in my voice, but she took in a slow steady breath and nodded. We went outside to where I parked my bike on the sidewalk. I unclasped the helmet lock and started working on the chin strap.

"I don't think I've ever seen you ride with a helmet," she noted thoughtfully.

"Helmet's not for me." I swept her hair over her shoulders and placed the helmet on her head.

"You've been riding around with it just in case?"

"Didn't know when you might need a ride. I'm not taking any chances with you," I murmured, embarrassed at my obvious bout of overprotectiveness.

"Wait." She stopped me from climbing on. "You got this helmet ... just for me ... without knowing if you'd even need it?"

"I'm not leaving your safety to chance, Storm."

Her delicate pink tongue peeked out as she wet her bottom lip.

I didn't do kissing—it was too intimate for my liking—but I found myself craving her taste. The feel of her lips opening against mine. The sweetness of her surrender.

The need hit me with such vehemence that I had to steel myself to keep still.

"Okay," she said softly.

That one simple word calmed me more than any drugs or alcohol ever could. It felt like hope, which was something I hadn't experienced in a long damn time.

The drive to her place took all of two minutes. I helped her off the bike, my nerves amping back up to a debilitating state. My fingers felt so damn shaky, I could hardly secure the helmet back to the bike.

"I know I've fucked up, Storm." The words tumbled out without preface like flood waters breaching a dam. "And I know it may have been too much for you. I get that. But I need you to know that I would never hurt you. I act the way I do because I prefer to keep people at a distance for my own messed-up reasons. It was never a problem until you came along. I've been so goddamn torn over wanting to be near you while needing to stay away. It's made me look like a fuckin' psycho, but I swear I'm not." I sighed, my eyes drifting up to the starless sky in defeat as I heard how pathetic I sounded. It was exactly what a certified creep would have said.

I shook my head and brought my gaze back down to the

frigid concrete at our feet. "All I've ever meant to do was keep you safe. I'm sorry that I managed to fuck it all up so badly."

I couldn't stand to look at her—to see the unease or pity undoubtedly etched in her kind eyes—so I was startled when her fingers trailed gently down the front of my jacket.

"Thank you ... for your honesty."

"I'm not going to tell you what to do about the job, but I will ask that you reconsider. Stay at Moxy. I can leave you alone. Hell, I'd rather quit running the club than know I was the reason you left." I grimaced. "Shit. I'm making this about me when it's not. I mean, it is, but it's not. I gotta go before I make a bigger mess of this."

I stepped toward my bike when her hand reached for mine. The simple touch seared a scorching trail of sparks up my arm and back down my spine. I finally brought my eyes back to hers, my breath frozen in my lungs.

"I'll think about it, okay?"

I couldn't speak. My voice had abandoned me.

All I managed was a brutish grunt with a nod before scrambling onto my bike and racing away. I felt strangely lighter and wondered at the cause until I realized it was because I'd left a piece of my heart on that sidewalk, wrapped in her tender fingers.

*Please, don't let this be an epic mistake.*

# CHAPTER 16

*Stormy*

*Present*

THANK GOD I HAD THE DAY OFF BECAUSE I NEEDED TIME TO think after Torin's unexpected confession. Not that thinking had helped. My trusting nature and learned wariness were at war with one another. How was I supposed to tell if I was repeating the same mistakes of my past?

Some part of Torin spoke to my soul on an elemental level. I couldn't deny that.

He was everything I shouldn't want, though, wasn't he?

Domineering. *Yet thoughtful.*

Gruff. *Yet tender.*

He pushed most people away. *And was devoted to those he*

*didn't.*

The man was a criminal. *Says the woman who entered the country illegally.*

Every argument my brain gave, my heart countered with an equally good point. When I peeled back the layers, it was evident that I was falling for Torin Byrne, and it scared me to death.

What if I was wrong about him? What if I gave him my heart just for him to rip it in two? How was I ever supposed to trust any man after what I'd been through?

It was times like these that I missed Honey more than ever. She'd have given me the perfect advice via a Southern metaphor about flowers or the weather, baked me some praline cookies, and made me feel like I at least had a tiny bit of guidance. Without her, I was stuck in a tar pit of self-doubt.

I spent all of Sunday distracting myself with important chores like sorting through old nail polishes and untangling charging cables. If nothing else, Blue Bell was entertained.

Monday was spent getting ready for work. I had to put more effort in than normal because it was Halloween, and we were encouraged to go all out. I didn't mind because a Halloween costume was one of the few things in my life that didn't require thought. One of the great things about relocating frequently was not having to come up with a new costume. I had an epic Harley Quinn costume that I reused every year with no one the wiser.

Halloween at the club would be insane, though it helped that it fell on a Monday. Every employee was slated to work, so tip share was divided among more people, but we'd still make more than usual. People were always more generous on fun holidays like Halloween.

I was looking forward to the night and cautiously optimistic about seeing Torin. I probably shouldn't have been, but I couldn't change how I felt. Mama used to say that feelings can't be wrong. The way things were going, we'd find out soon enough if that was true.

♦

I WAS GOING to eat my weight in ramen when I got home. Working nearly nine hours straight with only a few quick breaks left me beat.

"Last call, then we're home free." Candice, one of the bartenders, announced while I gulped from a now warm energy drink. I'd opened it an hour ago and never had a chance to take a sip. I desperately needed a boost, even if I was almost done for the night.

"Time's flown by, but my God, has it been busy," I replied.

The man at the end of the bar who'd been chatting with me on occasion piped in. "I don't know how you ladies do it. I'm tired just watching you race around this place."

"You get used to it, but holidays are extra crazy." I wasn't sure how familiar he was with the scene. He must have been comfortable hanging out all night mostly by himself, but he wasn't a regular. Maybe in town on business or something.

"Speaking of, it looks like someone's trying to get your attention." He motioned toward the stage where a man waved his hand drunkenly in the air.

"Duty calls." I plastered on my *bless your heart* smile and began my round of last call orders.

I'd gone by three tables when the music suddenly stopped, and Torin's voice boomed over the speakers.

"Club's closed," he announced harshly. "Those with open tabs, cash out and leave. Party's over."

I glanced at Candice, wondering if she had any idea what was going on, but she looked just as shocked as I did. Shrugging, I hurried over to the computer to start closing out the open tabs.

"Well, guess that's my cue. You ladies have a great rest of your night." The guy at the bar had been paying cash, so I didn't have to worry about cashing him out and tossed a quick, "You too," over my shoulder.

Out of the corner of my eye, I caught sight of Torin behind the man.

"Except you," Tor said in sharp warning. "You. *Stay.*"

Unsure if I'd heard correctly, I looked behind me, eyes widening at the way Torin had his hand firmly on the man's shoulder.

What the heck was going on? I wouldn't get any answers until the place was empty, so I whipped back around and finished closing out the tabs. Once I'd retrieved the final signatures and input tips, I stashed the receipts and reached for my drink as the last of the crowd dispersed.

Torin's hand clamped down on my wrist. "Don't fucking touch it."

"What? Why?"

"Hey, man. What's this all about?" the guy at the bar asked, looking panicked.

"Blaze, grab whoever's up front and tell everyone else to leave."

Guess Tor wasn't interested in answering questions.

Jolly strolled in from the back about then, leaning unbothered against the wall.

When the last customer was out, and the two guys up

front made their way back, Torin set the energy drink on the bar and glared at the man with a rage so palpable, the air around him vibrated with it.

"*Drink.*"

"What?" Sweat now dotted the man's forehead. "Look, I'm not sure what's going on here, but I think you've mistaken me for someone else."

"You wish. Now drink the fucking drink before I shove the whole goddamn can down your throat."

Torin wouldn't freak out for no reason. Did he think the guy had done something to my drink? I was always meticulous about keeping open beverages behind the bar on the back wall counter where they were safe. That was where it had been when I came over to close tabs, but I couldn't remember for the life of me if that was the case earlier.

The guy looked utterly petrified as he reached for the can and took a sip. I kind of felt bad for him only because I hated seeing someone in distress, but if he had tried to drug me...

"Fuck this," Torin growled. "Hold him."

Blaze and another bouncer each grabbed one of the man's arms, securing them behind the back of the chair at awkward angles. The man cried out and struggled but had no leverage to gain traction.

Hand over my mouth in horror, I watched as Torin pinched the man's nose shut, then poured the liquid down his throat. Forced to swallow, the man choked and sputtered, trying to gasp for air.

I didn't realize I was swaying until Jolly's hand firmly but gently clasped my arm.

"Okay, kid," Jolly said to Torin in his usual unhurried drawl. "You tend to this one. I'll take care of him."

I'd always considered Jolly one of those guys with a gruff

exterior who was all soft on the inside. I was starting to realize I'd been wrong. His voice had a steel edge I hadn't imagined he possessed, and I wasn't the only one who heard it. The man blanched.

"Take him to The Rack. Talk to Constantine and tell him this is a gift for Perillus."

"I'm familiar with The Rack, if you're talking about that gay sex club on the east side, but I don't know who Perillus is."

The faintest hint of a smirk carved across Jolly's face. "Not who. *What.*"

When the guys looked confused, Torin explained. "It's a *highly* secret extension of the club for extreme S&M. Before you get any ideas, I'm *not* a fuckin' participant. Con and I go back a long time."

Jolly left my side and started around the bar. "Come on, fellas. Time to have some fun."

"Guys, come on," the man stammered. "The girl is fine. No harm, no foul."

My stomach turned. I hated to think about what he'd planned for me, and somehow, envisioning his punishment only made things worse. I never could stand the thought of suffering on the part of any man or animal. It wasn't in my nature, no matter how vile the creature.

I reminded myself to focus on how this would hopefully save a future victim. Who knew how many others would suffer if he wasn't stopped.

Torin took my hand and led me back to the locker room for my stuff.

"I'm not sure about all this, Torin. What's going to happen to him?" My jittery fingers wouldn't cooperate as I tried to work the lock. It took three tries before the latch gave.

"You know he tried to drug you, right?"

"Yeah, I gathered. But his plan didn't work. I don't know…"

"You're too sweet for your own damn good," Torin muttered under his breath.

"Don't I know it," I clipped back more to myself than him.

After slipping on one arm of my jacket, I had to spin in a circle to find the other.

Where the heck did it go?

I started to giggle at the absurdity of my jacket playing games with me like Tom chasing Jerry round in circles. My laughter intensified.

"That was what I was afraid of." Torin's hands pinned me in place; his rough voice like velvet dragged slow across my skin.

I stopped breathing and peered up at him. "Say it again."

"What?"

"Anything," I breathed.

"Jesus *fuck*." It was even more guttural than before.

My eyelids drifted shut as I absorbed the euphoria that washed over me.

"We've gotta get you home and quick." He ushered me toward the front entrance of the building. "Think you can walk? There's no way I'm putting you on my bike like this."

"Yeah, I'm good. I'm *real* good."

Torin grunted.

He guided me on the short walk to my place, and I made it to within twenty feet of my building before my legs quit working. Silly knees went all wobbly like wet noodles.

I clung to Torin's arm the best I could, but it was no use. My brain couldn't convince my body to cooperate. Then I was flying in the air the same way I had as a little girl on our swing set in the backyard.

"Whee!" My head tipped back with the motion, then righted itself, my blurry gaze attempting to focus on the most breathtaking blue eyes I'd ever seen. A rich aqua that somehow shone at night just as brilliantly as during the day. Like a *Twilight* vampire. And he was strong enough, too. Oh, wow. Maybe he *was* a vampire. Except that scar on his eyebrow wouldn't be possible. I loved that scar. It made him look rugged. Just the right balance of pretty and masculine.

Torin huffed. It sounded kind of like a laugh. What was funny? I didn't say anything. Or did I?

I closed my eyes to try to think, but instead, it just made time skip.

One blink, we were at my front door.

Two blinks, and I was cuddling beneath the covers in my bed.

There were no more blinks after that.

WAKING up with a headache was the worst. It took the phrase "waking up on the wrong side of the bed" to another level. When your head hurt, it felt like losing the race before it even began.

I groaned as I recalled how I'd been drugged by a slimy jerk who I actually had the nerve to feel sorry for. Now that my skull was trying to crack open like an Easter egg, I wasn't so forgiving.

"You'll probably want to drink as much water as possible today."

My eyes shot open at Torin's voice in my bedroom, the

midday sun shooting tiny lasers into my retinas. "You're here."

"I am. I didn't want to leave you alone after being drugged." His voice sounded like it had been roasted over hot coals, making me wonder if he'd slept at all. "Do you remember what happened?"

"Yeah, mostly." I paused, reconsidering. "Up until we got to my building. That's all pretty fuzzy." I sat upright to see Tor where he sat in the loveseat that made up the entirety of my living room furniture. He looked like hell, though I suspected I looked worse.

I did my best to smooth back my hair as Blue Bell curled up in my lap.

"You have a cat." He didn't sound amused.

I bit back a smile. "I do. His name is Blue Bell."

Torin's eyes surveyed my ceiling briefly before circling around to where tufts of white hair covered his charcoal shirt. He swiped halfheartedly at the fur before giving up.

"Thank you ... for helping me."

My brain could hardly process how I felt—the man who'd been stalking me had saved me from being assaulted. I couldn't account for what had happened after I'd gotten home, but for some inexplicable reason, I wasn't worried. It was utter madness, but I felt safe with Torin here. I'd wanted to trust him from the beginning. I *had* trusted him, in a way. But my instincts hadn't served me well in the past.

Anyone with half a brain would be scared of a man who did the things Torin did. He was dangerous, no question about it. But was he dangerous toward me?

God, I hoped not.

My enigmatic boss slowly unfolded from the loveseat and stretched tall before helping himself to the fridge. He poured two glasses of filtered water, bringing one to me and downing the other in a single go. "Painkillers?" he asked.

"Medicine cabinet." I motioned toward the bathroom.

He brought me two pills and waited until I'd downed them. "I've taken you off the schedule until Friday so you have plenty of time to recover. Now that I know you're okay, I'll let you get some rest."

"Tor?"

He paused, looking back.

"How did you know?"

Twin pools of earnest aqua stared at me. "I was watching."

Watching me.

"You came from upstairs," I noted.

"Saw him do it on the security cameras."

He was watching the security cameras. Watching me. How often did he watch me like that? Should I have been upset? Maybe. But what mattered was how I *actually* felt, not how I *should* have felt. Maybe I was crazy, but all I could summon was intense relief. Somebody was looking out for me. I was safe. Wasn't *that* what counted?

I gnawed on my bottom lip before dipping my chin in a nod. "I'll stay at Moxy, so long as I feel safe."

Torin's chest expanded with a deep breath, then exhaled what looked like years' worth of tension. "Text me if you need anything."

I watched him slip out the door and wondered how someone who seemed to verge on uncivilized half the time could also be so dang sweet. The question was complicated on a good day but damn near impossible to think about with a hangover.

I took one more long drink of water and nestled back under the covers, not waking again until after dark.

# CHAPTER 17

*Torin*

*Present*

"You took him to Perillus? That's some serious *Pulp Fiction* shit. He won't be able to sit for a week." Oran's tone was more contemplative than judgmental. That was his MO lately. The energy he exuded had simmered to an almost eerie calm.

"Well deserved, I'd say."

"Mmm," he hummed his agreement. "She doing okay?"

My jaw clenched involuntarily. "I assume so." Stormy hadn't contacted me, and I'd forced myself to give her space, but fuck if it wasn't driving me crazy. I hated not knowing. "She's back at work tonight. Should be downstairs soon if she's not already." That was the sole reason I'd shown up early. So early, I'd gone up to my office to kill time, where Oran had found me.

"Good, I'd like to talk to her about Darina. That's why I stopped by. I figured I'd chat with anyone who might have been friendly with her."

Tension coalesced in my muscles. I was such a fuckin' nutjob where Stormy was concerned that I didn't even like the thought of my cousin talking to her. He might have set aside his Prince Charming act for the moment, but I knew how women responded to him.

"Yeah, I suppose we might as well go down and get that out of the way." I followed him out of the office, itching to see her.

I'd been hiding in my office Halloween night, convincing myself that it was best to let Stormy go, but after everything that had happened—after the things she'd said and how she'd looked at me—that ship left port and was long beyond the horizon.

Storm was going to be mine. End of discussion.

Oran talked to the bartender briefly. She and Darina hadn't spent much time together, so she had little to offer. Jolly was at the bar and had an emergency contact number for Darina, but that was it. Two other girls said that despite being friends at work, the missing woman hadn't told them much of anything about herself. By the time we finally got around to Stormy, the Friday evening rush had picked up.

"I know you only have a minute, but I wanted to ask you about Darina," Oran said, speaking up over the music.

"Of course!" Stormy said brightly. "I hate that she's still missing. You think she could have left on purpose?"

Oran and I exchanged a hard look. "No. Unfortunately,

we have information that something terrible may have happened to her. She managed to cross paths with someone..." He cleared his throat. "Well, heartless doesn't begin to describe them."

Right before my eyes, Storm's peaches and cream skin faded to a sickly white. "Hey, man. No need to upset her."

Oran's lips thinned. "I'm going to do what I can, but anything you might remember would be helpful."

"Definitely." Her brows knitted together. "Let me see ... We didn't exactly hang out, but I happened to run into her twice at the laundromat I use."

"You live down by 21st Street?"

"What?" Storm angled her head in confusion. "No. I'm right here just a couple of blocks from the club on 36th."

Oran's stare intensified. "She give you the impression she lived nearby?"

"Yeah, she lived somewhere right by me, but I didn't ask which building. We talked about how she used a nail salon one block over that I'd wanted to check out." Storm paused and glanced briefly at me. "Was her address not on her employment application?"

Oran's lips thinned. "The address she gave wasn't valid. Is there anything else you can remember from your interactions with her that would give me any info about her at all?"

"Not off the top of my head, but I'll give it some thought. I'm sorry."

"Don't be, this is all very helpful." Oran placed a hand on Storm's shoulder. "Could you take me by the laundromat and nail salon to show me exactly where you were? I'm happy to give you a ride so it won't be a pain."

"Absolutely. Anything I can do to help. I'm off tomorrow if that works."

"No, she's working," I blurted, sounding like I'd just emerged from the Cro-Magnon Era. I couldn't help it. I'd already envisioned chopping off Oran's fingers for touching her.

Storm stared at me with wide eyes. "It's my day off."

"Not anymore. We changed the schedule, remember?" I tried to sound nonchalant but knew it came off a little churlish.

Oran shot me a raised brow in his gray suit with perfectly styled hair and a face that wasn't covered in faded bruises from a fight.

*Yeah, asshole. Stay in your lane.*

"Is there a day that works better for you?" Oran asked me rather condescendingly.

"Sunday. We'll meet you wherever it is you need to go."

"Whatever, man," he said under his breath. "Storm, I appreciate all your help. We'll get together on Sunday." He cut a glare in my direction before excusing himself.

I grimaced as I pushed off in the opposite direction, hoping to lick my wounds in the privacy of the supply closet, except Storm didn't get that memo. The swoosh of her hurried steps chased me.

"What the heck was that all about?" Her voice wasn't as accusatory as it could have been, but I still felt defensive.

I pretended to scan the contents of a shelf. "He told you. He's looking for Darina."

"Torin Byrne, you know what I mean." She shut the door behind her and tried to look stern. "Why did you freak out about me showing Oran the places Darina had been?"

"I think *freak out* is a bit of an exaggeration, don't you?"

Lie. Deflect. Dismiss. Shit, was I gaslighting her?

"You forget you're talking to a Southern girl who knows all about being dramatic. Tor, I told you I don't want to feel threatened, and when you get all scary possessive, guess what?"

Fuck, she was hot when riled.

My eyelids lowered like a well-fed cat when I looked at my avenging angel. "You're right." I walked toward her until her back was up against the door. "I was feeling possessive. I know how appealing Oran can be. Women have always lined up for a chance with him. Is it so shocking that you might want the same?" I trailed my hand from her chin along her jaw and down the column of her neck, thrilled when her breathing grew shallow and lips parted.

"I'm only interested in helping him find Darina." Her voice dropped an octave, spurring me on.

"That's how his type lures you in. The well-dressed gentleman with good intentions. You'll never. See it. Coming." My hand continued down toward the outside curve of her breast. Her back arched, eyes dilating.

"What you don't realize," she said breathlessly, "is that I've had polished and sophisticated."

"And?"

"It's just a facade. I'd rather have honesty any day of the week."

I placed my palm over her ribs and trailed my hand down to her waist. "And what if honest turns out to be a little fucked up?"

Her hands came up to cup either side of my neck, giving me all the encouragement I needed to continue my path down to the apex of her thighs. I cupped her sex, the feel of her soft warmth sending my dick half mad with need.

"Who says we aren't all a little fucked up?"

That was it. I was going in.

Thank Christ for stretchy leggings—they were so much easier to get into than jeans. My hand was against her skin and sliding between her slick folds in seconds. "You don't get to say shit like that, angel. Not without making me need to reward you."

Stormy's body froze beneath my touch. "Don't call me that." She gave a couple sharp shakes of her head. "Anything but that."

Her visceral reaction stunned me. Why did she hate being called angel?

"Hey, *shh.*" I tried to soothe her, noting her pulse point thrumming at the base of her neck. "It won't happen again. Promise."

She gave an almost childlike nod. It was the most vulnerable I'd ever seen her, and it caused something to shift inside me. From the beginning, I'd wanted to possess and protect her. Those two desires came somewhat naturally to me. This new yearning she'd unlocked was different. It wasn't about physical protection. I wanted to take care of her —make sure she never had reason to worry and make damn certain that light in her eyes never dimmed.

A shiver cascaded down my spine as I licked my lips and prepared to do something I hadn't done since high school. I was going to kiss a woman. Not just any woman. I was going to kiss Stormy Lawson because she might not have been my angel, but she sure as hell had my heart.

Our breath was the first to mingle before my lips hesitantly grazed hers. I wanted to take it slowly, not out of fear but rather to savor the moment. I wanted her to feel the depth of meaning I placed in my actions because nothing I did was ever arbitrary. I lived each day with intent, and today, I gave Storm a piece of myself I'd never given to another.

My hands cupped either side of her face as my lips pressed ardently against hers. The way her lips softened against mine, her body melting into me, made me ravenous. I deepened the kiss, allowing my tongue to graze hers. Her taste was euphoric. Sweet yet sultry and so damn radiant it could have been pure sunshine.

We devoured one another, teeth grazing and tongues rolling. My lungs ached with each deeply held breath as I tried to take some part of her with me, even if just the air she breathed. What I couldn't possess, I memorized. Touch. Taste. Feel. I impressed every minute detail possible into my memory banks, hoping to keep this moment alive forever in my mind's eye. Because eventually, I had to pull away, though it made the savage inside me thrash violently against his iron cage.

"I should probably get to work," she murmured, her words breathy and lips delectably swollen.

"The boss won't mind if you need to take a minute." I cupped the back of her neck and pulled her in for one last press of our lips before letting go and opening the door behind her.

"It's the customers I'm worried about." She smiled shyly. "They'll start to riot soon."

"You know I don't let anyone disrespect you. Someone gets mouthy, I'm just one look away."

Storm bit back a smile and shook her head at me in playful admonishment before going back into the club. If only she knew the full extent of what I'd done for her. There was a reason the patrons who bothered her never did it again. They'd be dead if they did, and each one of them knew it. I'd made sure the message was well received after I followed them home.

Storm would likely be appalled.

Good thing my conscience was clean because I wasn't about to stop.

# CHAPTER 18

*Stormy*

*Present*

I REFUSED TO BE A VICTIM. I'D TOLD MYSELF YEARS AGO THAT I would learn from my experiences, but I was absolutely not allowed to play the victim. For that reason, I made an effort to look on the bright side of every situation. I didn't want the pain of my past to taint my future. I was a survivor.

That being said, I had no control over my reaction to Torin calling me angel. That term had history. It had meaning for me that Torin couldn't fathom, and the fact that he'd chosen to call me that had shaken me. But his response to my distress had been the perfect balm.

He was gentle and reassuring and respectful, all at the flip of a switch. The instant he realized I was upset, he didn't get defensive or try to convince me I was being silly. He listened. He understood.

Those two things were more attractive than any fancy suit or set of dimples.

And that kiss? Sweet Mother Mary, was that the best kiss of my life. I could have stayed in that closet, lips pressed to Torin's, and died a happy woman.

I didn't like showing my vulnerable side, but if that was the reward, I had to reconsider. It felt good to let down my guard. I let myself mull over my feelings as I worked that night and realized something huge.

I wanted to trust Torin.

I wanted to have a partner and know my heart was safe in his hands, but how could I when he did crazy things like freak out just because his cousin asked for my help? I had baggage with that sort of behavior that made me a little more wary than other women might be. He was still a little over the top, but even the little things scared me.

A thought I hadn't considered before occurred to me.

I could always tell him the truth—help him understand why I was so cautious by telling him about my past. I could let him see exactly what he was getting into by wanting to be with me. If it scared him off, problem solved. If it didn't, maybe we'd have a chance. Maybe, for once, I'd feel safe. And as a bonus, I wouldn't have to run. That alone made the notion worth considering.

I'd hidden for so long that exposing my past felt frightening. How would Torin react? There was a real chance he and his Irish family would be furious to know what I'd brought to their doorstep.

*That's only if danger ever does arrive. Though at this point, what are the chances?*

It was something to consider. Maybe sometime when my blood wasn't buzzing with endorphins. Torin Byrne didn't just light a fire inside me, he brought me into the light after years of darkness. I was starting to believe he wouldn't physically harm me, but he still posed a threat. My heart couldn't stand another stint in the shadows. If I allowed myself to let him in, he'd have the power to steal every bit of sunshine I'd fought so hard to hold on to. All the hope and joy I'd rekindled. That was an enormous risk to take. Was I willing to take the leap?

♦

TORIN REALLY DID MAKE me work the following night. I wasn't upset about working per se, but I didn't feel like allowing his possessive behavior to go unchecked was a good idea. If I was going to work on trusting him, he would have to do the same for me.

"You have plans for Thanksgiving?" he asked while I was getting the bar set up for the night.

"I'll be staying home. Why? Were you hoping to have me work Thanksgiving as well?" I lifted a brow, making sure he knew I disapproved of his behavior the day before.

"You know the club is closed that day," he grumbled with a touch of contrition.

"Do I? I figure I never really know where you're concerned." I finished scooping cherries into a container and dropped the empty jar in a trash bin.

"You're not going to let me live that down, are you?"

"I would if I knew you wouldn't go all caveman on me again."

His eyes dropped to his hands in an uncharacteristic show of uncertainty. "What if I backed off the Oran thing?"

"What exactly do you mean by back off?" I asked, my voice softening.

"If there's someplace you need to show him, I don't need to act as a chaperone. You two can go see whatever it is he needs to see." He flitted his fingers in the air dismissively.

A part of me wanted to shoot back a patronizing thank you for his generosity, but despite the absurdity, he was trying. I needed to acknowledge and encourage this unexpected concession rather than mock it.

"I'd appreciate that show of trust," I offered in a sincere, sober tone.

He casually leaned forward, reaching across the bar to extract a single cherry from the container and raised it to my mouth. I had to fight back a grin. Parting my lips, I took the sweet fruit on my tongue. His tropical eyes darkened with a raging storm of desire as he plucked the stem from the cherry. I took my time savoring the sugary treat and lavishing in the feel of knowing I affected him so profoundly.

For the rest of the night, we performed a seductive dance from a distance. Furtive glances. The accidental brush of a hand. A tease of skin on display. By the time I got home, every nerve ending in my body tingled with the need for release. Even more so when I opened the drawer to my nightstand and saw the note next to my vibrator.

*Think of me when you're using this.*

I couldn't help but grin as I shook my head. That man had no freaking boundaries, and that should have been a problem. What did it say about me that I didn't seem to care?

◊

Torin kept his promise and bowed out of my excursion with Oran. As expected, the outing was brief and purely informational. Torin's cousin was entirely too fixated on uncovering information about Darina to even think of hitting on me. I was glad he was so focused on finding her. It was far too easy to make a woman disappear. If anyone knew that, it was me.

A few days later, I was on a second outing with yet another Byrne family member. Rowan was a vivacious breath of fresh air that I took to instantly. She'd come by the bar a few times—even danced on stage once to piss off Keir before they ended up married.

The girl had balls, and I was there for it.

She might even have become my hero. I got the sense she blazed her path in the world on her terms, and I loved that. When I was given the opportunity to go shopping with her one day, I jumped on the invite.

"You know I'm dying to ask you about Torin," Rowan said as we strolled by racks of clothes at H&M. I was pretty sure she could afford way nicer stuff, but she didn't push to go anywhere fancier. Another point in her favor.

"Torin? What about him?" I didn't know where to begin, so I played dumb instead.

"I've seen the way you two are around each other. Your sexual tension is off the charts! You can't tell me nothing's happened between you."

Heat crept up my neck and blossomed on my cheeks. "I suppose I won't deny it, but that still doesn't mean I know what to tell you. Torin is ... complicated. Things between us are beyond confusing."

"Say no more." She lifted her hand and dipped her chin as though singing praise in a small country church. "If there's anyone who understands, it's me. Keir acted like he was equally likely to kiss me as he was to kill me. Hell, he married me without my permission after drugging and kidnapping me. That's *not* normal. None of them are, if you ask me."

I froze, my mouth gaping wide. Rowan took a second to realize I'd stopped before grinning on her way back to me.

"Are you freakin' kidding me? He really did all that? And you're still with him?"

She shrugged. "I told you. If there's anyone who understands, it's me. Sometimes life is complicated, and it sucks, but sometimes life is complicated in the most incredible way imaginable. I've never been happier since Keir came into my life. With a knife. After breaking into my parents' house."

I grabbed her hand. "Okay, that's it. We're finding a place to sit, and you're telling me *everything*."

She laughed and let me tug her along.

We sat in the mall food court for over an hour, completely forgetting about shopping. I ate up her words far more hungrily than the soft pretzel in front of me. Their story was fascinating. It helped me realize that unconventional wasn't necessarily bad.

"I appreciate you sharing all this," I said with a warm smile.

"Absolutely. I just hope it helps. I may not know Torin well, but I know Keir, and I'm learning more about their family every day. They're good people. Maybe not the most lawful, but still good. It took me a while to understand the difference."

Rowan didn't know, but she'd just touched on the crux of my dilemma. One of them, at least.

I was relieved to hear that Torin might not be as dangerous as my mind led me to believe, but that didn't change my situation, did it? Even if he was a good man, was I willing to bring so much danger to him and his family by having a relationship with him? Keir and Rowan and Oran and all the other Byrnes. Could I, in good conscience, drag them into my nightmare?

*Is that your decision to make? They're freaking gangsters. Maybe what you think of as dangerous is just another Tuesday to them.*

Time seemed to grind to a halt as the thought formed. Had I nurtured my fears so ardently that I failed to consider they might not be a problem for someone else? Or was I merely being selfish? I didn't want to rationalize away the dangers just because I wanted to be with Torin.

I would have to give it some thought because my past *was* dangerous. It had long, pointy talons that could shred my world to pieces. My present wasn't all that innocent, either, but was I willing to pit them against one another in a fight to the death?

The possibility chilled me to the bone.

# CHAPTER 19
*Stormy*

*Past*

"IVAN'S WIFE SEEMS NICE." IF YOU WERE INTO BEAUTIFUL AND aloof—she hardly said five words all evening. Her English wasn't great, but that hardly stopped the other wives and girlfriends I'd been introduced to in the past eight months. At least they smiled and tried to be friendly. I'd even become close with a couple. It felt so good to have female companionship again, especially since Damyon had been on edge ever since we'd returned from the trip to Paris he'd surprised me with two weeks ago.

"She was rather stunning, yet I noticed Ivan could not

take his eyes off you." His menacing undertones put me on alert.

I'd thought we'd put this sort of behavior behind us. He hadn't stepped a toe out of line for months. But his temper had resurfaced, and I found myself constantly monitoring his moods and my actions. The last thing I wanted was to set him off, but it was so hard to tell sometimes what might flip that switch. I'd even begun to question whether staying had been the right decision.

"He probably wondered why someone as devastatingly handsome as you had picked a country bumpkin like me," I teased, hoping to lighten his mood.

"Or he was enjoying the way your tits were on display." His icy stare drifted down to my cleavage. "I knew I should have made you change before we left the house. You looked like a whore."

My shoulders curled in as my hand drifted up to cover my chest. I wasn't sure anyone had ever said something so hateful to me in my entire life. I wanted to wrap myself in a blanket to keep the downpour of shame from soaking me to the bone.

"You don't mean that," I whispered, eyes cast down to the floor. My chest had filled out the dress, but I hadn't thought it was distasteful.

"I did not say you were one. Do not get melodramatic with me." He walked dismissively to the crystal decanter full of his favorite vodka and poured himself a drink. "When you take that off, I expect to see it in the trash where it belongs."

Tears pooled in my eyes as I walked away.

This was *not* how a relationship should be. I wrote off the incidents early on, but I couldn't accept this type of behavior if it was going to be a pattern. He was like two different men.

I adored the devoted man I first met, but this darker side of Damyon was terrifying. Hurtful. I needed some time to think. I needed my Honey.

Two hours later, I was curled up in bed when Damyon joined me. I'd been rehearsing what I wanted to say over and over in my head, but the words were still fragile and uncertain when I spoke.

"I was thinking, and I'd really like to take a short visit back home. I miss my friends, and that's been weighing on me. It's made me sensitive." I hoped that if I made it sound like the conflict between us was my fault, he might be more agreeable. No matter how perfectly I worded my request, however, I fully expected resistance.

"You have a credit card. If you feel you need to take a trip, you're welcome to make the arrangements."

I turned to face him in my surprise. I'd been certain he would be upset.

"I knew there'd come a time when you wanted to go back," he explained.

"Just for a visit. I'd love to see my family and friends and eat my weight in fried chicken." My voice was light and carefree. I wanted to reassure him in every way possible that he was making the right choice.

Damyon clicked off his bedside lamp and lay on his side facing away from me. "Do what you need to do, moya angel."

By turning away, was he showing me his displeasure? He'd used my pet name—my angel—and that was usually a good sign, but what if I was wrong? Could this possibly be a test?

When he was in this sort of mood, I overanalyzed everything he said and did, trying to gauge how he might be feeling and how careful I needed to be. I went round and round for what felt like hours before finally deciding to take the chance and trust that he meant what he'd said.

First thing the following morning, I booked a flight for the next day. The ticket was expensive, but Damyon had been insistent since we met that pinching pennies was an insult, as though he couldn't support me. He said it would make others think he was weak, so he was adamant I shopped at only the finest stores. A last-minute first-class plane ticket was nothing compared to the cost of some of the jewelry I now owned.

I had everything packed that night, and the following morning, one of our security guards took me to the airport. I was filled with so much excitement and trepidation that my stomach was a churning pit of nerves.

I'd hoped Damyon would take me to the airport himself. It would have gone a long way to reassure me he wasn't upset about the trip. Instead, he'd been eerily distant. His mood scared me, but what was done was done. I could only hope the small time apart would smooth things over between us.

Once at the airport, I wound my way through security, pulling my carry-on bag with my passport in hand. When it was my turn, I handed over the booklet and smiled at the balding man with skin so weathered it was almost leather. He muttered something in Russian.

"I'm sorry, I don't understand," I said with a pleading smile.

He shook his head, handed the book back to me, then waved me back to where I'd come from.

"What do you mean? Why can't I go through?" Trepidation sent my stomach plummeting into my Jimmy Choos.

Another member of airport security joined us as the people behind me in line grew agitated at the delay. The two men talked before the new guy took my passport, opened it to the main page, and said a single word.

"Expired."

"What? No, that can't be right. It's brand new." The dang thing was supposed to be good for ten years. When I looked at the date, I saw that they were right even though I specifically remembered looking at the expiration when I first received the passport and knew the date as shown wasn't what it had said back then.

The lady behind me pushed forward, muttering something harshly.

I stumbled back down the line, bumping into people in a baffled haze. How had this happened? What was I supposed to do if my passport was expired? Did I go to the US embassy?

Before I could come up with an answer, I emerged from the security line to see Damyon standing near the airport entrance, his arms crossed over his broad chest.

He knew.

He'd let me go because he knew I couldn't get anywhere. This had all been for my benefit, so I'd know he had me trapped.

*Dear God.*

I tried to swallow past the terror lodged in my throat. It was no use. Even if I could speak, I didn't know what I'd say. There were no words for this situation.

As soon as I was close enough, Damyon turned and led us out to his waiting car. What else could I do but follow? I had no friends or family here and no way to escape. The only thing I could do was try with everything I had to smooth this over. But how did I do that when all I wanted to do was scream at him and launch accusations? He'd planned this. Not last night or even last week. He'd planned this *months* ago when he'd first taken the passport.

We rode home in silence. It was the most suffocating, oppressive silence I'd ever experienced—like diving deep below the ocean's surface where the pressure pounded in your ears and made your lungs burn.

Damyon carried my suitcase into the house and left it by the stairs.

More silence.

I was about to haul the thing to our room when my heartbreak got the better of me. I turned tear-filled eyes to the man I'd given my heart to and whispered, "Why?"

That was it. That was all he needed, like a tiny tripwire detonating a bomb.

"*Why?* Because you belong to *me*," he screamed. His voice bellowed throughout the house and rattled my bones.

He charged forward. "I told you I would never let you go. Did you think I was joking?" His ice-blue eyes had always looked striking, but now I realized they were a warning about the soulless monster lurking inside him. The physical embodiment of evil.

I shook my head frantically, trying to save myself from the quicksand tugging me under.

Damyon's hand clamped viciously around my throat. "How dare you try to leave me. No one disrespects me like that. *No one!*" he shouted, his angry breath searing my face.

I couldn't breathe. I couldn't think.

Terror seized hold of me in a way I'd never experienced. I tugged at his fingers and mouthed the word, "Please," over and over and over. But it was no use.

The demon inside him had control with no plans of letting go.

My lungs felt drenched in hot oil. Black dots spotted my vision, growing larger by the second until I could barely see.

This was it.

This was how I died.

I knew it with a certainty as strength fled my muscles, then I was in the air, flying. I'd welcomed the hereafter, except instead of a bright light, there was only pain. My body crashed against something impossibly hard, then darkness.

♦

I DIDN'T KNOW what was worse, waking up to an excruciating headache or having the man who'd caused it hold me tenderly in his arms. I didn't want to face him—to face my situation. I cursed my luck for not hitting my head hard enough such that I didn't remember what had happened.

Forgetting would have been so much easier. But I did remember, and there would be no forgetting anymore.

What on earth was I supposed to do? The question alone made my head pulse. My body tensed against the pain, alerting him to the fact that I had woken.

"Moya milaya Alina, I am so very sorry."

My body shook with uncontrollable sobs.

"You have to understand how much you hurt me. I cannot stand the thought of you leaving me." His words intensified my sobs, which tightened the vise around my skull. Nausea churned up a riotous storm in my stomach.

"Oh God." I clamped a hand over my mouth and wriggled out from his hold.

He reluctantly allowed me to scurry away, and I made it

to the bathroom just in time. Over and over, I heaved into the cold porcelain toilet.

Damyon was there in an instant, holding my hair back and murmuring soothing words as he rubbed my back.

My Damyon was back—the Damyon I'd fallen in love with—but there was no comfort in it. Not this time. The flip of the coin from one persona to the other only made me feel worse. Betrayed. How could someone so kind and compassionate be such a monster? How could a man claim he loved someone, then hurt them so vindictively?

It wasn't right. Something inside him was broken beyond repair.

"You hit your head pretty good."

*I didn't hit my head. You slammed me against a wall. There's a difference.*

I nodded, knowing I could never say the words aloud.

"Sometimes a bump on the head will do this. I will have the doctor come by just to be safe."

I felt the tiniest modicum of comfort. His doctor was old but kind. I'd seen the man a couple of times to get my birth control shot renewed.

I peered down into the clear water of the freshly flushed toilet and stilled when another round of nausea roiled in my belly.

The nausea was from the headache, right? I couldn't be...

As if in answer, an ache radiated from my right breast. They'd been extra sore lately, and my bras had seemed snug almost overnight.

Sweet Jesus, no.

I couldn't be.

I'd had a shot only a month ago. My bleeding was irregular, but that was always the case with the shot.

*Please, God above, let this reeling nausea simply be a concussion. Don't let me bring a child into this mess.*

An hour later, the doctor stopped by and cleared me of any serious injury. There was no way he could have missed the horrid purple bruising around my neck, but he acted like it wasn't there.

I felt oddly embarrassed, which then triggered a slew of other negative emotions—primarily self-loathing. How dare I be embarrassed? I was the victim here. If anyone should be embarrassed, it was Damyon for what he'd done or the doctor for ignoring what was so obviously wrong. But neither of those things would change. This was my new reality, and if I didn't like it, I'd have to find a way out.

But first, I had to know the full extent of the trouble I was in.

Two days later, I did something I never thought I'd do. I shoplifted a pregnancy test. I didn't want to take it back to the house, so I asked my escort if we could pick up lunch, then begged off to the restroom. Thank God it was a single water closet with a lock. I didn't think I could do this with an audience.

I set the activated test on the edge of the sink and stared deep into the reflection of my eyes.

*Time to be strong, Stormy girl. No room for fear or doubts from this moment on.*

Tears streamed down my cheeks. The last I'd cry for a long time.

Two pink lines emerged on the test strip.

I was pregnant, and this was no longer about me anymore.

# CHAPTER 20

*Torin*

*Present*

I OVERREACTED ABOUT ORAN MEETING WITH STORM. I'D known it as the words left my mouth, but that was how it was with her. I couldn't think straight when she was around. Or when we were apart. She stole all capacity for rational thought, leaving me constantly on edge.

I needed to play this carefully, but that was foreign territory for me. I'd never had to finesse anyone before. To gain someone's trust. I hadn't given two shits what anyone thought of me since I was a high school kid, which felt like another lifetime.

Stormy's opinion mattered. If she didn't think I was

worthy of her, it would be my own damn fault.

"You were an angry bastard before, but you're damn near unbearable lately. What the hell's gotten into you?" Jolly hoisted himself into the bar chair beside me. The club was empty. We still had another hour until open, so no one else had clocked in yet.

"You know what—or *who*, rather." If there was anyone I let in at all, it was Jolly. I owed him so much more than my life. He was the only reason I wasn't completely unhinged.

"I've seen the way you two interact. She ain't exactly chasing you away with a stick, so what's the problem?"

I huffed out a sardonic laugh. Leave it to Jolly to make things painfully simple. "Let's see … I'm foul-tempered, possessive, and downright irrational where she's concerned. I'm amazed she hasn't already run for the hills."

"Well. Don't be."

"I can't, Jolly," I bit back at him. "How the hell am I supposed to quit being who I am?"

He shrugged. "I s'pose that's a matter of motivation. Anyone can change, if they want to badly enough."

Fucking goddammit.

I hated when he was right.

"You want a drink?" I grumbled as I made my way around the bar.

"Never said no to a drink before. No point in startin' now." He watched me get down the bottle of Jameson whiskey and pour us each a tumbler full before continuing. "You know, I was talkin' with Storm a while back."

"Yeah?" I peered at him before taking a drink, curious where he was headed.

"She had trouble hearing me—said she had hearing loss in her left ear."

Huh. How had I never noticed that? "Interesting, but not sure of your point."

"You know anyone else with that sort of issue?" He spoke slowly as though the subject had a deeper meaning.

I shrugged. "One or two guys at the gym, but that's from taking hits without gear on." Every fucking muscle in my body marbleized into solid stone. "You don't think...?" I couldn't even say it. The idea seemed preposterous. How could anyone lay a hand on a woman so radiant as Stormy? Yet there'd been the odd way she'd reacted to me calling her angel. Had someone else used the term before—someone who'd hurt her?

Jolly raised his hands in surrender. "I could be totally off base. Just an observation." Jolly wasn't one for idle gossip. He wouldn't have voiced the thought if he didn't think it had merit.

My glass hit the bar with enough force to slosh out half my drink.

"Well, she's not living with anyone now. No signs of a man past or present in her place."

"I want to know how you know that?"

"Not even a little."

Jolly brought the glass to his mouth and savored a sip, licking his thin lips after. "Love you like a son, but that girl is special. Don't fuck around there." His words were laced in warning, low and guttural. I wasn't sure he'd ever spoken to me with such chilling finality.

"You saved my ass, so I'll refrain from knocking loose your teeth, but watch your tone, old man."

Jolly grinned, a rare ear-to-ear affair. "Glad we understand one another. Now clean up that mess you made. We got work to do."

# CHAPTER 21

*Stormy*

*Present*

Torin had offered me a ride home the past three nights after work, which I accepted. He didn't ask to come upstairs, and I didn't offer. It was strange ... but nice. He was trying to be normal for my benefit. To help me feel safe around him.

Normal fit him like a suit sourced at Goodwill, but I appreciated his effort.

I'd spent more time than I liked to admit mulling over what Rowan had told me. I considered what I'd learned about Torin and how hard he was trying. Oddly enough, I realized that I wasn't sure I liked him changing for me. I'd been preaching honesty and transparency. Who was I to examine his true self and ask him to modify who he was? Especially when I had to admit that his surly, overprotective side was a little endearing so long as he didn't take things too far.

The more I thought about it, the more decided I became. I was going to give him a chance. A *real* chance. Tell him about my past and let him decide how we moved forward. Together.

How was it I was more nervous about the possibility of him rejecting me than I'd been about learning he was stalking me? I didn't know how to be logical where Torin was concerned, which was why I decided to give myself through Thanksgiving before doing anything irreversible. That meant one more day to change my mind. Then there'd be no going back.

If I'd been told two years earlier that I would consider baring my soul to a man who broke into my apartment and beat people to a pulp for fun, I'd have laughed at the absurdity. But it was true. I felt the pendulum of my life nearing a shift in direction. I prayed it was a shift for the better.

I closed my door on my way to work just as Luke returned home.

"Hey, Storm. You working tonight?"

"Yeah, but we're closed tomorrow, thank goodness."

"What are your Thanksgiving plans? You don't have family nearby, right?" he asked, brows knitted together.

"No family," I said with a twinge of sadness. "I'll be holding down the fort here, watching the Macy's Parade on TV and giving Blue Bell all the cuddles."

Luke pursed his lips and narrowed his eyes. "I don't like it. I'm going to a Friendsgiving tomorrow. You're coming with me."

"I'm not crashing your Thanksgiving."

"It's not Thanksgiving. It's *Friends*giving. And there's no such thing as crashing Friendsgiving. That's the whole point. It's for those of us who, for various reasons, aren't spending the day with family. You check the box. Besides, I won't take no for an answer." He raised a brow in challenge. "We aren't eating until three, so I'll grab you at noon."

"Luke, are you sure? I don't want it to be awkward."

"I'm *positive*. And trust me, nothing is awkward with this group. You'll love them."

I rolled my eyes with a smirk. "Fine. And thank you, I suppose."

"Hey, I'm just annoyed I hadn't thought to ask before." He opened his door. "Have a good night at work, and I'll see you tomorrow."

"Thanks!" What had I just been thinking about life being unexpected? I wasn't sure why I even tried. Fortunately, this change of plans would likely be a good one.

I made the short walk to work with a smile. We closed early tonight, which would help me get up and be ready on time tomorrow. I was surprised that I was looking forward to the gathering. I hadn't had Thanksgiving with anyone in years. The prospect put a grin on my face, though it died a tragic snarling death when I walked through the club toward the back and spotted one of the newly hired dancers draping her arms around Torin's shoulders. While she was topless.

Two thoughts entered my mind simultaneously. First, he was never going to get the glitter out of that shirt. And second, I HATED seeing her touch him.

He had his arms crossed, clearly irritated. I'd never seen him involved with any of the dancers, so it shouldn't have bothered me, but there was no denying I was madder than a one-eyed goose.

I marched toward them on a mission. "Desire, honey—" I started.

"It's *Destiny*," she said, clueless to my condescension, though she did relinquish her hold on Torin.

A feline grin split my face. "Yeah, that's what I meant. Jolly's looking for you. Said some customer came in yelling earlier." I leaned close and put my hand to my mouth as if not to be overheard but continued at a normal volume. "Something about you giving him chlamydia. You're gonna want to go talk to Jolly."

Little Miss Destiny gaped at me like I'd just farted all over her birthday cake. "I don't ... that can't be right," she sputtered with a horrified look at Torin before bolting for the back.

When I finally looked at Tor with a satisfied grin, he stared at me from eyes hooded with desire.

"That wasn't very nice."

I shrugged. "We can't all be perfect all the time."

He reached for my hand, hooking one of his fingers with mine and walking us backward. His eyes never left mine. His hold wasn't secure enough to actually pull me with him. I had to go voluntarily, which I did wholeheartedly.

I hadn't noticed, but we were only steps away from the door to the first private room. Rooms reserved for lap dances and ... other unlisted services.

My heart rate leaped to a gallop.

What was he planning to do? These rooms all had surveillance cameras that someone monitored while the club was open.

Torin closed the door behind me, his body remaining

inches from mine. "You, Stormy Lawson, wear jealousy like a goddamn crown. Never seen anything more beautiful."

My chin hitched upward. "She was out of line taking such liberties with her boss."

I'd never seen anything as captivating as the grin that lit his face. It knocked the air from my lungs.

"You don't have to explain a thing." He lifted his arms to either side of him. "Everything you see here is 100 percent yours. You want it, show me. Get on your knees and take what's yours."

"The cameras..." I started, wariness etched in my voice.

He brought his hand to my cheek, his thumb tracing my bottom lip. "You trust me?" he whispered, his eyes boring like azure beacons deep into my soul.

Did I trust him? That was the million-dollar question. It might have been reckless, and I might end up hating myself for it, but I knew the answer.

I nodded.

"Say it, Stormy. Tell me you trust me."

"I trust you, Tor."

An audible rumble reverberated from his rapidly expanding chest.

"Step back into this corner." The seductive timbre of his voice was enough to mesmerize me into motion. "It's a blind spot. The camera can't see you there."

I did as he instructed, lowering myself to my knees and attacking his belt with surprising fervor. I wanted this. I wanted to take him in my mouth and make him lose all control. I wanted to taste him like he'd tasted me and know that for the rest of the night while he worked, the kiss of my lipstick would mark where I'd been.

My tongue ran along my bottom lip at the sight of his

heavy cock swaying free from his pants. I hadn't actually seen it until now. It was so freaking thick, I wasn't sure how he'd fit in my mouth.

"Don't be nervous, baby. I won't do anything you don't want me to."

I nodded, exploring the feel of him in my hand. Thick veins ridged beneath warm, soft skin that begged to be licked … so I did. From base to tip like it was one hundred degrees outside, and he was a melting popsicle. I slurped and sucked and devoured every inch of him, my eyes peering up to witness his reaction. I wasn't disappointed.

Torin's hand cupped my head reverently. "*Fuck*, your mouth was made for my cock."

I used my free hand to clasp his heavy balls and give them a gentle tug.

Tor hissed through clenched teeth. "Not gonna last long, you keep that up."

I smiled wickedly, then swirled my tongue around his tip. Wanting to drive him wild, I forced myself to relax the back of my throat and allow him in until my nose brushed against his body.

Torin groaned deliciously. I could feel him swell against my tongue as I released him. His hand fisted in my hair but not with any real strength. He made sure I still felt completely in control, giving me the courage I needed to lose myself in my task. I dove in again, this time swallowing while his head was deep at the back of my throat. When his abs seized tight, I knew he was close, so I worked my fist and lips in unison.

"Oh *fuck*. That's it, baby. *Don't stop.*"

Seconds later, he gasped his release, and cum rocketed

down my throat. Gently, ever so gently, I gave him one last lick from base to tip, making him hiss with pleasure.

My chest expanded with a bubble of happiness from knowing how thoroughly I'd pleased him. Each of his words, his guttural moans, and the captivated look in his eyes were a shower of compliments coming from a man like Torin.

I wanted to pretend I still had a choice about how I felt for him, but it was more and more clear to me that my heart had already decided. I was falling for Torin Byrne.

But would he still want me if he knew my past? It was the last thing I should have been thinking about at that moment, yet the worry seeded itself deep in my psyche.

Tor helped me to my feet and tucked himself back into his pants but didn't make for the door. Instead, he cupped my face and brought his lips slowly to mine. Three ardent, passionate kisses later, we were both breathless.

"You fucking own me, Storm. Inside and out."

I didn't know what to say, but he made it easy for me, simply placing one last kiss on my forehead before leading the way back out into the club.

I intentionally kept my eyes averted from any onlookers, not wanting to see any knowing smirks. I wasn't ashamed, but I also didn't want our activities to be a topic of conversation.

After taking a quick minute in the bathroom to wash my hands and tidy my hair, I returned to the bar and got back to work. Jolly joined me not long after, leaning his elbows back against the bar with his eyes watching the room.

"Glad to see you're giving him a chance. Not many see past his armor."

I was shocked that Jolly was bringing up Torin. He'd been tight-lipped about the man so far.

"You see past it," I noted curiously.

"I knew him before. Know he wasn't always like this."

"You going to tell me what happened?"

"Nope. Not my story to tell." He finally brought his gaze to mine, and I was shocked at all he said with one simple stare—a world of worry and hope and pleading without saying a single word.

I responded in the only way I knew how. I squeezed his hand. A show of understanding and gratitude and apology all rolled into one because as much as I wanted to promise I'd never hurt Torin, I couldn't do that. My life was more complicated than most. Dating someone came with life-and-death consequences, which wasn't something I took lightly.

# CHAPTER 22
*Stormy*

*Past*

I KNEW TWO THINGS WITH CERTAINTY. ONE, I COULDN'T TELL Damyon about the baby. And two, I had to escape. Soon.

I spent every waking minute scheming. My biggest problem was figuring out how to get out of the country. Was the embassy in Moscow trustworthy? Damyon had half of the city in his pocket. As far as I knew, that could extend to diplomats. I decided it was too risky, if only because it would be the obvious answer. I had to go a route he wouldn't anticipate.

While I planned, I discreetly collected money at every opportunity. A few rubles here and there, every little bit I could stash away would help. For three weeks, I did my best to appear as though I'd accepted my fate. I put on the performance of my life, disguising my thoughts, emotions, and my subtly changing body.

I choked back the nausea. I smiled through the fatigue. I even had sex with him, going so far as to initiate so he wouldn't suspect my true intentions.

It was the longest three weeks of my life.

At least after my parents' deaths, I'd had Honey to reassure me and the comforts of home to soothe me. Here, I was all alone. I had no choice but to be strong, if only for the tiny life growing inside me.

Once the bruises around my neck finally faded, I went back at the yoga studio I'd joined. That was vitally important because it was the first step in my plan to escape. It was located in a nice part of town and frequented mostly by wealthy housewives, so my security was relaxed when I went to class. The studio had a back exit leading into an alley. I wished I'd been able to do more scouting to see what businesses kept their back doors unlocked during the day, but that wasn't an option. I knew I'd leave through that exit and try to work my way through the neighborhood as best as I could without being seen.

I would essentially be escaping with no more than the shirt on my back, but that was all I needed if I could get away. I mentally strategized every last detail possible. I knew what gas station I'd use to buy hair dye and what bus station would get me out of the city. I debated endlessly about what border country would be my best chance at freedom. I had decided after doing what research I could that going south to Ukraine would be best because anti-Russian sympathizers were more likely to help me across the border. How I'd find those select individuals was a problem I'd face down the road. My plan relied on a healthy dose of luck, but I had little other choice. As long as I could get out of Moscow, I had faith in my ability to get home. Eventually.

I decided on a dreary fall Sunday to execute my escape the following day. I wasn't sure I was ready, but waiting felt even more dangerous. I also worried that if I had a long lead time before walking away, he'd somehow sniff out my mounting fear and figure it out. I felt safer stealing away almost on a whim. It seemed less predictable. Less likely to cause suspicion.

The problem with a man like Damyon? He was suspicious of everything.

"I'm going to head out," I said, draping my yoga bag over my shoulder.

"Where do you think you are going?"

The words doused me in icy water. We'd both been in the kitchen carrying about our morning routines in our normal fashion. I had my yoga gear on and had told him the night before that I planned to go to class, so I wasn't sure why he was asking except to insinuate that I wasn't allowed.

Had I already done something to upset him?

Adrenaline spiked my heart rate to a frenzied pace.

"I'm going to yoga. I thought I mentioned it last night." I used every ounce of acting skills I had to sound blithefully unaware. Each muscle was loose with forced calm, my posture the epitome of unbothered.

Damyon came around the kitchen island, slowly stalking toward me. He was dressed for the day in a white button-down and black suit pants, his hair still damp from a shower. Even knowing what I did about the man, he was still breathtakingly beautiful. But now I saw that beauty for what it was—the cobra's way of mesmerizing its victim before it kills.

I flirtatiously peered up at him through my lashes, hoping to implement my own brand of enchantment. Sometimes he called me to him just for a kiss or a touch. He liked to know I was always within reach. I was silently praying this was one of those times.

He approached, towering over me, and lowered his lips to my ear. "Surely, you were not going to leave without this." He nipped my earlobe playfully, then displayed my phone in his palm. I'd left it on the counter while I was getting ready.

"Oops!" I grinned, taking the phone from him. "What would I do without you?" I raised up and kissed his cheek. "I better get going, or I'm going to be late. I'll see you after work." I flashed one last smile and turned toward to collect my driver when my bag snagged on something and stopped my progress.

Damyon stood with his finger hooked on the strap. His piercing eyes studied me.

"Your heart. It is racing." He tugged me closer, tracing his fingers over the pulse point at the base of my neck.

If it wasn't before, it certainly was now.

"You startled me before. I thought you were upset that I was going to class." True enough, and all too reasonable considering his hair-trigger temper. Wouldn't it be expected for a woman to get nervous around a man who *beats* her?

Unfortunately, logic wasn't part of the equation where Damyon and I were concerned.

He took the bag from me and began to extract its contents. A small towel for sweat. A water bottle. My wallet. A plastic bag of granola. A small bag of toiletries, including a travel-sized brush, a toothbrush, an emergency tampon, lip gloss, and a small bottle of painkillers. Damyon took the toothbrush from the zippered pouch and stared at it.

"Why would you possibly need a toothbrush at your yoga class?" The suspicion in his stare stripped me bare until I felt like a helpless child.

"It's just an emergency bag—like if I realized my breath was bad or something," I stammered, desperation taking over.

"Who do you think will be smelling your breath? Huh?"

The acrid taste of panic coated my tongue. "I don't know. I've always taken those things with me to the gym. Why are you questioning me about this?"

His glare turned cunning. "Do not try to make this about me. If I could trust you, I would not have to question such things."

"You *can* trust me."

"Then why the fuck are you taking a toothbrush to yoga?" he roared. "Is this some fancy new tongue yoga where you suck your instructor's dick? You think you can make a fool of me in front of the world?"

The trigger on his temper snapped, and once he'd crossed that line, there would be no going back. Not until the storm had run its course.

He grabbed my arm and shoved me toward the kitchen.

"Please, Damyon, don't do this. *Please*, no." I could try to tell him he was wrong or attempt to explain, but it would only make things worse. The one thing I knew to do was beg. For my life. For his forgiveness. For the end to be quick. Without the option of reason, the only other thing to do would be … to fight back.

I hadn't considered it an option because my chances

seemed so minuscule. He was so much stronger than me. But what if I didn't survive this fight to try another escape?

Instinct took over when I realized this might be my final moments. I didn't have to decide whether to fight; my body demanded it.

I stumbled around to the other side of the island so he couldn't reach me. "*Please*, Damyon. I love you. I promised myself to you. I would *never* cheat."

"You cannot lie to me. I saw the way your heart raced on your way to the door. You could not wait to get your lips around another man's cock." He sneered as he prowled closer.

A toothbrush and a racing pulse. Two things that could have meant nothing or anything, yet he'd convinced himself it was evidence of cheating. I'd tried so hard to keep him from suspecting I was going to run, and I'd been successful. He didn't think I was trying to escape. But his paranoia had driven him to an equally problematic conclusion that might mean my death.

I wanted to rage against the unfairness.

Damyon lunged for one side of the island. I ran in the opposite direction, but his hand clamped down on my ponytail in a quick end to his sadistic chase. He wrapped my hair in his fist and yanked my back against him, bringing his snarling lips to my ear.

"No other man will touch what is mine."

Tears of agony and frustration and hatred streamed down my face. "You're hurting me, Damyon," I cried helplessly through the pain.

He released me with a shove only to slap me so hard that all I could hear was a deafening tone and silence. I caught myself against the far kitchen counter, my thoughts suddenly disoriented and my vision blurred. I pressed my hand to my left ear, and when I let go, there was blood on my fingers. My ear was bleeding from the inside.

I peered over my shoulder in horror, only to realize he was speaking. As though time had stood still, then slingshot into motion, my brain seemed to register sound from my right ear all at once, helping me regain my bearings.

Damyon was on a rampage. I had to stop him before he killed me.

I spun around and grabbed the only thing within reach—a handheld can opener that happened to be on the counter. As he charged toward me, I whipped back around and used my momentum to slam the can opener across his face. Judging by the gaping slash that opened across his cheek, the sharp circular cutting pieces had made direct contact. His cheek was flayed open from his temple to the corner of his mouth.

Damyon bellowed in anger, stepping backward and slapping his hand over his cheek. Blood poured from beneath his fingers. He took a momentary peek at his hand to assess the extent of the injury.

My hand shook with a vicious tremble.

If I'd thought Damyon's stare was soulless before, that was nothing compared to the look of malignant hatred he now wore.

"I will make you suffer until the end of your days."

"I'm only trying to protect myself," I yelled back at him. "Can't you see you're hurting me!"

"As if a whore like you has feelings." He lunged, grabbing my wrist in one hand and prying the can opener free with the other. He cut himself with his effort, but it never even registered. He was too fixated on retribution.

Again, he struck me, this time with his fist. I crumpled to the ground, and the real beating began. He kicked me … over, and over, and over … until my body felt numb and my mind shattered.

He spoke to me, but his words didn't penetrate the fog.

I'd taken myself somewhere else.

A tire swing on a balmy Savannah night, swaying beneath a mossy oak tree. The thick shelf of greenery only allowed a glimpse here and there of the golden-hewn sky. It was sunset, and Mama would be calling me home soon…

Cold water splashed my face, making me cough and sputter as I regained consciousness.

My body was one solid ball of pain. I was on the floor in Damyon's office. When I looked over, he had a swath of gauze wrapped around half of his head, coaxing back my memories.

My eyes clenched shut in a refusal to deal with the horror.

"You know how my men show their loyalty to me?" he asked in a low, menacing tone. "They carry my mark. That way, everyone knows who they belong to."

Terror wrenched open my lids, demanding I do something. Anything. That was when I realized I was lying by the fireplace, and a roaring fire blazed next to me.

"Since you cannot seem to remember who *you* belong to, let me remind you." Damyon lifted a poker that had been resting among the logs. On the end was a glowing symbol. A brand. One I knew well—the joined letters of his name D and K in the Russian alphabet.

I'd never felt fear so acutely. I knew that because, until that moment, I'd never known what it was like to lose control of my bodily functions. Warmth radiated around my bottom and legs as urine soaked my clothing.

Damyon sniffed the air and smiled. "Now, you understand." He ripped at the neckline of my tank top, sheer madness in his eyes.

I wanted to fight him off. I wanted to run or do anything to stop what was happening, but my body was in so much pain. All I could muster were whispered sobs.

*"Please, don't do this. Please."*

"Too late, ptichka. You should have thought of that before you thought to betray me."

The scream that ripped from my throat felt like the bleeding of my soul as the scalding iron incinerated the flesh over my left breast. Never in my life had I experienced such agony. I'd never even imagined it was possible.

Too much for my damaged mind and body to process, my consciousness melted away, along with the pain.

"You will always belong to me." Damyon's whispered words followed me into darkness.

♦

EVEN AFTER MY PARENTS DIED, I could never imagine a time when I would be sorry to be alive. When I would rather not wake up than face reality.

I now knew the excruciating depths of that despair.

The desolation.

I was in a hospital. Bandaged. Alone.

Every inch of my body hurt, but only one question was on my mind. I voiced it when an older woman in scrubs entered my hospital room. "My baby?" I asked in a hoarse voice, one eye sealed shut. "My baby?" I murmured again, this time patting my tender stomach.

There was so much pain. How could anything survive such abuse?

We didn't have to speak the same language for me to understand the tormented look in the nurse's eyes. Slowly, she turned her head from side to side. "So sorry." Her words were heavily accented and laden with sorrow.

I didn't cry. Not really. I was too numb for that.

A single tear warmed my skin, commemorating the life stolen from me.

The nurse left me to grieve. I wished I'd had the luxury of such emotions. Instead, I sat still in silence and took inventory of my situation. It was dark outside my window, and judging by the dimmed lights and quiet hallways, I suspected we were well into the middle of the night.

Damyon must have been worried to have brought me here. I was surprised he wasn't standing vigil at my bedside. He had likely instructed the hospital to call him when I woke. Was he already on his way? And once he got me back to the house, then what? He didn't trust me before, so he certainly wouldn't now. I'd forever be his prisoner, assuming he let me live.

If I had any hope of survival, I had to escape. Now.

Damyon's absence was my sign from the universe—my one token of good luck—so I wasn't going to waste it.

Sitting up, I cringed at the pain lancing through my chest. I had to have at least one broken rib.

Once I was upright, I realized I was wearing padded panties, and judging by the squish, they were soaked. I peeked inside, wondering why they'd allowed me to pee myself.

I wished to God I hadn't looked.

Blood. So much blood.

Of course. I should have known. My body would have to shed what was no longer viable.

I scrunched my eyes shut and fought back the vomit burning my throat. I had to set aside all that had happened to process at a later time when my world wasn't on the verge of collapse. I had no time for grief or fear or pain. My life depended on my ability to escape.

I gently lowered my feet to the floor and dragged the IV pole to the scuffed cabinetry. Inside, I located a plastic laundry sack for patient belongings and piled in the extra pads left on the counter. I rummaged through every other nook and cranny in my room without finding much in the way of supplies.

I didn't have any clothes available, so I'd have to source some on my way out. Ready to make my move, I untapped the IV needle and pulled it from my skin. A peek beyond my room revealed that I wasn't near the nurses' station. While the hall was empty, I took my chance and walked as quickly as my broken body would allow. I didn't know where I was headed. I would have to figure it out as I went—that was the extent of my new plan. My life was riding on a wing and a prayer, as my mama used to say.

*Please, Mama. If you're up there watching, help me find my way back home.*

I rounded a corner and saw what looked like an exit sign over the door to a stairwell. One foot was across the threshold when I heard a woman's voice behind me. Slowly, I looked back. Her look of curiosity crumpled to one of tender sorrow.

She spoke softly. A question. But I didn't understand.

My eyes darted around, unsure what I should do. Was she going to try to keep me there? Could I evade her even if I wanted to?

Cold fingers gingerly took my hand in hers. I watched as she pointed at the bandages on my chest and colorful bruises blossoming all over my body. "You man do this?" Pure compassion shone from her hazel eyes.

A tear fell from mine as I nodded.

She gave a single nod in return, her face sobering before she urged me to follow her. I was wary to follow but felt I had little choice. Maybe my mama had been listening because this brave young nurse became my savior. She took me back to the nurses' locker room and gave me clothes to wear, helping me change when I couldn't bear to lift my arms over my head. She opened her phone and showed me a picture of a bus station, to which I nodded as vigorously as possible.

Two hours later, I was boarding the early morning bus to St. Petersburg with my plastic sack loaded to the brim with all sorts of provisions. The woman, who'd told me her name was Ulyana, drove me to the station, bought me a bus ticket, then gave me every bit of cash she had left.

I genuinely believed I met an angel in the middle of Moscow that night.

She understood. I could see it in the knowing depths of her eyes. She knew what it was like to be in desperate need of help. To have your life hanging in the balance. She knew, which was why her help didn't end there. The last thing she did for me before we parted was hand me a small piece of paper with what looked to be an address. I knew innately that she was sending me to someone who would keep me safe. Someone who would help me get home.

I didn't care how much it hurt; I hugged her with every ounce of my strength. Her courage and generosity were unmatched. I wanted her to know the endless depths of my gratitude.

Again, in the moment of my darkest despair, the pendulum shifted to send my life down a new path. It was a reminder to never give up—one I wouldn't soon forget.

# CHAPTER 23
*Stormy*

*Present*

I WOKE ON THANKSGIVING MORNING SOAKED IN SWEAT WITH my hand over my belly and tears still wetting my face.

*You're okay, Stormy girl. You're safe.*

I took several slow breaths and grounded myself.

It had been over a year since I'd had a nightmare. My concerns over what to do about Torin must have triggered it. I hated that I couldn't scrape that night from my memories.

I'd only been back in the US for about six months when I promised myself that I wouldn't live in fear of Damyon. Running from him was enough of a concession. I refused to surrender any more by allowing fear to rule my thoughts and actions.

"Not today, Satan." I threw back the covers and went straight to the shower. I scrubbed away the sticky bits of memory clinging to me and extinguished the scent of fear with a heavily lathered layer of strawberry-kiwi bodywash.

I felt like a new woman as I met Luke at the door an hour later.

"Ready?" he asked, his eyes glinting with green specks accentuated by a beautiful olive scarf over his jacket.

"I am, thanks. I didn't have time to make anything, so I'm hoping this bottle of wine will suffice." Southern hospitality dictated that I could never, not EVER, show up at a dinner party without bringing something to contribute.

"Alcohol is always a welcome offering. You know I don't cook, so I jumped on the cranberry sauce before anyone else could claim it." He held up a plastic grocery sack. "Two cans of jellied and a carton of the weird lumpy stuff, in case anyone likes that kind." His nose crinkled as though he'd been forced to take a big whiff of an old gym sock.

"Hey, I love the weird lumpy stuff! It's not truly cranberry sauce unless it has the little bits of cranberry in it." Honey made the absolute best Thanksgiving meal. Her cranberries were to die for.

His head tilted to the side, and his eyebrows rose to a peak in the middle of his forehead. "I believe this is where you'd say *bless your heart.*"

My jaw dropped in mock outrage. "Oh no, you didn't."

He burst out laughing and scurried toward the stairs. "Come on, weirdo, before we're late."

"You're lucky you're so cute," I muttered after him with a smirk.

He winked at me over his shoulder, and so began one of the best Thanksgivings I could remember, pre and post Damyon. His friends were fabulous. We laughed, teased, and encouraged one another. As promised, I fit right in and looked forward to hanging out with them again.

Between the glinting possibilities with Torin, my Moxy work family, and now Luke with his friends, I found myself wanting to stay in the city more than ever. Instead of dreading telling Torin the truth, I almost looked forward to it. I wanted him to understand. I wanted him to be the man my heart swore he was.

Luke and I spent all day at the gathering, only leaving after two rounds of hugs and professions of love by more than one tipsy individual. My stomach was full to bursting, as was my heart. I was so wistfully content that I almost didn't notice the feeling of eyes watching me.

We exited the subway, my arm hooked around Luke's, when I homed in on the sensation of being followed. I rolled my eyes to myself, knowing Torin was probably fuming about me being with Luke, especially when I had told him I would be home alone for the day.

Had he sat outside the building all day waiting for me to leave? If not, how else could he have known where I was?

I took a slow, disappointed breath.

He'd eased off his stalker tendencies now that we'd begun to form an understanding. His behavior hadn't caused me any unease. I'd even enjoyed his little show of power with the blow job the night before. The first threads of trust spanned delicately between us, but this was a huge setback. Stalking me all day was a big problem. Granted, our relationship was far from textbook, but this was unacceptable.

I didn't want to make a scene in front of Luke, so I ignored the shadow tailing us with plans of calling Torin as soon as I was alone. The conversation wouldn't be easy, but I couldn't let this go unanswered. The whole change in circumstances sat like a boulder on my chest. I'd gone from cautious optimism about our next visit to wary hopelessness.

"Thanks again, Luke." I forced a warm smile, despite the churning in my gut. "I had a phenomenal day."

He dropped a quick kiss on my cheek. "Told you it would be worth it. Now you're one of the crew." He grinned at me before unlocking his door.

"Have a good night," I replied as I opened my door.

My mood deflated quicker than a punctured balloon once I was alone. Frustrated, I yanked my drapes fully closed and changed into comfy clothes. I didn't even have a chance to grab my phone when a knock sounded at the door.

*Looks like I'm not the only one with a bone to pick.*

I'd like to see Torin try to be upset with me after pulling a stunt like watching me all day. I shook my head and steeled myself to stay firm. I refused to fall into the cycle of abuse and apologies. Either we were working toward trust and healthy behaviors or it was over. He needed to understand how important that was to me, and the only way to do that was for him to know where I was coming from.

While I hadn't planned to have my little unveiling that night, it looked like the time had come. I would do what I promised and come clean, but I'd also lay down an ultimatum. He would have to make some serious changes if he wanted to move forward with me.

I turned off the television and walked to the door, taking a single calming breath before opening it.

The possibility that someone other than Torin might be beyond the door never occurred to me. I only saw a gold tooth glinting from a wicked grin before a large hand clamped tight around my throat.

"YA nashel tebya." The terrifying stranger brought his face close to mine, vodka heavy on his breath. *"I got you."*

# CHAPTER 24
*Stormy*

*Present*

HE FOUND ME.

Damyon. The devil who haunted my worst nightmares.

Not the man himself, but the result was the same. This man would take me back to his boss, and the remainder of my days would be a living hell.

Fear choked off my airway even more thoroughly than the snarling man maneuvering me inside my apartment. The door slammed shut behind him.

"Boss will give me stars for this. His newest vor." His heavy Russian accent was even harder to understand with alcohol slurring his words.

I wanted to scream for help but couldn't make a sound, which was probably good because Luke would come bounding in and likely end up dead. I couldn't risk that. I would have to handle this on my own.

*STOP PANICKING. You absolutely do not have that luxury. You have to think.*

I gave myself a mental slap and focused on saving myself. The Russian brute was drunk off his ass. All I had to do was break free of his hold, then run.

Hours upon hours of self-defense classes flooded to the forefront of my mind. But before I could act on any one action, he released me just long enough to backhand me across the face. Hard.

"I knew we find you. Now we get out this shithole." His hands clamped down around my throat again, but this time, I was ready.

I yanked down on his wrists, using them as leverage to kick him in the groin. His arms instinctively recoiled, his body doubling over, but he still blocked my exit as he hissed a string of Russian curses. I whirled around to reach for the ceramic vase I kept by the window, but he snagged my oversized T-shirt before I could get to it. I was yanked back against him before he wrapped his arms around me, lifted me in the air, then slammed my body sideways onto the floor.

Every bone in my body rattled on impact. I had tried to protect my head but was stunned nonetheless.

"Stupid American bitch not know how to behave." His boot planted itself in my gut. The pain and flashes of memory had me heaving, acid burning my throat.

This couldn't be happening.

I refused to accept it. This drunk would *not* take me back to Damyon, not while I still had breath in my body.

My eyes shot to the baseball bat I kept under the loveseat. It was just within reach. I grabbed it and lurched to my feet as quickly as I could.

My attacker grabbed the end of the bat, his hand sliding off like a knife through butter. He gaped in surprise at his hand to discover he held a sheer knee-high stocking, which I had placed on the bat for exactly that purpose.

"Surprise, *asshole*." I swung at his knee like I was in the World Series and the bases were loaded.

He let loose a savage howl, swinging his fist into my face on his way down. He was vicious—relentless in his attack—but he wasn't the only one.

I refused to go quietly.

Continuing my momentum from his strike, I spun all the way around and slammed the bat into the side of his head with a sickening crack. The man dropped to the floor with a resounding thud.

I didn't think; I just ran.

Grabbing my purse on the way out the door, I bolted down the hall, nearly fell in the stairwell twice, then burst out the front entrance to the building. I didn't stop. I pushed forward as quickly as I could, though I had no idea where I was going. I just knew I had to keep moving.

Once I was a block away and the adrenaline began to subside, the pain kicked in. My hip. My ribs. My face. They all screamed at me to stop, but I couldn't. I had to get to safety. But where?

The first thing I did when I moved to a new city was prepare multiple emergency escape plans. What I didn't do was plan to run on a night when the entire city was shut down. I had a go-bag in my apartment as well as one tucked away in a locker I'd rented at the YMCA. Neither was of use to me now.

I wouldn't even consider putting my new friends in danger by showing up at their doorsteps. That wasn't an option. And it was too cold to spend the night outside, especially now that my body felt half broken.

Shit, *shit*.

What was I supposed to do? Where was I supposed to go?

Green neon lights caught my attention before I realized where I'd wandered. I'd taken myself on autopilot to The Moxy. That was when I remembered I had a key to the back door.

Tor wasn't the only one with a penchant for copying keys.

Like the bat and the vase, I was perpetually trying to set up future Stormy for survival. It had almost become a habit. When I learned Keir and Torin never used the alarm system because the cleaners were in during off hours, I decided the key might come in handy.

I could have kissed myself.

Slipping into the back alley, I got the key from my purse and breathed a sigh of relief when the lock turned over easily, and the door opened without the alarm panel beeping.

Thank *God*.

I just needed the night to figure out what to do, then I'd disappear first thing in the morning.

The locker room looked eerie in the silent darkness. I'd never seen the club so lifeless. I had to use my phone flashlight to find the light switch in the pitch black. When the fluorescent bulbs buzzed to life, revealing familiar surroundings, my system began to come down from its emergent panic. Like aftershocks following an earthquake, my entire body began to tremble. I needed to sit before I passed out.

With my back against the royal-blue lockers, I slid down to the cold floor, hugging my purse to my aching chest.

That was when it hit me that I'd left Blue Bell behind.

My precious, sweet Blue Bell.

The dam holding back my tears came crashing down. Sobs seized my lungs, wracking my body, one after the other.

I couldn't return to my apartment now that it had been compromised.

Blue Bell was gone.

My new friends were gone.

Moxy was a thing of the past.

And Torin ... how could I have even considered using him to shield me from Damyon? Coming between that monster and me was a death sentence. I never should have even considered telling him. As much as it shattered my heart, I would leave the city first thing in the morning, alone once more.

# CHAPTER 25

*Torin*

*Present*

"Any leads on Darina?" I asked Oran while we sat around our grandparents' house on Thanksgiving. I was asking more out of politeness than concern. That girl was long gone—part of the skin trade or at the bottom of the Hudson—but either way, looking was futile.

"Yes, actually."

Surprised, I lifted my gaze from my phone.

"Oh yeah?"

"Yeah. I was able to track down her last known location."

"No shit? Where was she?"

A muscle twitched in his jaw. "If you recall, Caitlin

followed her brother to learn more about who he was working with, which led her to Damyon. I'd thought maybe he'd been responsible for Darina's disappearance, but it turns out Damyon had gone to Lawrence Wellington's house the day she followed him. That's where she took Darina."

Fuck me sideways. That was unexpected.

Wellington was a shipping mogul who also happened to be the father of Rowan's ex-boyfriend. She'd seen Damyon at Wellington's house, which tipped us off that the two were somehow connected. It had been the start of an intense couple of weeks as we navigated the dangers. I'd thought that was all over, but it seemed Oran was in the process of reopening Pandora's box.

"Keir know about this?"

"I just sorted it out yesterday. Haven't had the chance to tell him, and no need to upset him on Thanksgiving."

We both looked over at our cousin just as his phone rang.

"Yeah?" Keir answered, piquing my curiosity. The last time we were together, his call had involved Storm, and the possibility that could be the case now had me on alert.

I was a fuckin' nutjob. No news there.

"No. I'll head over and check it out. I'm sure it's nothing." After a pause, he hung up.

"What was that all about?" Rowan asked as I moved closer to find out who had called.

"Alarm went off at the club."

"I'll go check it out," I volunteered, itching to leave. I'd given in a half hour ago and looked up Storm's location on my GPS tracker. She was at home like she'd told me she would be, so I wasn't worried about her, but I'd had enough family time for the next two months. I loved my family, but the chaos of two dozen adults and just as many rambunctious kids running around wore out my patience.

"We were about to head out anyway," Keir said. "I'll run in with you on our way home, just to be safe."

It worked for me, so long as I had an excuse to call it a night. We told everyone goodbye and were out the door in a handful of minutes. I followed Keir and Rowan on my bike. The frigid night air was perfect for waking me up after gorging on food all afternoon. If I didn't know better, I would have said the women had cooked for a whole damn army. With a mix of American and traditional Irish dishes, we had everyone's favorite and then some. If I'd sat at that house any longer, I'd have been at risk of slipping into a food coma.

After thirty minutes on my bike, however, I was wide awake. I parked on the sidewalk, noting that everything at Moxy looked as it should.

Keir left Rowan in the car and joined me at the front door.

"It's locked," I told him. "If someone got in, they went in through the back."

"I seriously doubt anyone's in there. It's Thanksgiving. Even the Albanians aren't out tonight. If I had to guess, I'd say it's those damn rats that keep multiplying in the back alley." He walked inside nonchalantly and flipped on the few light switches located at the front.

I wasn't about to take anything for granted, so I almost always had a gun on me, even if just conceal-carry .22. Gun in hand, I slowly made my way through the club with Keir behind me. I reached the back hallway and froze when I noticed a sliver of light shining from beneath the locker room door.

My gaze cut to Keir before we moved in sync to either side of the door. I strained to listen while Keir took out his Glock. Not hearing a thing, I took a deep breath and barged through the door, gun drawn.

I was ready for a showdown. I was ready to kick someone's ass or chase someone from the building. What I wasn't ready for was to find Stormy bloody and beaten, curled in a ball on the floor. She was shaking like a leaf, and I instantly lost my fucking mind.

"Storm, what the *fuck!*" I roared. It was a shit thing to do, but I couldn't help myself. I was mindless with rage. Someone had put their hands on my woman, and I was going to skin the bastard alive.

"*Easy,*" Keir hissed at me, though his admonishment barely registered.

"I'm so sorry, guys," Stormy whispered in a broken voice. The sound gutted me—ripped out my insides and made meaty confetti out of them. "I wondered if coming here might trip the alarm, but I didn't have anywhere else to go."

Keir started forward, helping me to break free from the shock and do the same.

"What's goin' on, Stormy?" he asked her gently.

Both of us crouched to examine her. Jesus, she was a mess. One eye swelling shut. Black tears staining her cheeks. An arm clasped around her middle as though attempting to hold herself together. I had to force myself to listen to her words before the rage took over again.

"It was my own damn fault. I had a feeling someone was following me on my way home, and I should have listened to my instincts." She wouldn't look at me. She wouldn't look at either of us. It wasn't like her. Something was horribly off.

"You need a place to stay?" My cousin's question startled me. Was he volunteering his place?

She nodded at him warily. "I can't go back there right now."

Fuck, no. She wasn't going back to her place or to his. Storm was coming with me.

I shot to my feet, my hand digging into my jacket pocket. "Here's the key to the bike. She's coming with me." No fucking way was I putting her on a motorcycle in her condition.

Keir stood, studying me curiously on the way. "Keys are still in the car, and I'm not taking Rowan on the damn bike. We'll call an Uber."

As long as I got Storm home safely, I didn't care if they walked home.

Keir stopped me before I could lower myself to carry her. "You sure you're okay to handle this? She's not up for an interrogation."

The fuck did he think I was going to do? Take her hostage?

"I'm not a total asshole, Keir," I hissed back at him. If he tried to stop me from taking Storm, things would get ugly fast.

He grimaced. "I want an update tomorrow."

I gave him a nod, then gingerly lifted my broken angel into my arms. She seemed so damn fragile. So unlike the spitfire ray of sunshine I was used to seeing.

A festering ball of rage swelled against the confines of my chest, aching to be unleashed.

*Not now.* I promised myself. *But soon. This shit will not go unpunished.*

# CHAPTER 26
*Stormy*

*Present*

My sobs had ebbed to a hollow numbness when the door to the locker room flung open. For a second, I thought Damyon had found me. My heart petrified into solid stone in the time it took for a bee's wings to flap.

The realization that it was Torin and Keir brought on a wave of relief I had no right to feel. The mixture of competing emotions had me feeling like a puddle of hopelessness pooled on the dirty concrete floor.

This was so incredibly bad—the exact opposite of what I'd wanted to happen. I'd just been coming to grips with the fact that it was better for everyone if I disappeared, and now

... everything was a complicated mess. Yet my relief at seeing Torin was undeniable.

My head screamed at me about consequences, but my agonized body and heart were adamant Torin equaled safety. They were convinced he would provide the stronghold I so desperately needed, helping to silence my fears for the time being.

Not that I had much say in their involvement.

The savagery in Torin's eyes made it clear he was now in charge. Any protests by me would be futile, and that was its own source of relief. Torin was taking me to his place. Nothing I said or did would change his mind or derail that plan. For once, I was forced to hand over control and simply ... breathe.

My relief was so overwhelming that when he lifted me into his arms, a part of me wished he'd never let go. The comfort of his presence even alleviated my physical pain. With such an intoxicating impact on me, it was no wonder I couldn't seem to cut ties with him.

"Hang in there, sweet girl. I'm taking you home." The whispered words blanketed my soul in warmth.

The second we stepped outside, Rowan came rushing over. "Oh my God. Stormy, are you okay?" She placed her hand gingerly on my shoulder like she wanted to do more but was afraid.

Keir put his arm around her and pulled her into his side. "She's had a rough night. We're going to let Torin handle it."

"Wha—" Whatever protest or question she might have had died a quick death after a single sharp look from Keir.

Tor ignored her completely, continuing to the car. "Someone needs to head over to her place and see if the asshole's still there."

Keir started to reply, but I cut him off. "*No!* You can't do that, please. It's dangerous. Please, don't." This night had already gone so wrong. I would feel wretched if the Byrnes went to my place and ended up in a showdown with Damyon.

Tor must have heard the sharp edge of my panic. "Hey, hey. It's okay. We don't have to go over right away."

"Promise me, Tor. Promise you're not going to send anyone over there tonight." I knew how these guys worked. They'd exchange one fleeting glance meant to say *ignore her,* then assure me everything was fine. It wasn't fine. The situation was more of a disaster than he could comprehend.

"I promise we won't send anyone over tonight, okay?" He eased me onto the passenger seat with the meticulous care of an archaeologist transporting the find of his career. He spoke earnestly enough that I decided to believe him and nodded.

"We can give them a ride," I told him as he buckled my seat belt. "They don't have to get an Uber. Who knows how long it'll take."

"It's Manhattan, babe. Car's probably already on its way." He closed the door, and as if on cue, a pair of headlights pulled up behind us. Keir must have requested the ride before leaving the locker room. Not a full minute later, we were alone with Torin in command behind the wheel.

"I want you to be honest with me," he said evenly. "Should I take you to a hospital?"

"No, I promise," I assured him quickly. "It's nothing some time won't heal."

Seconds ticked by as he stared at me, debating what to do before wordlessly turning his attention to the wheel and pulling onto the road. Neither of us spoke on the ride. I was afraid the truth would weasel its way out if I opened my mouth. I'd told Torin and Keir the attack had been random—just another unlucky statistic. The lie was my attempt at protecting them, but I still felt icky with betrayal. I was repaying their kindness with deception. My admirable motives did little to assuage the guilt.

*Imagine the guilt you'd feel if they end up dead while trying to protect you.*

Absolutely not. It wasn't an option.

I had to keep my lips sealed, recover as quickly as I could, then disappear.

Tor would be angry with me and even hurt. I knew that now that I'd seen more of the man behind the cold facade. He wasn't as hardened as he let on. Keeping people at bay wasn't the same as being mean-spirited. Torin was cautious and a bona fide skeptic, but he was also loyal and thoughtful and deeply passionate. Hurting him would be one of the hardest things I'd ever had to do, but at least I'd know he'd survive.

My eyes burned with the threat of another round of tears by the time we pulled up at his apartment building. When I tried to assure him I could walk, he ignored me and carried me to the elevator then up to his tenth-floor apartment.

Compared to my tiny place, his felt like the Taj Mahal. The high ceilings alone gave the impression of space, but the fact that my entire apartment would easily fit into his open floorplan kitchen was mind-boggling. I knew the man had money. He and his family ran several less-than-legal businesses, but he never actually looked like he had money. His clothes and belongings were understated. His bike, while nice, was a bike. He didn't drive a Lamborghini or flash a Rolex on his wrist, but his home proved he could if he wanted to.

The place was stunning yet suited him well. Modern with rich earthy tones and an emphasis on comfort rather than cutting-edge style. I was fascinated by the glimpse into his personal space. Unfortunately, I only had a second to take in what I saw because he swept me straight back to the primary en suite bathroom before allowing my feet to touch the ground.

He gently set me down, his penetrating stare commanding my attention. "I need you to tell me everywhere he hurt you." He spoke with measured control, white-knuckling the reins on his emotions. Only the slightest tremor in his voice broke through.

"Just my hip, rib, and my face. They're sore, but I'll be fine."

He took my face in his hands and stared fervently into my eyes. "I need to know everything, Storm." His jaw flexed with strain. "Did he force himself on you?"

I shook my head. At least in that regard, I could be honest. "He never had a chance. I got ahold of a baseball bat. The second he went down, I ran."

Torin brought his lips to my forehead, a shuddered breath brushing my skin. "*Good girl. I'm so proud of you.*" When he pulled away, his brows furrowed. "I just wish you'd have called me. Why did you sneak into the club?"

"Everyone's off with family, and I wasn't thinking. I was just suddenly ... there."

The look in his eyes begged for more understanding, but he let the questions go and nodded instead. "Let's have a look at your injuries."

I winced as I lifted my shirt to show him my ribs. He took over when he saw my discomfort, easing my arms through the sleeves and lifting the fabric over my head. His careful eye roved over my torso, fingers tracing my skin with a touch as light as a butterfly's wings.

"There's bruising already. Take a breath for me, as deep as you can without causing too much pain." He watched me carefully as I followed his instructions. "It should be okay, but we'll keep an eye on it. I don't want a broken rib puncturing your lung."

Moving his attention to my leggings, he lowered them to my feet, then assessed the blossoming bruise on the side of my hip.

"That one's not as bad as it looks. The rib hurts worse."

Tor nodded. "I'm going to run you a bath so you can soak. We'll need to ice the injuries later, but for now, I think heat to relax out the tension would be best."

"Okay," I said softly.

He slid my panties down my legs, then stood and unclasped my bra, all with the purest intentions. Not once did his eyes linger in a suggestive manner. Torin was in full protective mode without the slightest ulterior motive.

Another sliver of guilt wound its way through my conscience. Despite his unconventional actions, he'd been nothing but honorable since I'd met him. I hated knowing he'd think the worst of me when I left. It ravaged my heart in ways I hadn't anticipated.

"You soak," he instructed once I was in the bath. "I'll be back with some frozen peas. Best remedy out there for a black eye, trust me."

While he was gone, flashes of memory assaulted me—times when Damyon had tended to me in a similar fashion. Gentle. Tender. Sincere. The familiar scene poked and prodded at my fears, stirring them to life. I had to remind myself that this was different because Torin wasn't the one who'd caused the pain. He'd never once laid a finger on me or even been unkind in any way.

As fickle as the wind, my emotions came at me from all directions with no rhyme or reason. The longer I sat in the bath, the more unstable I felt. I hated the silence. The void left room for violent thoughts that sliced me open from the inside. When I could take no more, I stood.

"I'd like to get out now."

Torin looked at me with worry lining his face but nodded. He helped me out, gently patted me dry, then did something so unexpected that the tears I'd been fighting back finally trickled down my cheeks.

"Shit, am I pulling?" He lowered the brush he'd been using to tenderly work through my tangled hair.

"No." I sniffled and wiped my eyes. "I haven't had anyone do this sort of thing for me in a long time."

"You swear I'm not hurting you?" He took in my small smile before resuming. "I can't say I've ever heard you talk much about your parents."

"That's because they passed away six years ago." I waited for the awkwardness that always followed that revelation, but it never surfaced.

"Brothers and sisters?"

"Nope."

"You have a grandma you're close to. I've heard you talk about her."

I couldn't believe he'd paid attention enough to remember. "Yeah, that's Honey. She was the best grandma a person could ask for." I used the past tense intentionally. He must have noticed because he didn't push for more.

"You're surprisingly good at that, you know," I said after a while.

"What? Using a brush?" he asked with a nudge of humor.

"Yeah. You know how to start at the ends to work out the tangles. Guys don't always know that."

"I had long hair for a while. It was a phase," he added dryly. "I had enough curl that it was always tangled."

"You have any—"

"No pictures. It's not happening."

"How did you know I was going to ask that?" I stared at him incredulously.

He leaned in, bringing his lips near my ear as our eyes met in the mirror. "Because I know *you*, Stormy Lawson," he said in a resolute rumble.

Heat seared up my spine until my entire body blushed. I had to drop my gaze. I didn't want him to know that part of my reaction was rooted in shame. What he thought he knew was a lie. Even my name was a lie.

Unaware of my discomfort, Torin grabbed some pills and a glass of water. "Take these for the pain, then we'll get you settled in. You need to rest." He gently cupped the back of my neck and locked eyes with me. Torin slowly pressed his lips to mine in a devastatingly heartfelt kiss that left my head spinning.

"Do you want to head to bed or watch some TV?"

I didn't want to go to sleep. I had a feeling the memories would morph into nightmares. "No sleeping. Let's watch a little TV."

He nodded and led me into the living room. I waited for him to sit, then gently eased myself down next to him, fitting snugly into his side. He scrolled through a few channels before settling on a documentary about grizzly bears. The narrator's voice was so soothing that I could barely keep my eyes open minutes into the show. I shook my head to scatter the cobwebs, unsure what had come over me.

"The meds I gave you for the pain will make you sleepy. No need to worry, though. I'm confident you don't have a concussion."

"What? What did you give me?" Thoughts evaporated as quickly as they formed, leaving me dazed.

"Nothing bad, I promise." He handed me the remote and eased out from beneath me. "I'm going to run a quick errand while you rest."

"What? No, you said I'm not leaving." I thought about my words, noting something sounded off, but couldn't quite figure out what. "No errands, safer here. Go home tomorrow." I attempted one last time to persuade him to stay.

"Sleep, sweet girl. I'll be back soon." His lips touched my forehead one last time before my eyes fell shut without reopening.

# CHAPTER 27

*Torin*

*Present*

STORM WAS WORRIED THAT ASSHOLE MIGHT STILL BE AT HER place. I was worried he wouldn't be. I would never have left her so soon if I didn't have a good reason, and that reason was retribution.

Tonight, a man had surrendered his right to draw breath. I was going to rectify that situation, and it would be a hell of a lot easier if I didn't have to hunt him down.

I was more than happy to promise Stormy not to send anyone because I preferred to handle it myself anyway. I was a stubborn fucker. Always had been. Besides, Storm was out cold before I left the apartment and wouldn't wake for hours.

And despite her muddled argument, she would *not* be going home the next day, or the day after that.

I'd spent weeks telling myself to leave her alone, and the result of that had been a monumental fail. The one night I didn't follow her, she could have been killed. I had checked the GPS and saw she was home. It still hadn't been enough because I'd thought she was safe when, in reality, she was probably in the process of being attacked at that exact moment.

Fuck that.

Every fiber of my being had screamed that Storm was mine to protect from the first day I saw her. I was done trying to deny it. She was mine, and I was going to start owning that shit. And while it might take her some time, she'd come to understand it was the truth. Until then, I'd hold off on interrogating her over why the hell she'd been out when she told me she would be home all day. Where could she have possibly gone? Nothing was open on Thanksgiving.

I had to stop my runaway thoughts as they veered toward blaming her. None of this was her fault. She was the victim, and I would dole out punishment to the man responsible. If there was any justice in the universe, he'd still be waiting for me right where she left him.

The thought energized me as I walked from my car to her apartment. I came prepared with my gun as I carefully approached her apartment. The door was shut. When I tested the knob, I found it locked. That was unexpected. What kind of rapist creep locks up after his attempted assault is thwarted?

I used my key to let myself in, taking a quick inventory of the situation before entering. No one jumped out at me, and unless the man was hiding, it appeared he'd fled. There'd definitely been a struggle. Blood dotted the floor. But the disarray was more extensive—the place had been ransacked.

Unease settled into a concrete lump in my stomach.

The attacker had riffled through Stormy's apartment, yet a jar of tip money sat on the kitchen counter untouched. It didn't make any sense. This man who attacked her had come to after being knocked out and decided to stick around long enough to search the place but left without taking her money?

Every alarm in my body was going off in unison.

I thought about my conversation with Jolly—about the hearing loss and the way she'd recoiled when I'd called her angel. Had she been in an abusive relationship before, and could that person have paid her a visit?

My racing thoughts streamlined into one cohesive mission. No matter who the fuck had hurt Storm, it would never happen again, and I would brutalize anyone who tried.

A crucial part of keeping her safe, however, would be information. I needed to know everything I could about her and her past. I wasn't sure how she'd feel about that, but for the moment, it could wait. My immediate concern was getting her moved into my place. I peered around the room, debating where to start when my eyes landed on the kitty litter in the corner.

I'd forgotten about her cat.

Fuck, I hated cats.

*Get over it, asshole. You don't have a choice.*

My annoyance ebbed when an even more unsettling thought occurred to me. I'd seen no sign of the cat. What if it got out when the door was open, or what if the guy took the damn thing?

Jesus, I didn't want to have to tell her on top of everything that her cat was gone.

I sat on the loveseat, wondering what the hell I was going to do, when the cushion beneath me chirped. It wasn't a squeaking spring. Not fabric creaking. Something inside the chair definitely *chirped*.

I lowered to the floor and turned on my phone flashlight before lifting the front of the small sofa up. A wide hole had been shredded in the underside of the black fabric, and two glowing eyes watched me from within.

*Meow.*

"Hey, furball. You don't know how relieved I am to see you. Come on out." I got up and went to the bathroom, spilling some disgusting-smelling food pellets into a bowl.

It worked like a charm. The slim cat trotted out, tail high in the air as though not a care in the world, and dove into the food.

"Trusting little shit, aren't you?" I petted his head a few times despite myself. He was surprisingly soft.

A half hour later, I was ready to head back to my place. I had coerced the cat into a carrier I'd found in the top of her closet and packed some essentials for Storm and her cat.

Once I was back in my car, I called Keir.

"How's she doing?" he asked right away.

"She's asleep. Think she's going to be okay, but I need a hand with something."

"What's that?"

"I just went by her place, and something isn't sitting right with me. The guy was gone, and the place was ransacked, but her tip jar is still full, and the door was locked when I got there."

"Why would he have searched her place if he wasn't looking for easy cash?"

"Exactly. And why take the time to lock the door when he left? I don't like it."

"You think she knows this guy?"

I explained my suspicions to him. "She also has a tattoo covering a scar on her chest. Today was the first time I got a good look at it in the light. The ink does a good job of disguising it, but it's a burn. If I didn't know better, I'd have said it was a brand." I was surprised the steering wheel didn't crater from clenching it so tightly. Saying that word aloud —brand—filled me with rage.

Keir went silent. "You give me whatever info you have on her; I'll get a background check going."

"That's what I was thinking. We need to find this motherfucker and fast. I don't just want him in the ground. I want him begging me to put him there."

"Can't argue with that. I'll be in touch."

"Later." It felt good to take action. I'd rather cut off my own fingers than sit around and feel helpless. And in that vein, I had one more errand to run before I could go home. It was going to be a busy night.

# CHAPTER 28
*Stormy*

*Present*

I WASN'T SURE WHAT WOKE ME, BUT MY BRAIN WASN'T entirely prepared for consciousness. My eyes only half cooperated—hooded and burning—but open.

It was early, earlier than I usually woke up, but still light out. I was in an unfamiliar bed with a warm body behind me.

My brain was so fuzzy.

I should have been freaking out, but a mellow numbness kept all but a sense of confusion at bay. I tried to claw at my memories to figure out what was happening when a familiar rich purring vibrated against my tummy.

Blue Bell?

I lifted up just enough to see my sweet kitty curled in a ball on top of the covers.

Memories seeped in like floodwaters under an old door—the attack, Torin, his apartment. He'd said something about running an errand, but I'd been so tired it was all a blur. I remembered being worried. I begged him not to go, but he had, and he'd brought me my Blue Bell.

Emotion lodged in my throat as I snagged my furry baby and smushed his perfect little face against mine. "I'm so glad you're okay," I whispered. "I was so worried."

"Cat knows how to hide." Torin's sleepy voice was a warm caress. He curled onto his side and tugged me back against his body. It felt intimate and sweet—something I didn't associate with him—yet it seemed so natural between us.

Tears burned the backs of my eyes. "Thank you. Thank you *so* much."

He nuzzled his face into my hair and kissed the back of my head. "You can thank me by going back to sleep. It's too fuckin' early to be up."

I grinned, keeping my worries at bay for the moment. Blue Bell was safe. I was safe. And we were all snuggled up like the most perfect set of spoons ever made. For the moment, it was enough.

◊

THE NEXT TIME I WOKE, I was groggy and alone. I peered around the unfamiliar bedroom as my brain scrambled to catch up to reality.

I was in Torin's apartment. Damyon was likely hunting for me with rabid ferocity. My body was sore and stiff, but not as broken as I'd expected. And Blue Bell … My panic surged. Had I dreamed that Torin brought him to me?

I propped myself up and squinted at the comforter where my kitty had been curled up in my memory. Relief had me melting back onto my pillow when I saw cat hair covering the bed.

Oh, thank God.

The moment was short-lived, however, as my emotions burst like fireworks one after the other. Confusion and curiosity quickly replaced the relief and had me back upright.

Why had Torin brought me my cat? It was incredibly sweet, but he had no idea I was going to run. As far as he was concerned, I'd return to my place as soon as possible.

My eyes landed on my suitcase—another surprise. He hadn't just brought me a toothbrush and pajamas. The man had packed an entire suitcase—a big one.

Intrigued, I gingerly scooted off the bed and sat on the ground next to my bright-green luggage. He hadn't exactly folded anything but had done a surprisingly good job of including everything I would have chosen.

As I sifted through the contents, my hand bumped something hard. I lifted the clothes to reveal the one and only framed photo I'd had in my apartment. A small photo of me and my parents. Together and happy. It had been safely tucked away in my nightstand drawer, but Torin had seen it, known it was important, and brought it to me.

A shuddering breath brought instant tears to my eyes.

I'd thought that having Blue Bell with me was everything I needed, but this photo was beyond precious to me. How had he known that I'd needed this?

Emotions bombarded me from every direction. I wiped at my rapidly filling eyes.

"Shit, Storm. Don't cry," Torin said from the doorway behind me.

Surprised to hear him, I took a quick calming breath. "I just didn't expect this." I held up the framed photo. "Any of this. I don't know what to say."

"No need to say anything, but you do need to get dressed and eat some breakfast because the doctor will be here in thirty minutes."

"A doctor?"

"I want those ribs checked. Now, you comin'? Eggs are getting cold, and I hate cold eggs."

"Yeah, let me just step into the restroom, and I'll be right there." I rose slowly, doing my best to look unimpaired. Judging by Torin's frown, I wasn't as convincing as I'd hoped.

I ignored him and closed myself in the bathroom. He had my toothbrush and other toiletries already laid out next to one of the two sinks. I relieved my aching bladder, then freshened up. Torin had given me one of his undershirts the night before, which I kept on, but I swapped out my undies for a fresh pair.

On my way out of the bathroom, I lifted the neck of the shirt to my nose and confirmed it still smelled like him—a rich masculine scent that heated my insides like a shot of Fireball.

I slammed the door on my rioting hormones and joined Torin in the kitchen, where a very different but equally delicious combination of smells greeted me. He had heaped a mountain of food onto two plates at the bar—eggs, sausage, toast, and he'd even peeled an orange and placed a half on each of our plates. Honey, butter, and jelly sat on the counter with two steaming cups of coffee.

"I make them scrambled. Anything else is a pain in the ass. And I wasn't sure how you like your coffee."

"A dab of milk or cream would be great if you have it." I smiled shyly, touched at the trouble he'd gone to. "All of this is amazing. You really didn't have to."

"Wouldn't do it if I didn't want to," he said matter-of-factly as he slid the salt and pepper my way. "Eat." He sat in a bar chair and motioned for me to do the same.

Considering the Thanksgiving meal I'd had the day before, I shouldn't have been hungry, but I suddenly felt ravenous. We ate in silence—not totally uncomfortable, but not companionable either. It was hard to feel at ease when uncertainty perched like a greedy vulture over my shoulder.

"Guess I ought to get dressed," I said, standing after finishing.

Torin stacked my plate on his, then swiveled to face me, his hand casually lifting to hook into the hem of my shirt. Well, his shirt. I watched, a breathless anticipation filling my chest, wondering what he might do next.

"I had no idea," he finally said almost to himself.

A tendril of worry stiffened my spine. Had he learned something about my past?

"About what?" I hazarded to ask.

"That I'd like it so much."

"Like what?"

"Having you here in my space."

My head tilted a fraction as confusion set in. "Did you think it would bother you for me to be here?"

His electric-blue stare speared me in place. "I wasn't sure. I've never let anyone but family come over." His naked truth was spoken with such raw transparency, there was no room for doubt. He wasn't even exaggerating. I was the first outsider he'd let into his home.

While I stood reeling over the admission, he released his hold on my shirt and took the plates to the sink, severing our connection.

I'd never felt more ashamed or inadequate. Here was a man who clearly had trust issues, and I was about to prove him right in the worst sort of way.

Whether I told him the truth about me or not, the secrets I'd kept felt more and more like a nasty betrayal. That was why I prevented myself from forming attachments and a secondary reason for moving every six months. My past complicated everything.

I'd grown lax in Chicago and convinced myself that I no longer needed to run. And now, I was in danger of self-destructing before I ever made it out of New York.

# CHAPTER 29
## *Stormy*

*Past*

LEAVING RUSSIA TAUGHT ME THAT IT WAS POSSIBLE TO HAVE everything and nothing at the same time. To win and lose in equal measure, resulting in a cataclysm of emotion.

I was finally healthy and had been given my freedom. There was no descriptor adequate for that feeling. Elation. Relief. Boundless hope.

But at the same time, returning to the US without being able to go home highlighted all that had been taken from me. Eighteen months after losing my parents and going in search of my birth mother, I was no closer to finding her and had tacked on the devastating loss of a pregnancy and the knowledge that I might never see my remaining family again.

Everything I'd endured in Russia had all been for nothing. During the six months I spent recovering in St. Petersburg, that reality often plagued me, its poisonous barbs sinking deep into my flesh until the pain was insufferable. If it weren't for the fleeting moments of relief that enveloped me in warmth when I remembered I'd regained my freedom, I might not have survived those seemingly endless days.

At first, I wasn't sure I wanted to survive.

Those first weeks back in the US had been enormously challenging. But with time, those tiny pinpricks of hope grew into swaths of uplifting sunshine.

I had my whole life ahead of me.

As I stepped out from beneath Damyon's malignant shadow, I was able to see that the losses I'd suffered, though heartbreaking, were not all that defined me. I'd known exquisite joy in my childhood, and there was no reason I couldn't find that again.

I was forever changed as a person, but that didn't have to be a bad thing. The more I thought about it, the more adamant I became that I would determine my outlook rather than allow my circumstances to dampen my view.

I chose to be a survivor, not a victim.

Ulyana's contacts had been invaluable by helping to smuggle me into Estonia, then on to Canada. By the time I took my first steps back on US soil, the seeds of optimism had firmly taken root. I couldn't go home to Savannah, but I was free to start over anywhere else I wanted. I'd been smuggled into the country via Toronto and made my first temporary home in Detroit. Not exactly paradise, but everyone had to start somewhere.

I fumbled through the process of finding a place to live and getting a job while staying off the grid. I hadn't heard or seen any sign of Damyon, but that didn't mean he wasn't out there looking. I planned to move every six months to a new city and start over, at least for a few years until I felt safe enough to stay somewhere more permanently.

Columbus.

St. Louis.

Nashville.

Pittsburgh.

Indianapolis.

Chicago.

The Windy City. That was where I found myself after three years on the run. My six-month stint was quickly coming to an end, yet I was reluctant to plan my next move. The small studio apartment I'd been living in came furnished and allowed me to rent month-to-month, which wasn't always easy to find. The place had come to feel like home more than any previous apartment.

I'd even found a way to keep my connection with Honey alive, however tenuous. I allowed myself to send her a letter with a cashier's check once a quarter. She'd never had much money, so I liked to send what little extra tip money I could stash away. I kept the content of my letters vague but positive. I didn't want her to worry, but I also couldn't risk giving away any clues to my location.

The first time I wrote, it was out of guilt. I had to reassure her I was okay. Then it became a sort of balance check—a lifeline to my past that kept me centered. Each quarter, I took a day trip to a small town unconnected to me and sent a letter with no return address. Even if Damyon monitored her, he couldn't trace the letter back to me.

That was assuming he managed to locate her. I hadn't told him more than her pet name. She'd outlived all three of her husbands, my grandfather being the first of them. With each new marriage, she took her new husband's name and moved. She wasn't impossible to track down, but it also wouldn't be easy.

The fact that she was still unharmed gave me the confidence to consider settling down. I couldn't live on the run forever.

"What do you think, Blue Bell? Is it time to find a real home?" I hugged the sweet Siamese kitty to my chest. He was the other reason I'd been so happy in Chicago.

Smitten blue eyes peered up at me as though he was happy for me. Or maybe he was just pleading for more pets. He was a hound for attention. His owner lived above me, but the cat spent most of his time at my place, even keeping me company at night.

I'd been so tickled the first time he sauntered down the fire escape and through my window. Now, I didn't know what I'd do without him. He was even better than a tub of Blue Bell ice cream—that was how he'd gotten his name—the name I'd given him. At this point, his original owners were irrelevant. As far as I was concerned, they'd surrendered him when they stopped caring if he came home.

Home. God, I wanted a home again. I missed knowing my neighbors and hanging pictures on the walls and having friends over. Shoot, just *having* friends would be amazing.

I'd been meticulous about keeping people at bay wherever I lived. My guilty conscience about hurting people when I left demanded I not form attachments. I desperately missed having a support network. And on top of that, I liked the job I'd found at an old-school diner, unlike the last couple of nightmare jobs. I should have known the porn shop was a bad idea. I shuddered at the memory of some of the creepers who came through those doors.

"How about this?" I asked my furry roommate. "What if we rally for one more move, but then we stay put for a few years? I could give us six more months here, then we go somewhere and stay for a while—let ourselves have a real home."

Blue Bell purred even louder.

"Then it's settled. Blue Bell and Stormy are one step closer to a normal life."

My furry companion chirped.

"I agree, we should celebrate, but I don't have time right now."

He sneezed as if incensed by the notion.

I giggled. "Time to get ready for work. You try not to stress yourself while I'm gone." I set him on the bed where I'd been lying. He never even budged, falling instantly asleep without a care in the world.

❧

"That's the last of it. It's a good thing we're staying put for a while because we'll need a moving truck next time. I seem to be accumulating more and more *stuff*."

Blue Bell chimed in with a meow from his perch on the back of the tiny sofa.

"Yeah, including you. I couldn't possibly have left you behind."

As promised, I rallied for one more move after a year in Chicago, this time with my sweet Blue Bell. Did I steal someone's cat? Yup. Did I feel any sort of guilt about it? Not even a little. As far as I was concerned, he'd adopted me, and who was I to turn away such an honor?

"I'm going to check out the neighborhood while it's still light out. You be good while I'm gone." I zipped up my jacket and headed out to size up possible jobs nearby. I didn't like to go long without money coming in.

Not two blocks away, I came across a vibrant set of green neon lights outside a black building. The sign read Moxy, and it looked to be some sort of bar. The place would be convenient, only a couple of blocks from home, and bars tended to be ideal employers for me. They didn't ask many questions, which was good because I couldn't provide answers.

Social security number. Nope.

Driver's license. Nah.

References. No can do.

Stormy Lawson didn't have any of those. That was the name I'd chosen for myself when I started over. Stormy as a nod to my daddy, who always called me his stormy girl, while Lawson was random. I just liked the way it sounded.

The best I had to offer potential employers was a bright smile and the assurance that I would be reliable help. A Now Hiring sign was posted outside, and the green lights gave off a lucky vibe, so I decided to check it out.

I squared my shoulders, plastered on my charming Southern grin, and pulled open the solid black door. I was half right about it being a bar. To be more precise, it was a strip club. A nice one. I'd seen the full gambit, and this place wasn't so bad. In fact, I was pleasantly surprised.

It was still early for this type of place, so only a couple of girls were dancing. An enormous bouncer sat vigil at the front door. Good to know security was present.

"Hi, there." I beamed at him. "I saw the sign out front and wanted to see about applying."

He gave me a tough-guy chin lift. "Let me get Jolly." He pulled out his phone to shoot off a text, and a few minutes later, an older man appeared from the back. He motioned for me to join him at the bar. After a quick glance at the bouncer to confirm the gentleman was indeed "Jolly," I hurried over.

"We're looking for two nights a week right now. Can't guarantee more, but if you're good, it's likely you can get more shifts soon enough." He jumped right in without an introduction. Straight to the point. It worked for me.

Two nights wasn't much, but I could always get another job for the other days and go from there. "When would you want me to start?"

"Well, you'd have to audition first. I'm not puttin' you on stage until I see if you can move."

"Oh!" I laughed at the absurd notion. "I'm not here to dance. I'm looking to be a server. You don't want me up there, trust me." I winked with a grin.

He tapped his knuckles on the bar. "Makes that easy. We're not lookin' for anything else."

"Wait, are you sure? I'm super reliable," I assured him. "And folks up north always love a little Southern charm." I wasn't sure why I'd resorted to begging. I could manage a few more days of job hunting, but I couldn't shake the feeling that this place suited me.

Jolly shook his head, but before he could reply, a man seated on the other side of him spoke up. I'd just assumed he was a customer and hadn't paid him any mind until now.

"You know how to make drinks?" He looked over, and I was struck dumb by the most radiant blue eyes I'd ever seen. Multifaceted and warm like the images I'd seen of the

Caribbean. They almost seemed to glow from beneath his angular brow.

I had to give myself an internal shake. What was it with me and blue-eyed men?

"Yeah, I've waitressed and bartended before. I'd prefer to waitress, but I can do either."

Jolly gave the man a questioning look but didn't contradict him.

The blue-eyed man threw back the rest of his drink. "She can act as a filler, float between Candice and Lyla." He slid from the stool and walked away without another word.

I had to force myself not to stare at his retreating form. He was decently tall and lean with honed muscle visible beneath his snug, long-sleeved shirt. I couldn't even begin to describe how perfectly his chiseled backside filled out his dark-wash jeans.

*Sweet Mother Mary. Would you get ahold of yourself, child. The last thing you need is to get involved with a man—least of all, a man like* that. Honey's voice rang loud and clear in my head.

She was right.

"Well, guess that's that," Jolly grumbled. "When can you start?"

I gave him a Christmas morning smile. "You tell me when, and I'll be here."

# CHAPTER 30
*Stormy*

*Present*

Torin's doctor was a middle-aged man who looked like he'd been a heavyweight champ in a previous life. He was solid with mature muscle and easily six-five if he was an inch, and he moved with the carefree ease of a man of that stature—a man who rarely met with any challengers.

"That's a nasty shiner you're wearin' there, Miss Lawson." The man spoke with a breezy Caribbean accent that complemented his laid-back demeanor, though the disapproving look he shot at Torin wasn't so casual.

"You look at me like that again, and I'll give you one to match." Tor pointed at the man who was his senior in both age and stature. "Not that it's any of your goddamn business, but I didn't lay a finger on her. Not sure what would make you think otherwise." He muttered the last part, giving me the sense they knew each other well.

The man, who had introduced himself as Jonas, wasn't the slightest bit affected by Torin's threat. In fact, I detected a touch of amusement, as though he relished the thought of Torin attempting to challenge him.

"Still too easy to rile, little Byrne." Jonas grinned. "I thought I taught you better."

"Just do your job, old man," Torin shot back at him without any real force. Their dynamic fascinated me. And I quickly decided that I liked Jonas. A lot.

I smiled at the unconventional doctor. "It's true. I was attacked at my apartment. Tor had nothing to do with it. Just one of those random awful things that happen sometimes."

Jonas's eyebrows arched high. "On Thanksgiving, no less." He tsked. "Your luck must have run plumb dry, considering de timing. Thanksgiving day has one of de lowest crime rates all year." He spoke with slow, measured words as he looked me over, skepticism unmistakable beneath his melodic cadence.

My gaze shot briefly to Torin, whose fathomless stare already pinned me in place. "I'll hold off on buying a lottery ticket," I murmured.

"Ah, well. T'ings are bound to get better." He patted my shoulder gently and suggested we look at "those ribs," only it sounded more like "dose reebs."

He looked me over, running through a series of tests involving deep breaths, twisting, and bending—all of which hurt like a son of a bitch. Eventually, he gave me a clean bill of health, aside from bruising and contusions.

I excused myself to shower as soon as he finished, allowing the two men to have a moment alone. My hair hadn't been washed in days, and I needed a chance to do some thinking. I could feel myself wanting to fall back on the excuse of my injuries to stick around. Being cared for was an emotional luxury I'd long been denied. The allure was incredibly tempting, but I couldn't let it distract me or weaken my resolve.

I took a cold shower, letting the discomfort of the chill ground me and soothe my swelling. By the time I got out, my determination had returned, albeit somewhat less enthusiastic than before. I would go, but it was going to take a heavy toll. My spirit could only be chipped away so many times before the remaining piece was jagged and perilously hollow. Thinking I had finally found a place to call home, only to have it viciously yanked from my grasp, was so much more painful than if I'd simply stuck to my routine and kept on the move. And now that I knew Damyon was still on my trail, it looked like I'd never have a home.

With that depressing thought, I wrapped myself in a towel and opened the bathroom door to get clothes from my suitcase. I didn't make it far. Torin leaned against the doorframe across the room as though he'd been waiting for me.

I stilled. "Everything okay?"

He slowly uncrossed his arms and prowled closer without answering. The sultry wind from his brewing storm filled the room with electricity and heat and uncertainty. I watched with interest as he helped himself to my suitcase, selecting an outfit complete with bra and panties, then rose to join me.

How could a man who spoke so few words convey so

much with every little action? Nothing he did was unintentional or superfluous, yet it all seemed so effortless. So natural. As though self-assurance was just another strand of his DNA.

The effect was mesmerizing, intensifying exponentially as he drew closer. His fingers gently clasped my towel and tugged. Not hard. It was more of a command for me to let go than a move of force. He wanted me to follow his lead.

I shouldn't have. I needed to keep every barrier raised, both physical and emotional, but my body acted of its own accord and released the thick terry cloth. The burst of cool air on my skin sent a wave of desire flooding the highways and byways of my body. My nipples pebbled into tightly coiled buds as if desperately preening for his attention.

Torin drank up his effect on me, shoulders seemingly growing broader and pupils forcing out all but the outermost ring of his blue irises. He lifted his hand to trail his scarred knuckles over one peak, then gently plucked the sensitive flesh.

I gasped at the unexpected zing of pleasure, liquid desire melting my insides like hot tea over ice.

The clothes he'd held dropped to the floor.

"Maybe this wasn't a good idea," I said shakily, though each word was painful to say because, at that moment, I wanted him more than anything in the world.

Tor slowly lowered to a squat, his eyes lifting to mine once he was all the way down. "You don't even know what *this* is." His sultry words licked at my skin.

He held out the panties I didn't realize he'd kept in his hand and waited for me to step into them. I put a hand on his shoulder and followed his lead. He lifted the silk agonizingly slowly, his palms almost surveying my body like a conqueror taking inventory of his new territory. Then he hooked my bra in a finger before standing. I put one arm in each strap when he held it out for me, relishing the way his gaze stroked my skin as real as any physical touch.

"Turn." His voice grew as coarse as a long-forgotten gravel road.

I obeyed, my body seemingly his to command.

He brought his hands around to my front and ensured the bra cupped me just right, his fingers giving an extra swipe across each stiff peak for good measure before he secured the clasp at my back. I was so desperate for more of his touch that I wanted to weep when he began to slide on my leggings and shirt.

He'd chosen something comfortable, which was sweet, but I wanted to rip the fabric from my body and burn it to ash if it meant an end to his attention. Desire eviscerated every thought in my head beyond carnal need. I was seconds away from begging him to touch me again when the doorbell echoed in the air between us.

I startled a step backward and ran a hand through my wet hair, suddenly embarrassed. What the heck had come over me? Didn't I have any willpower at all?

"You expecting someone?" My voice was an entire octave above normal.

*Way to play it cool, Stormy.*

A tiny twitch tightened the corner of his eye. "Rowan insisted on coming over to check on you. Guess I should have specified a time." He grumbled the last part to himself before walking stiffly from the room.

♦

I was so touched that Rowan had come to see me. However, our budding friendship was the source of yet another stab of regret. Leaving the city would cost me dearly.

"Hey, sunshine! How are you feeling?" Rowan pushed straight past Torin, ignoring him completely.

"I'm surprisingly good, actually. It's so sweet of you to come by."

"Of course!" She gave me a whisp of a hug, scared the slightest touch might break me.

Behind us, Keir and Torin greeted one another with a pair of grunts. They said a few quiet words with their heads together, keeping me from hearing, then took their leave to sit at the kitchen table. Rowan and I settled on the sofa. She sat facing me, her entire focus directed at me.

"We don't need to talk about it," she said in a rush, "but Keir explained what happened, and I want you to know that I'm happy to help you get out of your lease or move or even give you a place to stay while you find a new place. I can only imagine you wouldn't want to stay there, and maybe I'm wrong, but just so you know, I'm happy to help however I can. And that's the last we need to talk about it." She raised her hand in a pledge.

"That's sweet of you. I haven't decided what I'm doing, but I definitely have some thinking to do." I'd become accustomed to a certain degree of evasion. It wasn't easy at first, but it had never bothered me like it did now. This didn't feel like harmless white lies anymore. My lies were blossoming into unadulterated deception, and the accompanying shame crippled me.

"Well, I know what it's like to feel unsafe. I told you how Keir and I came together, but there was a lot I left out. A lot of scary shit involving sex trafficking, my ex-boyfriend's psychotic family, and a scarred Russian man we thought wanted me dead. My life was unrecognizable for a while."

With every thudding beat, my heart ticked its way farther up my throat.

"Scarred Russian?" I asked quietly, almost too afraid to say the words.

"Yeah, from his temple to his cheek. And eyes so pale blue they could have been carved from ice. He was terrifying." A shiver ran through her at the recollection.

Bile burned the back of my throat.

It was Damyon. Not only had he been closer than I'd realized, he was already putting my friends at risk, whether he knew it or not.

I fought back the intense need to vomit. I had to learn everything I could from her. "Why would he want you dead?"

"We thought he did, but it turned out we were wrong. A mix-up over a sale of guns or something. It was complicated." Her eyes cut briefly to Keir, and I got the sense she wasn't sure how much she should tell. "Anyway, I didn't mean to worry you. You've been through enough."

I forced a thin smile, hoping to reassure her. We talked for another half an hour about nothing of consequence until Keir insisted they leave and allow me to rest. I was glad, but not for the reasons they might think. I needed to process what I'd learned.

Damyon knew about the Byrne family. It was only a matter of time before he put the pieces together.

"What were you and Keir talking about so quietly?" I asked once we were alone and making ourselves sandwiches for lunch.

"Work," he offered vaguely.

"The club?" I tried to pull more from him, knowing chances were good the work he was discussing was likely me.

"Yeah." His clipped answers made it clear that I wasn't going to get anywhere, so I decided to change tactics.

"Rowan was telling me about how she met Keir. Said some crazy Russian was after her?" She'd said more than that, but that was the only part I was interested in.

"Don't know why she'd tell you about that shit," he said with a hint of anger. "Last thing you need is more worries. Just ignore her. Everything worked out fine."

Great. Another brick wall. Third time's the charm.

"Okay then, tell me about Jolly. He said you two met at a juvenile detention center."

He spread mustard on a piece of bread, his blue eyes as calculating and cryptic as ever. "We did."

"What were you in for?"

His eyes darkened. I'd hit on a sensitive subject, but I wasn't sure why.

"Possession," he finally admitted.

"That where you started fighting?" I hated that he put himself in the ring and couldn't understand why he did it.

"I started training as soon as I got out."

"That's been a while. Long time to keep at it." He had power and money, so why did he keep getting in the ring? What did he get from fighting that kept him at it?

"Your point?"

I wanted to ask my questions to understand, but judging

by his clipped responses, I decided not to push. "You know why he goes by Jolly? Is it like calling a huge man tiny? Because he sure isn't very jolly at this point in his life."

With one simple shift in direction, the tension in his features instantly softened. "We called him Jolly because he was the spitting image of Santa."

Surprise drew my brows together. "Santa?"

"Imagine him a hundred pounds heavier with a full white beard."

My jaw dropped. "You're kidding."

"You ever know me to kid?"

"No, but there's always hope." I smirked playfully. "Did he come to you looking for work or the other way around?" I asked, hoping to keep the conversation going. Instead, I hit a wall.

Torin's lips thinned. "I went to him."

Our eyes locked. My stare begged to know why he'd asked to work with the man who'd essentially been his prison guard. His unrelenting stare told me it was none of my business. Before I could think of another question that might unveil answers about the mysterious man, he turned the tables on me.

"You haven't tried to reach out to any family or friends since last night. I haven't seen you go near your phone since you got here."

"I told you, my parents are dead."

"How'd they die?" He was more direct than most. I should have expected that.

"Boating accident." I took a bite of rolled-up pastrami, skipping the bread.

"Friends?" With a tilt of his head, he effectively had me under a microscope. "Seems strange that someone as outgoing as you doesn't have a whole horde of people close to you—family or not."

*You have to let people in for them to be close.*

Again, we engaged in a wordless contest of wills. This time, he was the interrogator demanding to know more, and I was as silent as the tombstone over my parents' graves.

His phone buzzed in his pocket three times before he relented and answered.

"Yeah?"

The caller spoke for several minutes without a break, and with each second that passed, a shadow darkened Torin's eyes. His unnervingly perceptive stare shifted from curious to downright accusatory, every ounce directed at me.

# CHAPTER 31

*Jorin*

*Present*

"I PULLED UP ANYTHING AND EVERYTHING I COULD ABOUT Stormy like you asked," Oran said after I picked up the phone. "I know you guys don't do full background checks on new employees, but you must not have checked her out at all because there's not shit on her anywhere."

"What's that supposed to mean?" I didn't like where this was headed.

"She's not just clean; she's a ghost. Stormy Lawson doesn't exist."

My pulse pounded in my ears as I tried not to overreact.

Oran couldn't dig up anything on Storm, but that didn't necessarily mean anything. "Could it be a nickname issue?" Maybe she didn't go by her legal name—loads of people didn't.

"The social on her job application is a fake, Tor. There were no Lawsons in the graduating class for the high school she listed. She said she was born and raised in Atlanta, but there are no birth records for a female Lawson that year that could have been her. I tracked down each one. She's lying to us, and we need to know why."

*Before you lose your shit, think this through.*

So Stormy lied. It wasn't a stretch to guess that she had history with an ex and was hiding from him. I was confident that was her reason, but why the hell hadn't she come clean at this point? I wasn't worried like Oran about Storm being dangerous to us. What bothered me was that she still trusted me so little.

"I have an idea of what's going on," I shot back at him. "It's not a concern."

"Considering the way Caitlin infiltrated our family, I think we have to investigate Stormy as a possible threat. For all we know, she could be working for a rival organization."

My hand clutched the phone so tight I was in danger of needing to replace the damn thing again. I wanted to tell my cousin he was a paranoid asshole, but how could I? His theory about Storm was technically as plausible as any other.

"I hear you, but I'll still be the one to handle it." My tone grew perilously close to a growl.

"You're too close, trust me. I know how easy it is to let your emotions fuck with your judgment when it comes to these sorts of things. Let me come over and talk to her."

Oran's interrogation of his now ex-wife had been ruthless. He'd been jaded toward women ever since, and I had no doubt he'd rip Stormy apart. She might have lied about her past, but everything about her trauma and the attack had been real. No one was that good an actor. She'd been genuinely scared for her life. I couldn't subject her to my cousin on top of that.

"I said I can handle it, and I meant it."

"It's not just you she's endangering, Tor."

"And *you're* making assumptions, which is exactly why I'll be doing the questioning." I hung up before I said something I'd regret. My patience was already worn too thin.

I began to pace, hoping to burn off some of the frustration eating my insides. Storm wisely remained silent. I could feel her wide, childlike eyes following me across the room. My raging emotions desperately fought to lash out, but I kept them in check. Barely.

I needed to address this with a level head, or I'd be no better than my cousin.

Stormy wasn't the deceptive type. My gut vehemently denied the insinuation that she might be out to hurt our family. The problem was that I'd been burned by people before, which made me question my judgment. I didn't want to believe my instincts could be so well deceived after all these years. Had I been completely wrong about her?

My anger sprouted scaly black wings and begged to be released. I yanked on its chain with a harsh command to be silent, the effort chafing away at my waning patience.

I stopped pacing and faced Storm, unable to hold back any further. "Who the fuck are you?"

Three seconds.

Three seconds was all it took to know I'd been wrong. About her. About everything. Because in three second's time, Storm didn't wither in response to my attack. She didn't look at me for understanding as confusion set in, and she certainly didn't drop her gaze beneath the weight of embarrassment after being caught. Instead, the spirited Southern spitfire across from me steeled her spine and lifted her chin defiantly.

"You know who I am," she said evenly.

"No, I thought I did. Turns out, I was wrong. I don't even know your fucking name."

"You know everything that's relevant. If that's not enough —" She stood, but I stopped her in her tracks, squaring my shoulders with hers.

"You think having an abusive ex isn't relevant?" I was dangerously close to yelling.

Storm's already porcelain skin drained to a ghostly white, but she didn't cower. She remained on the offensive. "What happened in juvie that made you so angry? Why don't you let anyone close to you except Jolly? Who is he to you?"

"This isn't about me," I bit through clenched teeth.

"My past is just as irrelevant as yours," she hissed.

"Yours is very fucking relevant if someone is after you."

"Why?" She spread her arms as wide as her injured ribs would allow. "Because you started *stalking* me and decided you had some fucked-up sense of responsibility for me? Well, let me make this clear. I don't owe you *anything*, Torin Byrne. Not my body, my heart, or my truth. If there's a monster in this room, it's not me, it's *you*. Don't try to pretend otherwise."

I was speechless.

Her rebuttal was so scathing that I felt seared from the inside, my skin flayed wide open.

After such an efficient decapitation, there was nothing left for me to say. No counterpoint or excuse would measure up. All I could do was scrape up my bloody bits off the floor and leave.

# CHAPTER 32

*Stormy*

*Present*

AS I WATCHED TORIN LEAVE THE APARTMENT, I WAS consumed with self-hatred. I saw my opportunity to right my wrongs, and I seized it. Leaving Torin would be better for him in the end—he and his family would be safer that way—but it shredded me all the same.

I'd never forget the look of unmitigated pain that flashed in his eyes before a chilling emptiness took over. It had almost been too much. I'd been seconds away from dropping to my knees and begging his forgiveness. Two blistering heartbeats from throwing my arms around him and assuring him it had all been a show. But I'd held strong, and I'd never been more equally proud and ashamed of myself at the same time.

Remorse thick as cooling tar blackened my conscience.

If it had been the right thing to do, why did I feel so wretched? How was I supposed to live with myself knowing I'd been so cruel?

I felt an intense need to escape before Torin returned, purely out of shame rather than a need to protect him. Tears ran like rivers down my cheeks as I walked numbly back to the bedroom. My bag was already packed. All I had to do was throw in a few miscellaneous items, get Blue Bell in his carrier, and I could disappear.

I battled against rising sobs, knowing they'd wreak havoc on my ribs, then decided I deserved the pain. I allowed the shuddering breaths to wrack my body. Melting onto the floor, I bellowed in agony, inside and out.

I screamed at the unfairness.

I threw clothing in fits of fury.

I smashed my fists on the ground to fight off the despair.

Eventually, my tantrum lost its thunder and faded into distant rumbles and bleak acceptance. Blue Bell joined me, curling up in my lap when he deemed it safe. My hair fell in a curtain around my face as I pet him. For a moment, I was able to shut out the world and pretend his gentle purring meant everything was okay. Then the front door clicked open and shut, followed by footsteps.

Torin had returned sooner than I'd expected. To what end? I wanted to peek at him to assess his mood but was too embarrassed. Instead, I sat motionless and listened to his steady footsteps as he passed behind me and sat on the bed.

"I was sixteen when I was charged with possession of cocaine," he started in an achingly hollow voice. "It wasn't mine. I had permission to use the family car for the afternoon and had taken some friends to the beach. We'd had a few beers, so when I got pulled over, the cop smelled alcohol and decided to search the car. They found a dime bag of coke under the driver's seat. I was handcuffed and arrested on the spot."

He took a long, even breath, making me realize I'd been holding mine, riveted by what he was telling me.

"I yelled and begged for my friends to fess up, knowing one of them had been responsible, but they wouldn't even look me in the eye. They watched me get taken away and did nothing." The disgust in his tone was understandable. I couldn't imagine being punished for something I hadn't done. "My dad was the only Byrne brother who didn't fall in line with the family business. He was of the opinion that my crime was hanging with the wrong crowd. He didn't reach out for help to get me off, hoping the sentence would be a wake-up call for his youngest and most undisciplined kid. I spent a year in that cesspool, and those guys I'd called friends let it happen to save their own asses. I may have been young, but I learned some hard truths I've never forgotten. *That's* why I don't let people in. Because I don't trust anyone. And I had no reason to expect you to trust me."

This wasn't supposed to be happening.

I should have been leaving, not growing more attached. Yet with every word Torin spoke, my heart rooted itself further in him and everything about this life I'd created in New York. Tearing myself away would mean severing parts of myself that would never grow back.

When I first came to the city, I'd already craved stability —a home and friends where I could settle in. Maybe I was meant to find Moxy. Maybe Torin and I crossed paths for a reason.

But what did that mean? Was I supposed to take the leap and come clean? I was terrified he'd get hurt, not to mention worried he'd be furious that I'd hidden so much from him.

*You've faced near death and total heartbreak multiple times and survived. You'll survive this too.*

It was true, but one thought bolstered me more than any other. If I told him everything, I'd know how he'd respond—one way or the other. The endless uncertainty would be over.

Torin had presented a chance at honesty and vulnerability and hope. A chance to have everything I'd ever wanted. Couldn't I summon the courage to meet him halfway?

Slowly, I turned and met his stare. The sight of my tearstained cheeks softened his features, but he didn't move. He'd done his part. The rest was up to me.

I stood and walked hesitantly to where he sat, then crawled onto his lap, straddling him. Torin held me in place, his hands clasping my backside. His nostrils flared as his fingers gently kneaded my flesh, but he made no other move. He only watched and waited.

My fingers toyed absently with the neckline of his shirt while I summoned my courage, eyes cast down between us. "I *do* trust you. That's what scares me," I finally admitted on a breathless whisper.

Voicing the words made my heart flutter like a drunken butterfly. I didn't get any more out when his hand cupped my jaw and forced my gaze to meet the savage intensity in his.

"Say it again," he ordered in a low rumble.

"I trust you."

His thumb swiped slow across my bottom lip, then tugged it down before his strong hand collared my throat. "*Again*," he demanded.

"I trust you, Torin Byrne." This time, the words came with more ease—confident and bolstered by a hint of challenge.

A feral growl wrenched from deep in his chest as he pulled my lips to his. He brought his hand around from the front of my neck to the back, holding me precisely where he wanted me while his tongue plundered my mouth.

What he did was so much more than a kiss. With each press of his lips and swipe of his tongue, he penned a binding contract between us. An oath I worried would shatter when he learned the truth about me. When he heard the name of the man who was hunting me and discovered the extent of my trauma, because it was so much more than what could be seen by the naked eye. More than the emotional damage.

I'd been robbed of my ability to bear children.

On top of everything else, that strike against me felt like the kiss of death. And maybe it was just my own feelings of inadequacy, but I couldn't imagine anyone thinking a relationship with me would be worth the trouble. And there would be trouble because Damyon was here in the city. It was only a matter of time.

Torin tore his lips from mine as though he'd heard my thoughts.

"I'm fucked up, Storm. I won't deny it. I couldn't be normal if I tried."

"I don't want normal." Normal would never understand me.

His hand fisted in my hair, and I felt him grow impossibly harder beneath me. "Don't say that shit unless you mean it because I'm already in too deep. I can't explain it to myself any more than I can to you. I just know that you're meant to be mine."

"You don't mean that." My heart began to crack as I whispered the words because I felt the end coming as the truth forced its way to the surface.

"Why the fuck not? You don't believe me?"

I shook my head. "Not that. It's just that … you wouldn't want me if…"

His grip in my hair tightened as he tugged my head back a fraction further. "*Why?* Why the fuck would I not want you?"

My vision blurred with tears. "Because I come with baggage."

"And I don't?" His hands released me before he stood and set me on my feet in front of him, his arms spreading wide. "You can tell by now that I'm no white knight, Storm. But I'll slay your demons because your demons are mine. *You* are mine." Each word was more adamant than the last, finishing with a fist pounding against his chest.

Energy buzzed the room the same way it did when lightning was about to strike.

My lungs felt like they couldn't get enough air. "I'm scared, Torin. At first, I thought I was scared of you, but now…"

"Now?" he demanded.

I met his stare, the first of my tears falling free. "I'm scared *for* you."

"What the fuck for, Stormy?" he asked in exasperation. "I'm not afraid of some ex-boyfriend asshole."

"It's not that simple." I shook my head, my words almost inaudible.

"What's so fucking complicated? Just tell me his goddamn name," Torin roared.

My legs collapsed beneath me, sending me to my knees.

"*His name is Damyon.*" I forced past my lips, eyes squeezed tightly shut. "*Damyon Karpova.*"

# CHAPTER 33

*Torin*

*Present*

STORM DIDN'T JUST SWIPE THE RUG OUT FROM UNDER ME; THE whole goddamn building was gone. I wouldn't have been more surprised if she'd said her ex was Genghis fucking Khan. At least then I could have laughed it off as a delusion. But this? Despite the insane unlikelihood, I didn't think she was joking.

How the fuck could sweet Southern Stormy have ties with the man who owned half of Moscow? It didn't make sense. The Russian Shadow—a name he'd earned in the streets—was the last person I'd expected. It was so outlandish that I couldn't figure out how I felt beyond my disbelief.

"How long have you been on the run from him?" The timeline would give me a clue about the severity of our problem. I would focus on finding a solution because I had no idea what to do about the rest.

"Five years," she said softly.

*Jesus.*

All that time—for her to be on the run—for him to keep hunting her.

This was a fucking catastrophe.

A blur of questions surfaced, but we didn't have time. If we were about to face off with Damyon Karpova, we'd already wasted too much time.

"Get dressed and pack an overnight bag. We're leaving." I had to bring in my family. They needed to know what we were facing and help me devise a plan.

Storm gave a defeated nod and rose to her feet. I hated seeing her so meek, but there wasn't time for gentle assurances. Our only hope of winning this war was with absolute ruthlessness.

Judging by her reluctance to tell me about Damyon, she knew exactly how dangerous he was. She'd also known that we were familiar with the man. How long had she known? Was that why she'd stuck around—hoping my family would shield her? Would that bother me if she had?

Fuck, I didn't know.

Setting aside my trust issues to sort out later, I called my cousins to arrange a gathering. We decided to meet at a basement property we rarely frequented—somewhere unlikely to be on Damyon's radar. For all we knew, he could already be watching us. I didn't want to tempt fate by appearing at one of our regular haunts.

Once we were both ready, I led Stormy to the car I owned but rarely used.

"For what it's worth, I'm sorry," she said, cutting the stifling silence. Her voice was wrought with remorse.

I wanted to believe her, but *Jesus*, she'd kept so much from me already.

*You don't owe me anything.*

Weren't those the words I'd spoken only hours ago? Did they not still apply?

She hadn't owed me anything, yet she'd given me the truth despite her fears. I didn't want to be the asshole who condemned her for it. I didn't want to, but … I had my own issues. Like I told her, I'd been fucked over before in more than one way. The instinct to push Storm away and protect myself waged a vicious battle inside me against my need to keep her close. I felt more conflicted than I'd ever experienced.

I stole a glance at the woman responsible.

She cried silent tears, each one causing a stab of pain deep in my chest. Despite it all, I hated to see her upset. What did that say about me?

"You never answered my question," I finally said in a calm tone, not quite acknowledging her apology.

"Question?" she asked in confusion.

"Who are you? If I'm about to go to war for you, I should at least know your name."

"You know my name. When I first met Damyon, my name was Alina, but that girl hasn't existed for a long time. The person you know as Stormy? That's *me*. That's the woman I am now."

Feeling her eyes on me, I met her gaze. The brief connection caused my lungs to clamp down. I had to force air into the useless organs and look away to keep my focus. She was so fucking disarming. I'd been worried about what kind of crazy shit I'd do because of my fixation on her, and now, we were about to find out.

◊

"Before we dive into this, we need to know whether the Russian knows about your connection to Torin." Jimmy Byrne, Keir's father, took the lead once we were all assembled. He was the only remaining founder of the Byrne family businesses that still took an active role, though he was transitioning out of leadership.

Aside from him, five of my immediate cousins and another half a dozen extended family had gathered. We all sat in folding chairs in a poorly lit basement. No table and the cell signal was spotty. It wasn't a great place to conduct business, but it was perfect for our current needs.

The entire family looked at Storm, who shifted uncomfortably in her seat.

"I don't think so, but it's hard to know." She shot me a quick glance. "I don't know what Torin has told you already, but I was attacked coming home from Thanksgiving dinner at a friend's place. I didn't recognize the man, but he recognized me and followed me to my apartment. He said it was luck that he found me, so I don't think they knew where I was hiding until then. But now…" She licked her lips and stared at her trembling hands. "I'm sure they've gone through my things and will have figured out where I worked. Beyond that, I'm not sure."

"Seems awfully coincidental that you just happen to have stumbled into our club when Damyon Karpova was after you." Oran sat near the back of the group, directly opposite Storm. His gray eyes impaled her mercilessly from across the room. "Care to enlighten us?"

"My parents died six years ago in a boating accident. I'd been adopted from Russia, and when I was going through their things, I found a document listing the name of the orphanage I'd been housed at. It was an incredibly hard time for me. I thought if I went there and learned more about my roots—maybe even found my biological parents— it might have filled some of the void created by their loss. From that point on, everything that has happened was thanks to chance. Damyon happened to have recently bought the old building the orphanage had been in and was there the day I showed up looking for information. And as for Moxy, I know it sounds like a stretch, but I had no idea who any of you were when I came looking for a job. I swear."

"Why is Karpova after you? You steal from him or something?"

I bit back a snarl. "Watch it, Oran. This isn't an inquest."

"It's okay," Stormy cut in. "I'm sure you all have tons of questions. I never stole anything from him, even when I left. We were together for almost a year. It started out amazing. Damyon was incredibly sweet and attentive. But as time went on, he seemed to form a sort of obsession with me. And … he had a temper." Storm peered at me warily, and it fucking gutted me.

I'd done the same goddamn thing he'd done, except I'd never have laid a finger on her in anger.

*How was she supposed to know you wouldn't?*

She had to have been terrified, yet she'd been so damn brave. She'd trusted me when she had every reason not to.

"So he was here looking for you in a city of millions and just happened to come across you one random night?" Condescension dripped from Oran's words.

"Just because he was here in the city doesn't mean I was the reason," Storm pointed out. "I don't know that he was actively searching for me."

"While that would be nice to believe, we already had a little run-in with your *boyfriend*, and he told us specifically that he was only here for one thing ... and one thing alone." He was right, but none of us had ever imagined the thing Damyon was after was a woman, let alone a woman waiting tables at one of our clubs.

Keir spoke up, thankfully in a less accusatory tone. "If he was here for you, Stormy, that means he must have had some idea you were in the city but no specifics. Any idea what might have tipped him off?"

Her brows furrowed as she chewed on her lip. She began to slowly shake her head, then stilled, her spine stiffening. "Honey," she breathed.

"Your grandma?" I asked. She'd talked about the woman as though she'd passed away. I wasn't sure how she could play into this.

She squeezed her eyes shut before opening them again and continuing. "I send my grandmother a cashier's check once a quarter. No return address, postmarked from a city I don't live in—somewhere close enough for a day trip but far enough to be unconnected to me. I've always been so careful —and there was a chance he hadn't tracked her down. I never told him her real name."

"But?" I prompted her.

"A while back, not long after I came to the city, a check I'd sent didn't get cashed. I was so worried that I took a quick trip down to check on her. I verified that she'd been in the hospital but had since been released. I never made contact with her, though I did park my rental across from her house and peek in her windows one night."

"He could have traced the rental plates back to New York," Keir deduced.

"Led the guy right fucking to us," Oran said menacingly.

"If that was the case, he would have taken her ages ago," I pointed out angrily. "The rental agency would have led him right to her."

"Not exactly," Storm cut in. "I used an ID someone left at the club to rent the car. He could have traced the car to New York, but no farther than that."

One of the more distant cousins stood, hands on his hips. "Why the fuck does this even have to involve us? He wants her, he can have her."

"That's what I'm sayin'." Another voice chimed in.

I rocketed to my feet. "That's not happening, so wipe the thought from your fuckin' minds." I'd hardly finished barking the angry words when Storm jumped up, slapped a hand over her mouth, then ran through a doorway into a dark closet.

The sounds of her vomiting echoed in the air around us.

I'd never been so goddamn furious with my own family. I had to clench my fists to keep from slamming one into someone's face. Jaw flexed tight, eyes spitting fire, I made a sweep of the room with my violent stare.

"That woman is going to be my *wife*, so I expect you to fucking treat her accordingly. Is that understood?" The snarled words had everyone's attention. Those who had stood sat back down with their hands raised in surrender.

My point made, I swiftly strode from the room to check on Storm. She hadn't made it far. I found her just past the doorway on her hands and knees, one hand attempting to hold back her hair. The smell of vomit on the concrete floor filled the air, but I didn't give a shit.

"Let me help, sweet girl," I murmured, gently scooping her hair into my hands and rubbing her back. "No one's sending you back to him. You're safe."

Her body shook with silent sobs. "I'm so sorry, Torin. I'm so sorry."

"I know you are. And I'm sorry, too. But we're gonna get through this, you hear me?"

She wiped her face with the back of one hand and lifted her warm brown eyes to mine. Storm nodded, giving me a look filled with such gratitude and hope that I felt like I could have toppled a fucking mountain.

"You good to go back out and finish this shit?"

"Yeah."

I helped her to her feet and led her back into the room. A chorus of hushed murmurs instantly quieted, but I kept a steely gaze on my family in case anyone forgot themselves. Before taking my own seat, I scanned the room for the lowest-ranking family member. "Aidan, go track down a bottle of water."

The kid didn't hesitate.

"Alright," I said, addressing the room. "Now that we're all focused on how to proceed rather than dwelling on the past, let's talk action."

Uncle Jimmy was the first to speak. "Tor, I know you want to go on the offensive, but is there any chance the

Russian would walk away when he learns she's under our protection?"

I knew he thought he was being reasonable, but it pissed me off.

Heads nodded, and murmurs resumed.

"The guy's a psychopath," I argued. "He's not going to see reason, especially where Stormy is involved."

"I get that, but we're no worse off for trying, right?"

Three others piped up, demanding we give diplomacy a try.

"I'd say we have a duty to the rest of the family not to launch an attack," one of the older cousins pointed out. He was a more distant relative but held more clout than the others. "Moving on this guy without cause would be an act of war. Who knows where things go from there. I'd say we need to make sure there's no other alternative."

"We don't even have a way to communicate with the man," I pointed out in a clipped tone.

Had they not heard me when I told them Storm was about to be my wife? Did they not see her bruised and swollen face? Would they want to talk it out if their wives were at risk? Fuck no.

"We could send a message via Boris." Oran. Fucking Oran.

I wasn't sure what I'd expected when I'd called everyone together, but it wasn't the show of timid uncertainty I was witnessing. I'd known Oran would be an issue. He was still licking his wounds after his cunt of a wife betrayed us. The others had no excuse.

Keir finally decided to chime in. "We can go that route, but it'll take more time. We've never formed any sort of alliance with the Russians. They'd be more apt to talk to us if we went through the Italians since they have connections. It's a touch more complicated but probably our best option."

Heads nodded all around.

It was decided, and I'd been outvoted. They were making a huge fucking mistake.

With Keir's blessing, we spent the next half hour discussing diplomatic measures and strategy. I had nothing to add to this bullshit, so I kept my mouth shut. None of them would see things the way I did, so I would bide my time and handle the matter on my own. I wasn't about to sit back and wait to see if Damyon attacked before I took action.

As much as I hated to admit it, he and I were similar. We were both single-minded in our pursuits and ruthless when it came to our desires. The only way to stop him was to kill him, and the only way to kill him was to flush him out. I'd find a way to do it.

Damyon wanted what was mine.

I'd burn down the entire city before I let him have her.

# CHAPTER 34
*Stormy*

*Present*

GUILT WAS AN INSIDIOUS VINE THAT CHOKED OUT THE LIFE OF every other emotion. I suffocated on the inside as I sat in that room. So many lives were at risk because of me, and I still hadn't told Torin everything. It was no wonder my stomach had revolted.

By the time the meeting adjourned, I wanted to crawl into a hole and never come out.

"We have one quick stop to make before I take you to Keir's place for the night." Torin opened the car door and helped me in, still mindful of my tender ribs.

"Just me? You're not going with me?"

"I'll be back there later. I have a few things I need to do, and I don't want you left alone." His voice rang with malice so cold and calculating it sent a shiver down my spine.

"Please, be careful," I said softly once he sat behind the wheel.

Torin didn't respond.

Minutes later, we pulled up in front of a jewelry store. My stomach clenched tight again. I'd heard him from the other room when he'd told the family his plans to marry me. Surely, he hadn't meant so soon, had he?

With Torin, anything was possible.

We walked inside the jewelry boutique. It wasn't a big box shop. The sign out front advertised custom pieces and repair, and inside were several glass displays showing off the decidedly unique artistry. I wasn't sure what to think.

"Luther." Torin nodded to an older man who joined us from the back. "I'm going to need that piece now. I hope it's ready."

Ready? Had he already commissioned something for me? When had he had the time?

Curiosity helped distract from my worry as I watched the man set out a cloth on the glass counter and unveil a gorgeous gold necklace.

At least, I thought that was what it was. The length was right, but the rest was confusing. It had no clasp, just a beautiful circular medallion the size of a dime on one end of a chain.

"It's the Byrne family crest," Torin said, handing it over for a closer inspection.

I studied the intricate detail and noted an inscription on the back. *Mo rúnsearc.*

"What does it say?"

"That you're under our protection." He kept his eyes lowered as he encircled my neck with the chain. "The length is good."

"It still needs a clasp," I pointed out.

Torin's azure eyes met mine. "It's not the sort of thing you take off." His meaning settled deep in my chest, filling me until my lungs burned. This was Torin's way of making a pledge. Of telling his family and the world that I was his.

"It's perfect," I breathed through the swell of emotion. Pride. Elation. Worry. Shame. I experienced the entire gambit in the span of a heartbeat but settled on gratitude when Torin's lips pressed passionately against mine.

He'd been incredibly understanding and supportive despite a harrowing series of events that most people would have deemed insurmountable. Not Tor. He charged ahead fearlessly, my heart safely in his hands. His steadfast commitment gave me the courage to believe that maybe, just maybe, he truly would stand by me through it all. Despite the danger and uncertainty, Torin was devoted to me in a way I never imagined possible.

A sense of hope and burgeoning pride filled me as the jeweler soldered on the necklace. I promised myself that I'd tell him everything soon—tomorrow even. I just needed things to settle a tiny bit before I dropped another potential bomb. Or two.

We said our goodbyes to the jeweler, then returned to Torin's car. The fall sun had already dropped low enough that only a soft glow penetrated the late afternoon blanket of clouds. Mother Nature had set a somber tone for the night, and I felt it seep deep into my bones.

"I'm going to check on the cat after I drop you off, just so you know." Torin's statement stunned me because A, I'd been a horrible cat mom and not considered Blue Bell at all; and B, Torin *had* thought about him, knew I'd been distracted, and was assuring me in his own surly manner that he had it covered.

"Thank you. Blue Bell and I both appreciate you thinking of him."

His eyes cut briefly to me. "Not doin' it for the cat, babe."

Warmth unfurled in my chest. "I know," I said softly. "How long do you think we'll stay with Keir and Rowan?"

"No clue. I don't think there's any way to predict how this will unfold. I'm taking it one damn hour at a time."

I couldn't help but sigh.

*Me, too, Tor. Me, too.*

# CHAPTER 35

*Torin*

*Present*

KEIR HAD A HEADS-UP THAT WE'D BE COMING, BUT HE DIDN'T know much more than that. I wasn't looking forward to the questions he would undoubtedly ask. Not after his lack of support in the meeting. I would have avoided him entirely, dropping off Storm and bailing, if I wasn't painfully aware that I needed help. I could have tried elsewhere, but Keir was my best bet and the man I'd most prefer at my back.

The minute we arrived, Rowan swept Stormy off to get her set up in a guest bedroom, leaving Keir and me alone.

"Let's have a word," he instructed in a cool, calm tone.

I followed him back to his office, closing the door behind us.

"There's no convincing you to hold off on whatever it is your planning, is there?" The question was purely rhetorical.

"You know better than anyone how dangerous this guy is and what it's like to have him after your woman." For a time, we'd thought Damyon was a danger to Rowan. He'd been so damn desperate to protect her that he'd married her on the spot.

He studied me, probably curious at my sudden possessiveness toward Storm, but he didn't call me out. "I do, but we need to respect the family."

"You think that back in the day, your father would have said this was a fucking democracy?" My words took on a harsh edge. "He and Uncle Brody made all the decisions for this family. They didn't invite other opinions or worry about hurting anyone's feelings."

Keir's eyes flashed in warning.

I'd intentionally struck at a sensitive topic. With Uncle Jimmy transitioning away from leadership and Uncle Brody's recent death, a vacuum of power had stirred up tensions among the next generation of Byrne men, Keir and Oran among them. An intricate dance had played out in the past year as everyone jockeyed for positions while trying not to upset Jimmy before he was out of the picture.

I'd had the misfortune of not only being born the youngest in my family, but my father was the least involved in the family business. All four of my siblings had chosen to distance themselves from our less-than-legal lifestyle. I never did fit their mold. I was an old-school Byrne, through and through, never meshing well with authority. I knew I wouldn't be in line for leadership anytime soon, and it hadn't truly bothered me until now.

"What exactly do you want to do?"

"Strike before he has a chance to prepare. But in order to do that, I need to find the bastard." I didn't mind doing the dirty work but had hit a brick wall in my search for the man.

Keir sighed. "I took a photo a few months ago," he said somewhat reluctantly. "It was a picture of the car Damyon had been driving when I saw him with our stolen guns. I gave it to Oran to see if it might help him learn more about the situation and what happened to Darina."

"He able to find anything?" My pulse thudded in my ears.

"Yeah, but not in the way I expected. The plates led to a dummy corp that didn't give us any info, but Oran noticed from the photo details that it was taken on a Wednesday night. He already knew from looking into Lawrence Wellington that the man goes to the Olympus club every Wednesday night like clockwork, so he called in a favor and got a look at the guest registry. Sure enough, Damyon was in attendance that night."

"I didn't think guests were even allowed." The insanely secretive social club was so private that it was almost mythical.

"Oran has learned a lot in the last year hobnobbing with society and has put that information to use. The club allows guests, but only if approved, which means they have to give certain information beforehand. The given address was in Russia, but a Manhattan marina was listed as a local residence."

"Why the hell didn't Oran bring this up in the meeting?" I snapped in no small amount of frustration and excitement.

"He's working on something. He hasn't told me

everything, but I know he's trying to keep it under wraps and doesn't want his activities publicized. He may have thought you would jeopardize his plans."

I wanted to bitch about him needing to trust us, but I bit back the angry comment, knowing it was the epitome of hypocrisy, considering I rarely trusted anyone. And after what Oran's wife had done, I couldn't blame him for keeping secrets.

Keir continued. "He also got a phone number. I don't know if it's legit, but you could start there."

I gave one sharp shake of my head. "Don't care about phone numbers. That's not the kind of message I want to send."

His chest slowly filled with a long sigh. "I'm not going to like this, am I?"

"It hasn't been so long that I don't remember what you did to the man who hurt your wife. You going to deny me the same?" I glared at him, daring him to point out that Stormy wasn't my wife.

Smart guy kept it to himself. "What do you need?"

I stared into Keir's eyes. It wasn't something I did often. Not the open sort of look I was giving him now—a wordless view into my soul.

"I need to know you've got my back," I told him plainly.

His expression never hinted at what lurked behind his dark stare. "My father and I have only ever come to blows once. We've had words and shouted and said things we shouldn't have, but only once have our arguments gotten physical, and that was after you were arrested. I was furious that he wouldn't do anything to get you out. He insisted it wasn't his place—that making a move would have gone against your father's wishes, and he didn't have the right. I lost it and swung at him. I was twenty and thought I could take him, but Pop had me in a chokehold faster than I imagined possible." He paused, a flash of emotion hardening his features. "I had your back then, and I have it now. Never doubt that."

I held out my hand, unable to conjure any words. We clasped wrists in a show of solidarity that shook me to my core.

"I didn't know." That was all I could muster.

"Now you do." He tipped his chin. "I have Stormy covered. Call if you need me."

I nodded back. "I won't forget this."

"I'd kick your ass if you did." His casual reply hinted at a challenge.

"You could try..." I smirked and walked away, relieved to know we were all good.

# CHAPTER 36
*Stormy*

*Present*

A CLOSING DOOR WAS A METAPHOR FOR SO MANY DIFFERENT things, but in this case, watching the door shut behind Torin carried a genuine risk of death. The voice in my head was screaming at him not to leave. I didn't even know what he was up to, but I knew it involved Damyon, and that would always be dangerous.

I would never want anyone to end up hurt because of me.

But this was a different sort of fear—a suffocating foreboding that threatened to capsize my entire ship. If Damyon hurt Torin, I'd never forgive myself. Just the thought had my heart wrung so tight it had already begun to bleed. I could hear the drips echoing in my ears.

Desperation sank its barbed claws into me and begged me to stop him, but I refused. I had to. I'd told Torin I trusted him and had to stand by that. I had to trust that he would come back to me.

If I'd had any doubts about my feelings for him, the intensity of my fear dashed them away. I cared deeply for Torin. I'd thought I'd loved Damyon, but how could you love an illusion? I'd only ever seen the mask he wore to disguise his rotten soul. Torin wasn't like that at all. He was the opposite—a coarse, offensive exterior meant to deflect people so they couldn't see the generous, loving man he was underneath.

And now he'd gone to war for me.

Whatever happened to him would all be because of me.

The emotional burden was so exhausting that I could barely eat and excused myself to bed early. Rowan was endlessly patient, but I needed to be alone. My tears needed a pillow to call home.

I had just turned off the bedside lamp when my door quietly opened and closed.

"It's me," Rowan said as she crossed the room. She didn't ask if she could join me; she simply curled up behind me and hugged my body into hers. I hadn't realized how much I needed her comfort until she was there, and silent tears finally poured from my eyes.

We lay still in the darkness for several long minutes.

"I saw him, you know. Damyon," she whispered after a while. "I can understand why you're scared."

"I heard. I'm so sorry that my being in the city brought him here."

"It's not your fault he is who he is. You weren't the one who raised him, and you didn't force him to do bad things. That's all on him."

"It's hard not to."

"I know," she whispered. "That's what I keep telling my therapist. I'm just passing along what she said."

A small smile teased at my lips. "I suppose I'll need one of those when this is all said and done, assuming I survive."

"Don't talk like that, Stormy." Rowan gave me a squeeze. "You'll be just fine. This isn't the first time these guys have gone up against a scary bastard."

"I hope you're right," I breathed shakily.

"Okay, hun. I'll let you get some rest. Come get me if you need me."

"Thanks, Ro."

"Anytime, Storm. Us girls have to stick together."

It was so true, and I'd never in my life been so grateful for a friend.

# CHAPTER 37

*Torin*

*Present*

THE MARINA OFFICE CLOSED AT SIX, BUT I WAITED UNTIL AFTER dark before breaking in. The wood doorframe of the waterfront building was rotted enough that a good shoulder was all it took to circumvent the lock.

The place was tiny. Real estate this close to the river came at a premium, and they obviously hadn't wanted to consume any more than necessary. A bar height counter divided the room—one side for receiving customers, and the other was dedicated to a workstation for two employees. Each had a desktop computer that was password protected. I didn't have time to screw with that, so I searched the office for anything else I could find that would tell me which damn boat belonged to Karpova.

I looked through all the desk drawers, then turned to the filing cabinets lining the back wall. What I'd hoped would be client dossiers ended up being utterly worthless historical financials and nautical maps. I poked through every nook and cranny of that place looking for information and came up empty.

Eventually, I sat back in one of the desk chairs and slowly spun, debating the merits of going boat to boat Girl Scout style, when I noticed a blinking light on the phone. They had a traditional multiline office phones, and the message light was on. Even better, a sticky note with a six-digit code peeked out from under the phone.

God bless stupid people.

I picked up the phone and hit the message button. The scribbled passcode worked. I listened to two messages about employee scheduling before I was given an option to listen to saved messages. The third message was from a man with a heavy Russian accent requesting a fueling service for the Karpova vessel in slip 14.

Bingo.

I'd had my share of bad luck in my life. It was goddamn time the tables turned.

A few minutes later, I boarded the large yacht, which appeared to be unoccupied. I systematically worked my way through the boat, using my phone as a flashlight in one hand and keeping my gun ready in the other. No one was getting the jump on me.

It wasn't the biggest yacht I'd ever seen, but it was large enough that I needed to keep moving. I didn't stall until I came across a lavish office. On the desk were documents written in Russian. Even better, I came across stationery embossed with a symbol that looked like it could be initials. I pulled up the Russian alphabet on my phone. The K was the same, but the D explained my uncertainty as the Russian equivalent looked substantially different from the English version. The symbol was the initials DK.

This had to be his boat.

The question was, what did I do now? I hadn't had a specific plan when I arrived because I didn't know what I'd find when I got here. After a thorough search of his personal space, I knew exactly what I would do.

I took a sheet of his expensive-ass stationery and wrote a short note. I put it and a rubber band in my pocket before heading back to my car for supplies. While I hadn't known how the night would end, I had come prepared for multiple contingencies. Besides, it never hurt to have a little C4 on hand. You never knew when you might need it.

I grabbed my black duffel and walked calmly back to the boat, where I rigged the explosives in the engine room. A diesel machine like the yacht wouldn't light up on its own. It wasn't the same as shooting the gas tank in a car. This type of rig required something more sophisticated to bring it down, and C4 would do the job nicely.

Once I had everything as I wanted it, I stopped on the way out at the sign on the main pier walkway that advertised slip 14. I used the rubber band to secure my note to the wooden post.

*She doesn't want you anymore. Go home before you embarrass yourself. Torin Byrne*

I waited until I was passing the office to trigger the explosives. The entire neighborhood shook, and light flared all around me.

It felt fucking incredible.

I lifted my middle finger in the air, knowing security cameras likely captured my exit. I wasn't interested in hiding. Let the fucker come for me. I'd be waiting.

$$\diamond$$

ALMOST AN HOUR LATER, I was walking into the lobby of Keir's apartment building when my phone rang with a call from an unknown number. I answered, curious if my suspicions were correct.

"Byrne here."

"Mr. Byrne. I appreciate you taking my call." It was Karpova, probably trying to send his own message by getting my number so quickly.

"Not at all. I was expecting you."

"You can hardly blame me. That was quite a message you sent, but my question for you is, what next? I have nothing more here that you can threaten or take, but you..."

I had to hand it to him. He had the intrigued psychopath tone down to a science. Keir could be eerily stoic, but this guy was in a whole other class.

"There's always your life," I reminded him.

"I would like very much to see you try." Genuine eagerness licked at his words.

"I doubt that. I'm a man of conviction. As you've seen, I follow through with my threats."

"Mr. Byrne," he started with a hint of impatience setting in. "Give me my wife, or you will live to regret it. I can promise you that."

His *wife*?

I had to fight back a crippling wave of shock. He couldn't know how profoundly he'd shaken me.

"So you can beat her to a bloody pulp? I don't think so. Didn't your mother teach you better than that?"

"You have twenty-four hours to give me my *fucking* wife. I will not tell you again."

The line clicked dead, the sound of his fury buoying me.

His wife.

Stormy had married fucking Karpova and hadn't told me. He wasn't just an ex. He was her fucking *husband*. Why the fuck hadn't she told me? What more was she holding back?

If I had any chance of keeping her alive, I needed to know the goddamn truth—all of it.

I looked at the elevator and contemplated going upstairs, but I was too keyed up from my night and Karpova's little revelation. I'd end up saying something I'd regret. Instead, I went back to my car and set out to relieve the tension pulsing behind my temples.

*His fucking wife.*

# CHAPTER 38

*Stormy*

*Present*

DESPITE MY EXHAUSTION, I WOKE UP THREE TIMES IN THE night, hoping Torin had returned. He never did. I had no missed calls or texts. Feeling a twinge of panic filter into my bloodstream, I decided to check in with him.

**Me: U ok?**

I made sure the ringer was on and lay in the dark, hoping for a reply. The next thing I knew, I was waking a fourth and final time to the smell of breakfast cooking.

Torin hadn't replied.

I quickly got moving in the hopes that he might have come back and slept on the couch to keep from waking me. I found Rowan and Keir together in the kitchen. Rowan stood at the stove frying sausage while Keir sat at the table, sipping coffee. Both had their eyes on a small kitchen television showing a news program.

"Good morning," I greeted them.

Both were so engrossed that they hadn't noticed me join them.

Rowan startled, then flashed an exaggerated smile. "Hey, Stormy. Sleep okay?" She turned the dial off on the stove and came to join me at the island.

"I did, thanks. Did you guys hear from Tor? As far as I can tell, he didn't come back last night."

Rowan and Keir exchanged a look that chilled the blood in my veins.

Keir was the one to answer. "He texted saying something came up, and he'd be back later today."

Well, that didn't seem so bad. I looked at Rowan questioningly. Was I missing something? Her brows knitted together before she looked back at the TV. I followed her gaze. The newscaster spoke while a previously recorded video of firefighters dousing flames on a large boat played in the background.

"What happened?" I asked, confused about the implications.

"Tor happened," Keir drawled slowly. "That was Damyon's yacht." As he spoke, the news replayed grainy footage from a security camera showing a massive explosion from a distance.

I slapped a hand over my mouth, watched the video replay one more time, then ran for the bathroom. Rowan followed me. She pulled my hair back as I emptied the contents of my stomach and gently rubbed my back.

"It's okay, honey. He's just fine. No one was hurt." Seeing a break in my heaving, she handed me a wad of toilet paper. "Let me get you some water."

Seconds later, she returned with a glass of cool water. I sat back on my knees and took a deep breath. My stomach was already settling now that it was empty, though my emotions were still a mess.

"I'm so sorry. I'm not sure what the deal is with me. The same thing happened at the meeting last night." I usually didn't have stomach issues. When I looked up at Rowan, her eyes were wide. "What?" I asked warily.

She lowered herself to sit with me on the floor. "Um, is there any chance that ... you could be ... you know —pregnant?"

I shook my head. "Before I escaped Russia, I was seen by several doctors. I'd been badly beaten. They told me the damage was too severe, that I'd never be able to have children." My chin quivered ever so slightly as I explained.

"Oh," Rowan said on a remorseful breath.

"Yeah. And besides, I had my period ... what day is it?"

"You still have a period?" Her gaze narrowed.

"Yeah, why?"

"Did you ever go to any doctors here once you got back?"

"No." Aside from the difficulty of finding a new doctor constantly and money being tight, I hadn't had any reason to get checked out. I hadn't been with anyone since Damyon. Not until Torin entered the picture.

I suddenly started to think about when exactly my last period started. It had been early October...

Holy shit.

We'd just had Thanksgiving. That meant I still hadn't had

my November period. How could I have forgotten? I'd had a lot on my mind with Torin, but...

Rowan must have noticed my breathing change because she began to rub my back again. "Hey, now. It's gonna be okay. Breathe, Stormy."

"I think you may be right," I whispered. "I hadn't ... I don't know ... I thought it couldn't happen, so..." My hands trembled as I waved them in the air. I was at a total loss for words.

*I might be pregnant.*

A flood of memories and phantom emotions from the past swarmed me until I couldn't breathe.

"Hold up, Storm. Let's not panic until we know for sure. I can run out and get you some tests."

I clasped her hands in mine, eyes wide. "Please don't tell anyone. Not yet. I need to figure this out first."

"Of course." She nodded readily.

"Promise me, Ro."

"I promise I will not breathe a word of any of this. It's no one else's business."

I nodded shakily.

"I'm going to run downstairs right now to the store. You need an answer, and I don't want you to have to wait."

I didn't step foot from the bathroom the whole time she was gone. It felt like no time yet an eternity as my entire perspective shifted.

Pregnant.

If that was the case, it changed everything. I would no longer only be risking my own life to stick around and face Damyon. I would be risking my baby's life, and that wasn't an option. If Damyon got ahold of me and discovered I was pregnant with another man's child...

My entire body shuddered.

I remembered the cramping and pain. I remembered the blood—so much blood—and the devastation. I couldn't live through that again. The grief of losing a child was too much. Not when I knew I could prevent it. All I had to do … was run.

I'd done it before, and if there was any incentive worthy of keeping me on the move, it was a child. If I truly was pregnant, no sacrifice would be too great.

I took the tests from Rowan with an eerie sense of calm. Judging by her concerned expression, she sensed the change in me but didn't comment. Five minutes later, my entire world changed.

Two pink lines.

I was pregnant.

Again.

I walked back into my room, where Rowan anxiously waited for me on the bed. The second she laid eyes on me, she shot to her feet and rushed to wrap me in a hug.

"It's gonna be okay, honey," she urged softly. "You'll see."

"I know." I nodded, giving her a squeeze. "But please, keep it between us for now. I need to wait until the time is right." I hated to intentionally mislead her, but I had no choice. If Torin knew I was pregnant with his child, he'd never let me leave.

Panic screamed at me that staying put meant I'd be served to Damyon on a silver platter. The only way to stay safe was to hide. It had worked for five years, so it would continue to work. I berated myself for ever considering the notion of settling down. Fear clawed at my heels, urging me to go now.

I wished I could summon Torin's confidence about taking down Damyon, but I knew the man too well to underestimate him. Damyon Karpova was a monster hell-bent on getting me back. Nothing would stop him until he did. Nothing.

*Go now.*

"Of course. You tell him in your own time." Rowan's gentle smile sent a stab of pain through my chest.

Guilt. Remorse. They were debilitating at best, but nothing compared to how I'd feel if I didn't do everything in my power to keep this child alive.

*Go now.*

"I think I'm going to lie down for a bit."

"Take all the time you need. Keir is working out, and I'll be in the room across the way dancing for a bit. I'll keep the door closed so I don't bother you, but you're welcome to grab me anytime."

My reassuring smile was genuine because she'd given me the perfect window of opportunity. She and Keir would be preoccupied for a while. I could slip out of the apartment and have a head start on my escape before anyone knew I was gone.

*Go before it's too late!*

Thirty minutes later, I walked out the front door, leaving everything else behind.

This child's life would not end in tragedy.

I would *not* make the same mistake twice.

# CHAPTER 39

*Torin*

*Present*

I'D MET GROWN-ASS THUGS WHO COULDN'T THROW SHADE THE way that cat could. It was like the damn thing knew something had happened when I showed up at my place without Stormy.

He sat on the dresser, ears back and tail swooshing, while I tried to go to sleep, which was hard enough when my own guilt set in. I nearly shit myself when I woke up to find him looming over me.

"I get it," I grumbled, rolling away from him. "I overreacted, but that was a pretty huge oversight on her part. You gotta at least give me that."

The cat started laughing at me.

My eyes flew open. How the fuck was the cat laughing? Cats don't laugh.

I whipped my head around just in time for the little monster to cough up a giant hairball on my pillow.

*Jesus fucking Christ.*

He wasn't laughing. He'd been puking.

"*Motherfucker*, that stinks. You hairy piece of shit. You had to do that on my goddamn pillow?" If Storm didn't love that thing so much, I would have tested the nine lives theory and sent him flying over the balcony. Instead, I stomped into the kitchen for paper towels and cleaned up the mess.

I needed to get up anyway and go see Storm. She'd probably been worried while I'd had my head up my ass sulking. I couldn't help it. I had a hair trigger when it came to honesty. The second I detected a lie, my first reaction was to cut and run. Most of the time, that practice served me well. I didn't need liars in my life.

But the world wasn't black and white, and not every lie was necessarily bad. Storm was just as gun-shy to trust people as I was. As much as it hurt to have her keep something so important from me, I couldn't be angry, and I needed to tell her that.

I tossed some food into the cat's dish, hoping to bribe the thing into cutting me some slack, then jumped in the shower. I was only in for a minute when my phone began to wail.

It was the new alarm I'd set up. Storm had breached the digital perimeter I'd designated around Keir's building.

I was out of the shower in a heartbeat. Water dripped all over the floor as I checked the app and verified that her GPS location was on the move.

The fuck was going on? Keir had promised to keep her with him in the apartment.

I dialed Storm's number, but the call went to voicemail. Next, I dialed Keir.

"Yeah?"

"Where are you?" I barked.

"On the treadmill. Where the fuck are you?"

"You're in your apartment?"

"Yeah, I told you we'd stay here. What the hell is going on?" His voice sobered.

"GPS says Storm is on the move. You sure she's still there?"

I heard him start walking before I even asked.

"Shit," he hissed. "Her room is empty." Heavy footfalls echoed in the background. "She's not with Rowan, and I don't see her anywhere else."

Fear unlike any I'd known clamped tight around my chest. "You think Karpova could have walked in there and taken her without you two knowing?"

I'd never forgive myself if he'd taken her while I was off wallowing in self-pity.

"I wouldn't—" Keir paused, and I could hear Rowan's voice in the distance. "Why the fuck would she do that?" he asked her.

"Do what?" I demanded.

Keir sighed. "Rowan says it's not her place to say, but she thinks Storm may have run."

Run? From me? Why?

I couldn't for the life of me fathom what she was thinking.

"I'm on it." I tossed the phone on the counter and threw on some clothes.

This game of cat and mouse ended now, one goddamn way or another.

# CHAPTER 40
*Stormy*

*Present*

"Mommy, why's she wearing sunglasses inside?" A cute little girl in pigtails and a mermaid swimsuit stared at me while her mother shoved their belongings into a locker.

The woman sat tall and spun around, lifting horrified eyes to me. "I am so sorry," she said before tugging her daughter close. "Cici, what have I told you about talking about people?" The hushed whisper almost made me smile. Had my heart not been in my throat, I would have.

Properly chided, the poor little girl chewed on her lips and turned away, sneaking one last peek at me.

She was right to be curious. I'd been so intent on my

mission that I'd forgotten to take off the darn things. On my way out of Keir's place, I had nabbed Rowan's hat, sunglasses, and coat. I didn't want anyone to recognize me before I made it out of the city. I didn't even take a chance with public transportation. A ten-minute cab to the YMCA, five minutes to grab my emergency bag from the locker room, and then I would be gone. Nothing but a bitter memory to everyone I'd befriended.

My vision blurred with tears.

Maybe the sunglasses weren't such a bad idea. I left them on as I unlocked my locker and grabbed the black Swiss Gear backpack. A glance inside assured me everything was as I left it months ago. I slung the bag over my shoulder and closed the locker door. A strangled cry wrenched from my throat at the sight of Torin on the other side.

"Mommy, boys aren't allowed in here," the girl whispered loudly.

Torin tore his gaze from me. "I need to talk to my friend for a minute."

The woman seemed to understand it wasn't a request. She nodded, gave me a worried look, then tugged her daughter from the room. I stood inhumanly still and prayed that a sinkhole might open and swallow all of Manhattan. Anything to escape Torin's wounded stare.

"Why, Storm?" His chill penetrated my clothes and sank deep into my bones.

I slid off the glasses with my trembling fingers.

I was so damn scared that I couldn't string words together. My lips parted, then shut. What was I supposed to do? What did I tell him? I couldn't see a way out without telling him the truth, but that terrified me. Would he become enraged? Would he try to hurt me?

Growing impatient with me, Tor pushed again. "You so afraid to tell me you were married that you'd rather leave?"

"What? No, I ... that's irrelevant." Completely thrown, I scrambled to catch up. Torin had learned I was actually Damyon's wife. How? What had happened in the night? At least I now had one less secret to unload.

He scoffed. "Your husband sure doesn't agree."

"I don't care what some piece of paper says," I shot back at him, a tendril of anger sparking to life. "I'm *not* his."

"Then why, Storm? Why're you runnin' from me?"

"It's not you."

"Sure feels that way. I told you I'd protect you."

"But what if you can't?" I pushed, feeling my emotions fraying at the edges.

He took an angry step forward. "You won't even let me try."

"Because it's not just my life at stake," I cried back at him, my hand falling inadvertently to my stomach.

Torin was too observant not to notice. His gaze flicked down.

In the time it took a human heart to squeeze out a single beat, a lifetime of emotions crossed behind his eyes. So many, so fast, I couldn't tell what would win out.

*Please, don't hate me, Tor.*

My eyes squeezed shut as a wave of fear—a devastating, new sort of fear unrelated to Damyon—threatened to swallow me whole.

"You said you couldn't," he murmured, still grappling with shock.

The tears began to flow. "The doctors told me I couldn't." The words were barely audible as my throat constricted impossibly tight. I hadn't even had time to process how I felt about the fact that they'd been wrong. That my body hadn't been damaged beyond repair. I'd been given another chance.

"You were gonna keep my child from me?" His face contorted into something harsh and merciless.

He would never understand. How could he? He'd never known fear like me.

"You're blowing up boats … He'll be so angry … It'll get us killed."

"You said you trusted me," he shot back.

"And what about you? You going to trust me?"

"Doesn't look like I can. You disappear if I turn my back."

"Don't throw stones, Torin. I'm not the only one running."

"What the hell does that mean?"

"It means you're running every day of your life. You push people away. That's running, Tor, just a different kind. Why? What keeps you getting back in that ring to fight? You don't need the money. Who are you really fighting?" By the time I finished, I was pointing and shouting, desperate to defend myself.

The door to the locker room creaked open. Neither of us budged, our turbulent stares locked on one another. The intruder must have sensed they were interrupting and slowly backtracked, leaving us alone again.

Torin swallowed harshly before speaking in a brittle tone that cleaved my heart straight from my chest.

"There was a guard at the detention facility. I was still small at sixteen, and he was so much bigger than me. When he started to do favors for me—extra food or extended rec time outside—I figured he was a good ally to have. Until he decided payment was due for the services he'd provided."

Torin lifted his gaze to me, holding nothing back. All the

hatred and terror. The helplessness and agonizing pain—both mental and physical. He showed me the jagged pieces of his soul, still tainted by the sticky residue of the nightmare he'd experienced.

I'd known Torin was damaged. That was no secret. But to hear how devastating the trauma had been was more than I could bear.

I had to lower myself to the bench beside me before my legs followed my heart and plummeted to the floor.

"I take it you get the picture without the need for more detail."

I nodded, fighting back a particularly vicious wave of nausea.

"You wanted to know my history with Jolly," Tor continued. "The assaults had been going on for about a month when Jolly started to catch on. He saw the way I tried to avoid the other guard. Jolly's not a fan of perverts. One day, he strolled over and asked point blank if the other man was forcing himself on me. I took a chance and told him the truth. That was the last day I ever saw my tormentor. Two weeks later, rumors surfaced that the man had been found washed up on a riverbank. When I started working for the family, the first thing I did was give Jolly a job with a hell of a lot more pay than he'd been getting. He's been with me ever since. You wanted my truth, Stormy Lawson or Alina Karpova, or whatever your name is—you have it. You know more about me than any other person on this planet. Take it or leave it."

He turned to leave, and panic engulfed me.

I couldn't let him go, not like this. Not at all.

He'd taken the risk of a lifetime by telling me what he had

and endangering his family for me, so I could summon the courage to expose my greatest shame and deepest sorrow.

"I was pregnant before," I blurted, the words sticky and uncomfortable on my tongue. "I was pregnant with his child, and I…" A sob escaped. Then another.

I had to keep going and get it all out.

"I couldn't protect it," I forced between heaving sobs in a voice ravaged by heartbreak. "My baby … I lost my baby…"

# CHAPTER 41

*Torin*

*Present*

I KNEW THE ASSHOLE HAD BEEN ABUSIVE. THAT WAS BAD enough. I hadn't fully considered the breadth of the possible implications. I had avoided thinking about the particulars of what Stormy might have suffered through because it was too damn maddening. Storm didn't have that luxury. She'd had to live every agonizing minute.

I felt like an insensitive prick.

I knew better than anyone what it was like to have a past that haunted you. To feel tarnished compared to those around you because they'd never known depravity. That sort of darkness marked a person. Changed them. And those of us who had experienced it were more apt to sense it in others.

Pain recognizing pain.

I realized at that moment that trauma had been the intangible thing that had drawn me to Storm. We'd carried our burdens differently, but we were the same underneath. We knew what it was to feel broken.

I forced myself to set aside my reeling thoughts and listen to the rest of her story.

"Damyon never knew about the pregnancy. I should have left him before it happened, but I didn't, and that's my greatest shame in life. When I found out the baby was coming, I knew I had to go before he figured it out. I planned and waited for the right opportunity, knowing I would only get one chance. Only, I waited too long." Her fragile voice thinned until it was only a whisp of memory.

Seeing her in so much pain was hell. I would have taken it from her and carried it myself if I could have. Anything to bring the light back into her eyes.

"He got it in his head that I was cheating." She shook her head to herself as though still in disbelief. "The beating was beyond anything he'd done before. It landed me in the hospital. When I woke, I learned that the baby was … gone. I knew my life would be next if I didn't find a way to leave, so instead of waiting, I got up off the bed in my gown and left."

"You walked out onto the streets of Moscow in only a hospital gown? How did you survive?"

Warmth flooded her eyes as she smiled. "I only made it to the end of the hall when a nurse stopped me. She didn't speak much English, but she had gathered what I'd been through and that I was sneaking away. She took a risk and saved my life that day. She got me dressed and fed and on a bus to stay with friends of hers in St. Petersburg. I owe her everything." She hugged the black bag to her chest and peered up at me. "I'm terrified, Torin," Stormy whispered. "The last time I stuck around, it cost me my baby's life. I can't let that happen again. I can't."

I dropped onto the bench and wrapped her in my arms where she belonged, breathing a deep sigh of relief. Holding her—feeling her melt into my touch—soothed my soul better than any drug.

"I will rip out his spinal column with my bare hands before I let him harm you or our child." No exaggeration. I meant every goddamn word.

"It's not that easy, though. I want to believe I'm safe, but I know how ruthless and calculating he can be."

I pulled back and brought her gaze to mine. "I get it. At this stage, you know him better than you know me—not that I ever want you to know that side of me—but you saw me in that ring, remember?" I waited until she nodded. "I've known evil. I've learned how it thinks and studied its weaknesses. Evil. Will. Not. Touch. You." Each clipped word was reinforced with absolute conviction because despite the fear campaign Damyon had employed, I knew he was flesh and blood just like the rest of us. A mortal man with a God-like ego that would be his downfall in the end.

Stormy flung her arms around my neck and clung to me with such force that I could have walked on water had she asked me to. "I'm sorry I hid the marriage from you."

"I wasn't happy about you keeping a secret, but I don't give a fuck about the marriage itself. You can't be married to a dead man."

"Thank you for understanding and for being patient," she whispered.

I huffed on a sardonic laugh. "If you think I'm patient, we might want to have your head rechecked."

She pulled back and gave a small shrug. "My standards are a little skewed."

"Hey, if it works in my favor." I smirked, drawing a smile from her.

"How did you know where to find me?"

I let my finger hook beneath the chain at her neck. "It has a state-of-the-art tracking chip inside the disk. I'm not leaving anything to chance." I waited for her to balk at what I'd done, but she nodded instead.

"I'd wear just about anything if it keeps him away."

"Baby, not even the devil himself can steal you from me."

# CHAPTER 42
*Stormy*

*Present*

IT WAS FUNNY HOW TIME CHANGED A PERSON. SIX YEARS AGO, men who opened doors for me and brought flowers delighted me. That sort of thing now seemed so inconsequential. But Torin's oath? It had my heart soaring into the stratosphere. It was archaic and a touch paranoid, yet exactly what I needed to hear.

I wrapped my arms around his middle, pressing my ear to his chest. The reassuring thud of his steady heartbeat kept the tempo until my own heart fell into step.

"All right, sweet girl." Tor chuckled when I didn't let go.

"Let's get out of here. We're on a tight schedule today, and my girl still needs to see a doctor."

"Doctor? My ribs will be fine." I pulled back in confusion.

Tor's eyes softened. "Different sort of doctor," he said, placing his hand gently over my lower belly.

"Oh," I breathed.

I would have to start blaming the hormones for my mood swings because they were seriously out of control. A flood of overwhelming joy hit me with such force that I had to fight back tears while Torin made a call.

"Jonas, we need to get Stormy an ultrasound as soon as possible ... No, not as in early this week; as in now ... It's an emergency in that she was beat up a few days ago and just discovered she's carrying my baby." His tone took on a challenging edge. Having met Jonas, I doubted he was much affected. "And Jonas, make sure it's a woman ... Yeah, I know I am." He ended the call and slid his phone back into his pocket.

"You're what?" I nudged, curious what the imposing doctor had said.

"A pain in his ass," Torin muttered. "Too bad for him, I don't give a fuck."

I grinned as he led us back out of the YMCA. Torin's bike was parked near the front entrance. Illegally, I might add. He seemed to believe the world was his parking lot.

Hands going to his hips, Torin stared at the bright green racing bike with a scowl. "When I left to come for you, I wasn't expecting to bring you back pregnant."

"I'm pregnant, Tor, not dying."

"Don't even joke about that." He sighed, then threw his leg over the bike. "Enjoy the ride 'cause it's the last time my unborn baby rides anywhere without a seat belt."

"At least you have the helmet with you. Now, you just need one for yourself." I clipped the chin strap over my head, fighting back a smile.

"I'm worried about you, not me," he grumbled.

"Yeah, but who will keep me and the baby safe if you're not around?" I climbed on behind him, sensing him stiffen, then relax.

"Well, *shit.*"

He muttered the words under his breath, but I was close enough to catch them. I grinned as I hugged him tightly. I was still worried about a multitude of things, but those fears suddenly weren't so daunting. Not with Torin at my side. I never imagined it would feel so rewarding to have everything out in the open. Someone as fiercely independent as Tor could have easily been horrified about an unexpected pregnancy, but he'd actually seemed to welcome the idea. He'd even been pissed at the possibility of being kept from his child.

As he drove us through traffic at well under the speed limit, I wondered if he'd feel differently given some time for the news to sink in. From my perspective, after thinking I couldn't have children, the pregnancy was an incredible blessing. But Tor hadn't spent five years coming to terms with infertility. He might not have wanted kids at all, and now he had no choice.

The more I thought about it, the more my worries grew.

If the prospect of a child diminished his desire to be with me, would he be less inclined to protect us from Damyon? A world of insecurities bombarded me until I slammed a mental door on those thoughts and refused to entertain them.

Torin had made his thoughts about me clear, and I

trusted him to stay true. He was allowed to have his own set of fears. That didn't mean he would stop being devoted and caring.

By the time we pulled up onto the sidewalk in front of a glass skyscraper, I was feeling relatively sure-footed on my emotional tightrope.

*One foot in front of the other.*

Jonas had texted Torin with a doctor's name and suite number. I didn't know what to expect. Tor had said we needed an ultrasound, but I wasn't sure that would be possible on such short notice.

"I can't be far along," I said nervously. "This may not even be necessary." My previous pregnancy hadn't provided an opportunity to learn anything about the process, and I didn't have any family or friends who'd been pregnant while I was growing up. All of this was foreign to me.

"You absolutely need to get checked. They'll do an internal ultrasound to check for a heartbeat, tell us what prenatal vitamins to get, and start your file to monitor the baby's growth." He said it all casually as though he'd worked as a nurse for years and had spouted the information a thousand times over.

I gaped at him as the elevator doors opened. "How on earth do you know all that?" I'd never considered that he might already have a child out in the world, but now...

He smirked while ushering me into the waiting elevator. "I have four older siblings, three of them sisters, and all have children. I couldn't help but learn more than I ever wanted to know about babies."

Torin Byrne, brooding boxer and gun-toting gangster, had a side gig as Uncle Tor. I could hardly wrap my head around it.

"How did I not know about this? You never talk about siblings or family outside of your cousins."

"They're all very suburban. I'm the only one who went into the family business, so I don't see them as much."

A chime indicated we'd reached our floor before the silver doors opened.

"You're a lucky man, you know that?" I said as we stepped into a sterile gray hallway.

Tor's fathomless gaze met mine. "Luckier than I was before, that's for sure." He took my hand and led me to an OB/GYN suite around the corner. The door was locked.

"It *is* Sunday, after all," I told him.

"Here," called a female voice. "I'm here!" A woman in jeans and a Jets hoodie charged around the corner and squeezed by us to unlock the door. "Come on back. I'm Nicole Bromstead. Jonas said you two needed an ultrasound?"

"Yes," Torin answered. "We just discovered that Storm is pregnant. As you can see, she was attacked a few days ago, so we want to make sure everything is okay."

The woman halted and looked back at me, finally taking in my bruised face. "Oh dear. Yes. Of course." She started to turn away, but I stopped her with a hand on her arm.

"Just so you know, he did *not* do this." I glanced briefly at Torin. "I was followed home from the subway." I knew the assumption was easy to make, and I hated for anyone to think that of him.

Her brows knitted together. "I'm so sorry. What a very tumultuous few days for you."

I smiled reassuringly. "I'm doing a lot better, thanks to this guy."

"Good!" She patted my hand, quickly rebounding.

"Okay, come on in here. I need you naked from the waist down since it sounds like you're not far along. You can use this drape to cover you." She set a folded paper drape on the table, then booted up the machinery. "I'll put the game on out here while you're changing and pop back in a minute. Jets were up ten-zero at half!" Her excited announcement hung in the air after she swept from the room.

"She has an awful lot of energy," I whispered, starting to undress. "I think I like her."

Torin rolled his eyes. "You would."

Ten minutes later, I was on my back, my knees spread wide with a dildo-looking device up my hoo-ha, and a death grip on Torin's hand. The machine made some static sounds like a microphone being jostled around in a bag of groceries, and the display was a swirl of black and white splotches. I couldn't make sense of any of it.

Then the distinct beat of a rhythmic pulse filled the room.

It replaced all the air in the room, leaving me breathless.

That was my baby. *Our* baby. The sound of its tiny heart thrumming inside me. And I could see a defined white peanut-looking shape on the screen floating in the middle of a black circle.

"Here," Dr. Bromstead said, pointing at a tiny flickering dot. "That's where the heartbeat is coming from." She used the mouse to draw a line from one end of the peanut to the other. "Looks like you are seven weeks and five days along, which puts your due date at July fourteenth. Congratulations, you're going to be a mommy."

I burst into tears. Heaving, cathartic crocodile tears that probably made me look insane.

"Is everything okay?" the doctor asked.

"Everything is fine," Torin told her. "But can I have a minute alone with her?"

"Yes, of course. I'll just be out here watching the game." She pulled out the wand from inside me and set the equipment aside before scurrying out.

I pressed my hands over my face, embarrassed that I'd suddenly come unglued. Torin pulled them away and stood over me. Seeing his normally turbulent stare full of wonder and adoration, I nearly lost it again.

"Tell me those are happy tears," he murmured.

"Yes, mostly," I said with a hiccup. "I didn't think it was possible, so I'm in awe that it's actually happening. I'm a little sad that I can't share this with Honey because I know she'd be tickled, but also I'm worried about what you're thinking. I don't want you to feel forced into anything."

Torin swept my hair off my forehead, his hand resting on my cheek. "I've never thought much about kids—no reason to when I couldn't even stand having a woman in my home—but all that changed when you showed up. I'd want this kid no matter what because it's something you and I made together, but the fact that it makes you so happy seals the deal. I'd do just about anything to make your eyes shine like that."

If my heart swelled any more, it would burst through my straining rib cage.

"It's a damn shame no one else gets to see this side of you, Tor. You really are incredible."

He grunted, making me smile. "Not sure you'd say that if you knew what else I was thinking."

My eyes rounded when his grew hooded. "We can't," I hissed." The doctor's right outside."

"Pretty sure she knows we fuck, babe."

"Doesn't mean she wants a front-row seat."

With one long sidestep, he was at the end of the table, where he tugged on my ankles and had my legs around his middle in one swift motion. "I just learned this amazing woman is going to be the mother of my child." He unclasped his pants with one hand, never taking his eyes from mine. "We were together once. She wasn't supposed to be able to have kids, but it happened like fucking fate. I haven't been inside her since." He leaned forward, pressing his cock against my folds. "I wouldn't give a fuck if the president of the United States was on the other side of that door. The only thing that matters is right ... *here.*" Torin angled his hips and pressed inside me.

He took care to move slowly, giving my body time to adjust, but my heart struggled to keep up. I'd faced nothing but uncertainty and fear for weeks. Years, even. Torin's words were everything I didn't know I needed to hear.

I clung to him, his body snug against mine, as his short, possessive thrusts picked up speed. "*Yes, Tor,*" I breathed.

His angle and proximity were perfectly aligned for his body to make contact with my clit at the exact moment his cock laid claim to my G-spot. The onslaught of sensation built up a cataclysmic ball of pressure in my core almost instantly—faster than I ever imagined possible.

"*Fuck, my girl takes it good.*" His lips teased the skin on my neck.

I clung to Torin Byrne with all my strength. Not because I had to or needed to, but because I wanted to. I wanted every complicated inch of him—the sweet and possessive, the jealous tendencies and sincere devotion, his protectiveness and everything between—because he wasn't one without the other. He was the sum of his imperfect parts, and I wanted all of them.

*"Only for you, baby."* My orgasm overtook me as I spoke, each word more breathless than the last.

Torin's release seemed to consume him with the same unexpected speed as my own. His body stiffened and arched with two slower, emphatic thrusts and a shuddered exhalation. And in perfect Torin style, he topped off a frenzied fuck with a breathtakingly tender kiss on my neck as if to ensure that no matter how gruff or domineering he might seem, underneath it all was pure adoration.

# CHAPTER 43
*Torin*

*Present*

I PULLED BACK AND BREATHED DEEPLY THROUGH MY NOSE, trying to slow my heart rate. As I did, the sight of Stormy's tattoo peeking from her top caught my attention. I slid my finger inside the shirt's collar, pulling it and the cup of her bra down until the entire tattoo was visible.

Stormy tried to sit up. I got the sense she was trying to sidestep the subject, but I refused to let it go.

"He gave this to you, didn't he?" I suddenly recognized the shape for what it was—initials. The same initials I'd seen on Damyon's stationery.

"The last time I saw him before I woke in the hospital and ran."

I wasn't sure what made me more furious—the fact that the bastard had branded her, or the fact that she was clearly embarrassed about it. She wouldn't even meet my gaze.

I was going to tear that motherfucker limb from limb.

But for now, I didn't want my fury ruining our afternoon. This was the first day we saw our son or daughter, and I didn't want my temper marring our memories.

"And the tattoo?" I asked, hoping I'd steered us into safe waters.

Stormy smiled. "They're fire poppies. They grow from charred soil—one for each of my parents." Her chin trembled.

"And one for the baby?"

She nodded. "And the bee is for Honey. I wanted to cover up the ugly with the most beautiful parts of my life."

I'd never known anyone who could find a silver lining like Storm could. Her ability to celebrate the positive was extraordinary, even when it was only one tiny clover in a giant mound of shit. I supposed it made sense, though. Only a woman with her ability would be willing to give me the time of day.

I didn't believe in soulmates, but goddamn if the universe wasn't arguing a sound case.

My lips came crashing down on hers. Storm giggled, but my voracious kiss quickly devoured it. I was contemplating round two when my phone began to buzz.

*Fuck me.*

Too much shit was in the works to ignore the call.

"Yeah?" I answered gruffly.

"Everything's set up for the meeting. Your place in two

hours." Keir had spent the morning helping me coordinate the family.

"Good. We'll be by your place in a few to grab her things." I hung up and took Storm's hand. "We need to go. I'll explain once we're home."

We thanked the doctor on our way out, and I told her to get my billing info from Jonas. An hour later, we were parked in front of my apartment building.

"Leave the helmet on." I helped her off the bike while quickly surveying the area for threats.

Being out in the open made me beyond uncomfortable. I should have taken my car, but I'd been in a rush to get to Storm, and the bike was by far the fastest mode of transportation. I hadn't considered how exposed we'd be on the way back. Damyon was likely already monitoring my apartment building.

I could have gone to Moxy or someplace random like the skating rink we'd used for the fight to meet with my cousins, but both were too isolated. Too easily surrounded. There was safety in numbers, and my fifteen-story apartment building was a perfect stronghold. We had the high ground, which was always an advantage in war.

And war was coming.

Damyon had said I had twenty-four hours to hand over Stormy. That time was almost at an end, and I was confident he intended to follow through because it was what I would have done. If I were in his shoes, I wouldn't even wait the full twenty-four—hit the enemy unaware. That was why we were taking every precaution.

I ushered Stormy upstairs and got her situated in the guest bedroom with Jolly, who I'd brought in as protection. Ideally, I wouldn't have let her out of my sight, but she didn't need to hear the shit we'd be discussing. It would only make her worry more, and I wouldn't be far. Someone I trusted would have eyes on her at all times without distraction. Even if I was only one room away, I wasn't leaving anything to chance.

# CHAPTER 44

*Stormy*

*Present*

"I wish I could be there with you, but Keir wouldn't even let me finish my sentence when I tried to ask." Rowan's call was an unexpected relief. I'd only been in the back bedroom a couple of minutes when my phone lit up.

"I'm just glad you'll still speak to me after I ran out on you like that. I kind of freaked out a little." God, I was so embarrassed. I knew I shouldn't be. She understood the complications of my situation, but it was never great having an audience when you panic.

"Girl, if you had any idea of the wild stuff I did when I thought I had no other option, you'd think I was unhinged."

She paused, her voice dropping low. "Did you talk to him ... about ... you know?"

I had to laugh. "Yeah, we talked. I told him everything, and I think that maybe, things will be okay, assuming we can get all this chaos sorted out." That was the catch, and it was a big one.

"Oh good! I'm so relieved. That sort of thing is scary enough without relationship complications."

I stole a look at Jolly as I considered telling her about our doctor's visit but decided to hold off. That was big news, and I wanted Torin to be able to share it with his family and friends. The older man didn't seem to be paying attention, but I'd learned from working with him that he was aware of more than he let on.

"We'll have time to sort things out," I assured her, keeping things nice and vague.

She started to respond when an ear-piercing siren split the air. With the phone still in one hand, I slammed my hands over my ears as best I could and jumped to my feet.

"You stay put," Jolly hollered. "We're not going anywhere until we're told."

"Ro, something's going on." I had to yell over the siren. "I'll call you back."

If she replied, I didn't hear it. I could hardly hear my own thoughts.

Jolly stood and positioned himself between me and the door. Tor had said something like this might happen, but it didn't make it any less terrifying. What felt like an eternity passed before the door flew open.

Torin's stare clocked me for a cursory once-over, then cut to Jolly. "Building communications center sent a message. It's a gas leak filtering into the ventilation system. They want the whole building to evacuate."

"Is it Damyon?" I lowered my hands from my ears as fear anchored me in place.

"Without a doubt."

Jolly glowered. "He'd poison a whole damn building full of people to get us out?"

I swallowed. "I wouldn't put it past him to burn the thing down rather than let me go."

"We talked about him pulling a stunt like this," Torin said, his tone all business. "Everyone knows what to do." He waited for us to nod before leading the way into the hall.

"What about my cat?" I blurted. We'd never specifically discussed a gas leak. Was I supposed to leave poor Blue Bell?

Jolly grabbed my wrist and yanked me with him. "Jesus, woman. We've got bigger problems. Let's go."

He was right, of course. I was just too terrified to face them.

Damyon was here for me, and I could only pray that Torin found a way to stop him.

# CHAPTER 45

*Torin*

*Present*

IT SEEMED DAMYON AND I WERE AS SICKENINGLY SIMILAR AS I'd suspected. He hadn't waited the full twenty-four hours to come for Stormy, but I had discussed the possibility with my cousins and had a plan.

Granted, my plans had centered around the chance of a fire or explosion that wouldn't necessarily compel our evacuation, but Damyon had been thorough. We had no choice but to make our exit.

Every ounce of my attention was laser-focused on what needed to be done. The wailing alarm didn't even register as I directed our escape. Keir and Oran were both present and would normally have taken the lead, but they had respectfully taken a back seat and let me run the show. Six of my cousins had come to the apartment, and we had a dozen more nearby. The goal was to keep Stormy safe, but it was equally important to me that no one else ended up dead in the process.

"Is the car in place?" I asked Keir.

"Ready and waiting."

"Good, I'll lead the way." I grabbed Storm's coat and hat. "I want her in the middle surrounded by us at all times." Everyone nodded, guns drawn. "Then let's head out."

I gave Storm one last kiss before we left the apartment. "This will be over soon enough. Stick to the plan and try not to panic, okay?"

She nodded, her large brown eyes wide with worry. "Please, be careful."

"I will," I assured her, bringing my lips to her ear. "I can't afford to be anything less. There's two of you counting on me now." My hand grazed her stomach.

Her shaky smile filled me with determination. She trusted me with her life and the life of our unborn child. That meant the world to me. I wouldn't let her down.

Everyone in the apartment filtered into the hall and walked quickly but carefully to the stairs. We weren't the only ones evacuating, and the chaos made visibility difficult. I wasn't sure if that was good or bad. People gave us a relatively wide berth when they saw we were armed, minimizing the immediate crowding.

We proceeded around in circles down ten flights of stairs before reaching the ground level, where everything would get more complicated. I paused at the stairwell exit and scanned the landing. Not spotting anyone loitering with guns, I led our group away from the crowd and to the small coffee shop in the lobby. The place had its own separate back exit leading to the side alley where it received deliveries and had dumpster access. All we had to do was go through the shop to where the car would be waiting.

I placed a quick call to our driver as we walked through the empty shop. "How's it look out there?"

"All quiet."

"We're on our way out."

"I'll unlock the doors once you're in sight."

I ended the call and stopped at the back exit, turning back to talk to my family. "As you know, our only experience with Damyon proved that he's good at what he does. There's no sign of him so far, but that doesn't mean he isn't here. I don't believe for a second that this gas leak is a coincidence, so be on your guard."

Everyone nodded. I took a deep breath, then reached for the handle.

The black SUV was in view about twenty feet from us. I'd only opened the door a couple of inches, so I couldn't see much else. Not that it mattered. This sort of situation only allowed for so much control. The rest would have to be luck.

"Three, two, one," I counted down quietly before pushing open the door and leading the charge. Time passed in slow motion as I approached the car, reaching for the door just as a bullet exploded into the metal by my hand.

I recoiled, my cousins clustering in a group behind me, forming a protective circle. Before we could run for cover, another round of shots rang out. The result was chaos.

Oran went down to the ground.

Keir flew into action, dragging him back toward the safety of the coffee shop while Oran's brother covered them.

Their departure divided our group in half. I reached for the car door again.

"*Stop.*" The barked command vibrated with totalitarian authority.

I looked up to see Damyon stepping from the doorway across the alley. A quick scan revealed three more shooters in the windows above and four men entering from either side of the alley.

We were surrounded.

Adrenaline lit my body with an electric need to strike at the enemy, but I had to hold back. No one was shooting at the moment, and I needed to keep it that way.

"You measure time differently over there in Siberia?" I asked with practiced indifference.

Damyon strolled closer, clearly not impressed by our threat. "As if you were planning to hand her over." His condescending smile was infuriating. This guy seriously thought his shit didn't stink. Well, I had news for him. He wasn't so goddamn special.

I would have shot him where he stood, but that would have been too easy an out for him. Damyon needed to suffer for what he'd done. I had plans for him.

"You might be surprised what I'm willing to do."

"Really? Then step aside. Let me have my wife." His Russian accent was almost comical, reminding me of every movie villain since the Cold War.

"How about we let my family go, then you and I can talk about what happens next?" I kept my body angled toward Damyon, shielding the small form huddled behind me. Her body shook, but I didn't let it distract me.

"You are willing to send them away and face me all alone?" He studied me as though I were a rare two-headed snake he couldn't figure out. Was I a defective mutation or a newly evolved species posing a special danger?

"What choice do I have? I'd rather some of them make it out of here alive, and you clearly have the advantage."

"You see that, yet you are not willing to walk away? You will sacrifice yourself, yes?"

"Damyon, we both know the score. You aren't going to leave me alive to come after her."

He gave an impish smile and shrugged. "You are too right. It cannot be allowed."

I nodded gravely. "Let them go, and it's over. You won."

"Winning would mean I had faced someone worthy of calling an adversary. You are nothing but a waste of my time." His gaze lifted to a point above my head. The look was a signal.

A frenzy of action exploded in a span of seconds before returning to relative silence just as quickly. Gunfire rang out, echoing harshly off the tall buildings around us. Empty hands lifted to the sky, and bodies dropped to the ground.

Damyon was right. It was a slaughter more than a fight, only ... not in the way he'd intended.

Every one of his personal guards was dead. Boris's men were the only Russians left standing, and their guns were aimed at Damyon. He'd been double-crossed and was completely surrounded.

Seeing his loss play out in real time, Damyon lunged. I'd shifted while the shots rang out, allowing him enough access to grab ahold of Storm's wrist and yank her out from behind me. In one swift motion, he spun her around and pulled her against him like a shield, a glinting switchblade at her throat. Panic made his unnaturally pale eyes look downright demonic.

He bellowed at Boris's men in Russian before shifting into English, spittle flying in the air. "Pick up your weapons, you *fucking cowards.*"

I tsked, slowly shaking my head. "It's so hard to get good help these days." I looked at the half a dozen Russians standing idly in the area. "Gentlemen, give my compliments to Boris."

They nodded, then disappeared, leaving Damyon alone in the lion's cage.

I continued unhurriedly, a cat toying with its supper. "You promised Boris you weren't here for business, Karpova. He wasn't too pleased when I brought him information about the new skin trade arrangement you'd made here in town. It's understandable that this would all come as a shock to you. How could you have known that I knew? Your home office is a pile of charred splinters at the bottom of the marina. You thought my attack on your boat was personal, but everything I did was strategic. Did you actually think I was stupid enough to *accidentally* let my car get caught on marina security footage?" I shook my head in mock disappointment. "All of it was strategy, but your ego was too inflated to see it. And now, you've backed yourself into a very painful corner."

The look in his eyes reminded me of an injured cat cornered by a pack of dogs. Escape was impossible, and he knew it.

"You think you're so clever, but all I ever wanted is right here," he hissed. "If I go to hell, I will take her with me."

I chuckled, truly amused. "Good luck with that."

Damyon stilled. I could almost see the wheels in his head chugging along as he processed his confusion. He spun his captive around, accidentally yanking off her wig in the process.

Shae flashed a wicked grin.

Lightning fast, she swept his legs out from under him, then used the ground as leverage to disarm him by breaking his wrist with a sickening crack.

The great Russian Shadow wailed in pain as I approached and stood over him.

"You may own half of Moscow, but this is *our* fucking city. You're *nothing* to us."

# CHAPTER 46

*Stormy*

*Present*

Shots rang out from somewhere down below, but up on the roof, it was impossible to tell who was firing or what had happened. My imagination played out every horrifying situation possible. I would have gone to the railing and tried to learn more if Jolly would have let me.

His scathing glare told me to forget about it.

We hunkered down behind a large block of ducting where Jolly could peek around the corner at the door, but someone exiting the roof stairwell wouldn't see us. I felt like I'd lived and died three lifetimes up on that roof.

My hands were so sweaty they tingled, and my heart was ten miles into a marathon sprint.

When Jolly's phone began to buzz, I had to fight back the urge to yank the phone from him.

"Yeah?" He nodded. Once. Twice. "Will do." Conversation over.

"Was that Torin? What happened? Did anyone get hurt? Oh God. Is everyone okay?" My rapid-fire questions flew at him without pause.

Jolly raised his hand as if to interrupt. "It's over. Went down exactly as planned, and he wants to meet you back at his place."

My lungs seized. It wasn't a sob or a gasp. More like the greedy intake of air after fear had strangled off my supply. I flung myself at Jolly, holding him in a death grip.

"Oh my God. I was so worried." My eyes squeezed shut with relief.

Jolly patted my back somewhat awkwardly. "All right, then." He huffed when I didn't immediately release him. "We gonna go see your man or stand up here blubbering all day?"

I laughed as I pulled away, tears of happiness and relief burning the backs of my eyes. "Lead the way." I waved him ahead, following him to the door. I was more than ready to see Torin alive and well for myself. It had been the worst kind of torture to branch off from the group and head up instead of down, knowing the danger they'd be in because of me.

The siren had stopped, though the emergency lights continued to flash. We descended five flights to the tenth floor, my heart soaring higher with each step down. I was elated to reunite with the man who had quickly become the center of my world.

When we stepped into the hallway, we saw a fireman walking toward the opposite stairwell. He turned around when the door closed behind us. I assumed he was about to tell us we had to evacuate, but when his soulless eyes met mine, fear overtook me.

I clamped my hand around Jolly's arm in a vicious hold and froze. "It's *him*—not a fireman." My words were rushed and breathless, saturated with panic. "He's the man who attacked me in my apartment."

I wanted to vomit and scream and run, all at once.

But I didn't do any of those things. There wasn't time. The man across from us already had his gun in his hand and was raising it with his violent stare fixed on Jolly.

I knew what I had to do before I'd even formed the thought. Instinct took over.

I shouldered Jolly with all the momentum I could muster on short notice right as the shot rang out. Not a second later, pain ripped through my shoulder. My body recoiled as Jolly's shots exploded, three in quick succession.

"Jesus *Christ*, woman," the older man shouted, turning to see me stumble to the ground.

My gaze was still trained thirty feet away at the far end of the hall where the other man had collapsed into a motionless heap. I wanted to think he was dead, but I was terrified he might not be. I kept myself propped up on the uninjured arm so I didn't lose sight of him. The effort was a strain as my head began to spin.

"Torin's gonna skin me alive. Why the hell'd you go and do a thing like that?" He crouched to look over the wound.

"You risked your life for me, but I can't do the same?" I asked, my breaths shallow.

"Damn selfless … son of a … don't listen to no one…"

Jolly muttered curses as he took out his phone. "Tor, we got a little problem."

# CHAPTER 47

*Torin*

*Present*

"WHAT THE *FUCK* DO YOU MEAN SHE'S BEEN SHOT?" I WAS
going to crawl through the phone line and wring his fucking
neck. Every bit of the soaring sense of victory I'd felt seconds
earlier was now peppered with buckshot and crashing to the
ground.

"It was her own damn fault," he barked back at me, not
helping his case. "She did it to protect me, but she's gonna be
okay. It's only her shoulder."

"*She's fucking pregnant, Jolly.*" The words exploded past my
lips, resounding off the marble in the apartment lobby. I'd
already started on my way to the elevators.

"Shit," he grumbled.

*You got that goddamn right.*

"I'll call an ambulance on my way up." I hung up. Anything else he said was only going to piss me off even more.

When I stepped off the elevator on the tenth floor, I was greeted by a dead fireman bleeding out on the carpet. What the fuck had happened here?

I kicked the gun away from his hand.

*Okay, so not a fireman.*

I placed a call to Keir. "We've got a dead soldier dressed as a fireman up here. Spread the word to be on the lookout for others."

"Got it."

"How's Oran?" I felt a little bad that I hadn't stuck around to check on my cousin, but I wasn't too worried about him.

"Bruised but fine. Kevlar took care of it." Every one of us who were out in the open had been outfitted with vests.

"Good. I've called an ambulance. Stormy was shot."

"The fuck?"

"Exactly. I'll call you later." I hung up and dropped to my knees next to Stormy. "Jesus, baby. That's a lot of blood." I took over holding Jolly's shirt over the wound for compression, my heart pounding like the relentless bass of club dance music.

"It's okay, really." She smiled through the pain.

How fuckin' sweet was this girl that she was reassuring me when *she* was the one who'd been shot?

"Jolly was supposed to protect you. Not the other way around," I chided her gently.

"Yeah, but it's Jolly. He's like family to you."

Fuck if I wasn't insanely, maddeningly in love with this woman.

I leaned down and pressed a kiss to her forehead. "Thank you, baby. That's crazy sweet of you, but if you ever do something like that again, I'll spank your ass raw."

Storm started to laugh, then winced. "Is he dead?" she asked, pain lancing through her words.

"Not dead but secure."

"Promise me you'll end it, Tor. I want this to be over." She lay her hand over mine and looked at me with such desperate yearning, it ripped me in two. I hated the thought of Damyon not suffering for what he'd done to her. He deserved to endure the same months of torment he'd inflicted upon her. But hell if I could tell her no, and I wasn't about to lie to her. Not when she'd already given me so much of her trust.

"Fine," I said through teeth clenched so tight, my jaw ached.

Her whole body visibly relaxed. "Is Shae okay? I was worried sick about her."

"Crazy woman was fighting back laughter before unveiling herself. I think she had a little too much fun disarming him."

Stormy smiled, but her eyes were drooping. The blood loss was getting to her. I was five seconds from calling 911 again to bitch out someone—anyone—when the elevator doors pinged open, and two men with a stretcher stepped out. They took a look at the fireman, then Storm, then back at the fireman, unsure what to think.

"He's not actually a fireman," I called to them. "And he's beyond fixing. Now get over here and help her."

After a moment's pause, they followed my instructions.

They were good at their jobs, getting her stabilized and loaded up in a matter of minutes. I rode with her to the hospital, my hand clasping hers the entire way.

◊

THE ER DOCTOR updated me not long after we arrived. He said Storm wasn't in any danger, but he needed to perform surgery to remove the bullet and clean the wound. I didn't care how much he reassured me. I wasn't going to breathe easy until I saw Storm alive and well with my own eyes.

Keir and Rowan soon joined me in the waiting room along with Jolly, Micky, and that asshole who came by the club for Storm. I didn't even have time to kick the guy out before four people joined him, all twittering about Storm like they knew her. Then Shae appeared with Pippa, Bishop's woman, and Conner's wife, Noemi. The three women had grown close in recent months. In five minutes' time, the waiting room was a fucking circus.

I would have been annoyed, except I knew Storm would be beside herself when she saw all the people who had rallied around her.

Just as the doctor had said, Stormy was taken to recovery two hours later. She'd done well in surgery, and the baby's heartbeat was steady and strong. As I waited to be called back to see her, I tried to wrap my head around it all. Stormy. The baby. Damyon's capture. It had been one hell of a week.

"Family of Stormy Lawson?" A man in scrubs stood at a set of double doors.

The entire room stood up.

"Here," I said, making my way to him. "I'm her husband."

Someone behind me began to cough and choke. I ignored them.

"Storm is awake now. We can only let family back, and only one at a time." He peered over my shoulder, brows raised. "They're not all family, right?"

"Nope, none of them."

"Except me," Shae chimed in, joining me with an obnoxious grin. "I'm her sister."

I arched a brow at my cousin but didn't contradict her.

The doctor gave a nod. "Right, well, still just one at a time. I take it you'd like to go back first?" he asked me.

"Definitely." *I'd like to see him try to stop me.*

Shae leaned in as the doctor turned and whispered, "If we're making up shit, and you get to be her husband, then I can be her sister."

"Hope you know you just volunteered for watch duty should I need to leave since you're now the only other person allowed back there."

"Wouldn't have it any other way." Shae winked.

"Good, because I don't want her left alone for a minute."

I turned to catch up with the doctor, following him down a maze of corridors to Stormy's room. She was reclined in the bed when I entered, her right shoulder area wrapped in layers of gauze. She gave me a doped-up smile the second she saw me. It wasn't her usual electric grin, but it was still damn good to see.

"How are you feeling, beautiful?" I dropped kisses on her forehead and cheeks before pressing my lips to hers. The tiny amount of contact loosened the rope knotted tight around my chest.

"I'm all good," she said in a drawn-out Southern twang.

"Those meds treatin' you right?"

"Mm-hmm." She nodded, her eyes closing, then reopening on an extended blink. "I'm gonna need another tattoo, though."

"Oh yeah?" A smile teased the corners of my lips.

"Yup. One on the other side for my new scar."

My smile turned to a grimace. "You may have a new scar, but I promise it's the last. No one will ever hurt you again."

Clarity forced away the haze in her eyes. "It's over, then? You finished him?"

"Not yet. I've been here with you."

Worry lines creased her forehead.

"Is that what you want, sweet Stormy? You want me to go now and end it?"

Her childlike nod was more than I could bear. "Okay, baby girl." I gave her another kiss. "Next time you see me, it'll be over. I'm going to send Shae in. She's your sister now, in case you weren't aware."

A spark lit Storm's eyes as her smile returned. "I've never had a sister."

I chuckled and shook my head. "Well, now you do." I walked back to the waiting room and sent Shae back to keep an eye on my girl. After learning that Stormy was doing well and that only family could see her, the room had thinned out to Keir, Rowan, Pippa, and Noemi.

Keir took one look at me and turned to the ladies. "You three think you can make it home without getting into trouble?"

Rowan shot him a glower with one brow arched high on her forehead. "I bet we can manage."

Keir grunted and walked over to join me. "I believe you're in need of a ride."

"I can manage if you'd rather get the girls home safely."

"And let you have all the fun? I don't think so." He spoke quietly so the women couldn't overhear.

"Not sure how fun it'll be. I promised Storm to end it quickly. Of course, I never said it had to be painless."

Keir flashed a rare wolfish grin. "Sounds like plenty of fun to me."

♦

CONNER and another cousin had taken Damyon out to an abandoned meat processing plant that we owned and used for miscellaneous purposes. Nefarious and illegal purposes. It was one of my favorite properties because I rarely left the place feeling unsatisfied.

Keir and I made our way past the front offices and into the main facility where the beltway of hooks overhead could easily identify the old assembly lines. Remote, well-insulated, and forgotten—it was the perfect place to conduct business.

A heavy metal door led to a small room with no windows and thick walls. My cousins waited inside for us, along with Damyon, who was tied to a chair with a rag duct taped in his mouth.

"Thanks, guys." I nodded appreciatively. "We'll take it from here."

"Storm okay?" Conner asked.

"Yeah, everything's fine. She's out of surgery and doing well."

"That's great, man." He gave me a clap on the back. "You need anything else, let us know."

The two slipped from the room.

"I take it no one ever told you that real men don't hit women." I stalked closer to Damyon until I hovered over him. "Stormy's strong as fuck. To make her as scared as you did ... I can only imagine you must have been brutal." Images of her curled up on the floor where we'd found her at Moxy flashed in my mind, fueling my fury. "I'd like nothing more than to hurt you in every way you hurt her—every bruised and bloody lip—but a year's worth of abuse would take more time than I have to give."

Without warning, I leveled a devastating right hook at his cheek, reveling in the feel of his jaw breaking under the force of my fist.

While his face was still turned to the side, absorbing the strike, I leaned in close. "But that doesn't mean I can't have some fun."

I stood tall again as he straightened himself, wanting him to feel powerless beneath me the way Storm would have felt in his presence.

Damyon tried to speak. The sounds were unintelligible through the rag, but he continued trying, his attempts growing louder and more enraged.

I slowly shook my head. "Your time for words is over. I don't give a flying fuck what you have to say."

His head jerked as if trying to spit at me.

Chuckling, I tore open his shirt, pulling it over his shoulders to expose him from the chest up. He was tatted, as I knew he would be. Black ink only. I didn't give a shit about any but the two stars near his shoulders.

"Keir, think you could grab the can for me?"

"You got it."

I began to pace around my captive slowly. "Not sure if they told you, but this place was a meat processing plant back in the day. Great insulation. Even without A/C, it's always pretty cool inside. This room especially, which is ironic. It looks like it could be an industrial fridge and feels that way, but that's not accurate. You see, these operations end up with a lot of waste byproduct that has to be disposed of." I looked around the room and up at the concrete ceiling that contained circular openings at regular intervals. "This room housed the industrial incinerator. It's located right beneath the smokestacks you may have seen when you arrived."

Keir returned, setting a red gas can at my feet along with a rag and a box of matches.

The Russian never even flinched. I knew because I kept my eyes glued to him, wanting to soak in every ounce of his fear. He was ballsy; I'd give him that. His anger overrode his fear instinct at the moment, but that would make it even more satisfying when he eventually cratered.

I went to a tool box we kept by the wall and took out a pair of large pliers, then returned to the gas can. I unscrewed the lid and removed the pour spout. Once I had the rag wound around the end of the pliers, I tipped the can just enough to wet the rag.

"That's a nasty burn mark Stormy has on her chest." Malice darkened my voice. "Seems only fair you know what she suffered since you were the one who put it there."

I stepped away from the gas can then took out a match. Elated anticipation flared in my chest with the scrape of phosphorus bursting into flame.

Damyon's body coiled tight before he forced the muscles to relax.

*That's right, fucker. This is gonna hurt.*

The match never had to touch the rag before the flame lept from one to the other, flaring hungrily as it consumed the rag.

I leaned in. "You never deserved these in the first place," I goaded quietly before bringing my makeshift torch to the star tattoo under his right shoulder and holding it in place.

Damyon yanked against his bindings. Judging from the fury in his frigid eyes, my comment riled him more than the pain. The man was fucking deranged. Nostrils flaring, he stilled, eyes boring into me, as the skin bearing his inked star puckered and singed.

Maybe I was deranged too, because I wasn't remotely disturbed at the sight. Quite the opposite. A smug smile teased at the corners of my lips, relishing a small taste of justice as I moved the flaming torch to the star on his left side.

Sweat began to dot his forehead.

The Russian maggot tried to put on a stoic front, but his shields faltered as the rank odor of burning flesh filled the room. After a few minutes, any remaining ink under the disfigured skin was no longer recognizable. Effective, though too quick for my liking. But the fun wasn't over.

Again, I squatted down and used the gas spout like a straw, covering one end to create suction that would hold a small portion of gas.

"And what about your knees? Do they have stars as well? I know you lot like to boast that you kneel before no one." I lifted my gaze to his. "I suppose that's still true since you can't kneel when you're dead."

I flicked the plastic spout at Damyon's legs. He jerked as a spray of gasoline dotted his clothes.

"I promised Stormy I'd put an end to this." I flicked another splatter of gas at him. "And that's what I'm going to do because I keep my word." Dip and flick. "And remember, you have her to thank for that. If it were up to me, I'd have drawn out your punishment to make up for every time you laid a finger on her. Burn off each of those worthless tattoos one at a time then let you watch as I chopped off that pathetic dick of yours." More splatter. "The possibilities truly were limitless."

I stood, this time allowing a small trickle of gas to pour over his head. "But Stormy is more important than you'll ever be. She's pregnant with my child, after all."

*Point. Set. Match.*

I knew what it was to be obsessed. I knew how Damyon thought—the intensity of his emotions. Nothing in the world would hurt him more than knowing the woman he desired had been claimed by another man. I'd been anxiously awaiting the moment I would unveil those words, and fuck if it wasn't glorious.

The asshole roared and raged against his bindings, a vein bulging from his forehead.

I grinned and picked up the box of matches.

"There are consequences to all our actions, Mr. Karpova." I struck a match and watched it flare to life before flicking it at him.

The match extinguished as it tumbled down his shirt, then fell to the floor innocuously.

Damyon's chest heaved up and down with ragged exertion, his vengeful stare locked on me.

"Consequences keep us accountable," I continued coolly.

The scraping strike of another match filled the room.

I tossed the tiny scrap of wood in his direction. The straining man tried to lunge at me. The match dropped to the floor and extinguished like the previous one.

"You have a lot to answer for."

Scrape.

Flick.

*Fire.*

Damyon jerked as the tiny flame took its first breath, then fizzled out.

"Tell the devil hello for me."

Scrape.

Flick.

*Flame.*

The match found its mark and whooshed to life.

His eyes widened as realization began to set in. This fire wasn't going out.

The flame leaped from one dot of gasoline to the next, slowly expanding across him one inch at a time until it found a rivulet that had trickled down from his head. With a whoosh, the greedy flames engulfed him.

In the end, none of us are all that different.

Damyon screamed and flailed like anyone would in his position. His wide eyes pled for mercy in the only way he could, but there was none to be had.

I watched him writhe with zero remorse as the consequences of his actions consumed him.

# CHAPTER 48

*Stormy*

*Present*

"I CAN'T BELIEVE YOU DID THAT FOR ME." MY WORDS CAME out sluggish, but I couldn't seem to break free of the quicksand slowing me down. Everything felt sticky and clumsy.

Shae leaned a hip on my hospital bed and grinned. She was so beautiful with her blue eyes and sharp features that contrasted my own. When the guys told me the plan to dress her up as me, I couldn't imagine anyone ever confusing us. But with the wig, sunglasses, and makeup to match the bruising on my face, she'd made an eerily good body double.

"Are you kidding? I was thrilled the guys let me

participate. Usually, I get stuck on the sidelines. That was the most fun I've had in ages."

"I like you, but you're a little crazy." Crap, I wasn't supposed to say that out loud.

Shae threw her head back and laughed. "I think you're pretty great, too. Anyone who can get through Torin's barriers is someone special, that's for sure."

"He's special. Like super special." My eyes drooped shut, and I had to fight to get them open. "I mean ... not like that kind of special. He's special special." I wasn't making sense. I could hear my words and recognize that I sounded drunk, but I couldn't do anything about it.

"All right, sis. I think you need to get some rest."

With one last burst of effort, I clasped her hand in mine. "Thank you, Shae. And tell the others. Thank you so much."

She patted my hand, her eyes softening. "We were happy to help. You're one of us now, gorgeous. Welcome to the family."

No energy left, my eyes drifted shut with a long-forgotten sense of peace wrapping me snug in its arms. When I woke again, Shae was gone, and Tor sat in the visitor's chair beside me.

"Hey, you," I said with a smile, relieved that my stupor had begun to wear off. "How long was I out?"

Torin was on his feet and at my bed in a heartbeat. "A few hours. How're you feeling?" He swept his fingers across my forehead, tidying stray strands of hair down behind my ear.

"Better, I think."

"Any pain?"

"Not really. I'm sure it'll come. But for now, I feel pretty good."

The tension in his shoulders visibly relaxed. "I'm glad. I hate seeing you in here."

"They say how long until I can go home?"

"A couple of days, if there's no sign of infection."

"That's good. Blue Bell will be so worried. We've never been apart like this." My eyes shot open, a burst of adrenaline snapping me wide-awake. "The gas! Is he okay? I completely forgot about it."

"He's fine," Torin assured me calmly. "The authorities have cleared the building to be re-occupied and said that the initial leak was short lived."

My left hand came to rest over my chest as I breathed a sigh of relief. "Thank goodness."

"You don't need to worry about anything but recovering. I have everything under control." He took my hand and set it palm up before placing a platinum ring in the center. Damyon's wedding band. "It's all done," he said softly.

A wall of emotions pressed against my chest, making my lungs tingle with the urge to cry, but I refused to give way. I refused to cry any more tears for that monster.

"Thank you," I breathed. A tear broke free when I looked at Torin, but it was the good kind. A tear of gratitude to be surrounded by people who would risk their lives for me. Joy to know I had my whole life ahead of me and a man who would do anything to ensure that life was everything I wanted.

The beautiful, grumpy bastard muttered, "He shoulda had it worse."

I grinned wide enough for a red carpet photo shoot. "Kiss me, Tor."

The aqua and azure swirled in his eyes with heat as he leaned in and did as he was told. First gently, then more ardently. Soon, it was no longer a kiss; it was a reassurance, an oath, a benediction, and everything between. By the time we separated and Tor lay his forehead against mine, we were both out of breath.

"Tell me you're mine, Stormy." His voice was so raw and vulnerable that I wanted to wrap him in my arms and never let go.

What we had wasn't conventional or even rational, but I felt more secure and free with Torin than I ever had before. My heart found its home in him before I even knew what was happening.

"I owe you my life," I started quietly. "But you stole my heart long before that. I love you, Torin Byrne, and I'm yours so long as you'll have me."

"*Fuck*." The single exhaled curse bore such emotion that I would have thought he was in pain had his eyes not bore into mine with exalted joy. "Love doesn't even begin to describe what I feel for you. You're my fucking everything, and I'll want you with me every damn day of my life."

He kissed me again, but only briefly, thanks to a not-so-subtle cough announcing the arrival of the new shift nurse.

"It's time to get you on your feet and test out a trip to the bathroom." She arched a brow at Torin. "You can wait in the hall if you'd like."

He didn't budge an inch. "I'm good." Somehow, in two short words, what he really conveyed was "I'd like to see you try to force me out of here."

I bit back a grin. "He can stay." And I had no doubt he would.

He'd stand by me through every trial and tribulation and celebrate each of my victories as though they were his own.

He'd be by my side, figuratively and literally, devoted to the end.

It was a good thing patience was my strong suit.

I giggled to myself.

Tor narrowed his eyes at me.

"It's the drugs," I replied with a shrug. "They must have given me the good stuff." I wasn't sure he bought it, but he let it slide when the nurse stepped between us to lower the bed.

I stayed in the hospital for two more days before they agreed with much persuading to release me. Torin had told me we were going to his place, which made sense because it would be easier for him to care for me there, and that's where Blue Bell was. I didn't expect to find all my things already moved.

"This is my stuff," I said dumbly, staring at a box labeled "kitchen shit." "Did you move me in with you while I was in the hospital?" My tone was incredulous, though I shouldn't have been surprised. If I'd thought about it at all, I could have guessed he'd do something like this.

"Sure did."

"But you didn't think to mention it?"

"Seemed obvious." He shrugged. "My girl isn't living anywhere but with me."

Hearing him call me his girl had me melting into a gooey puddle on the floor. "Okay," I whispered.

His heated gaze snapped to mine as he peeled back the flip top of a can. I was immediately distracted when Blue Bell came running, meowing loudly.

"Hey, boy! Mama missed you." I gingerly lowered myself to one knee only to have my cat run straight past me and into the kitchen. "What the …?" I watched in shock as Torin set down a plate of wet cat food and *cooed* at my cat. Yes, cooed.

"What on earth is going on here?" I gaped.

"He didn't like that dry crap you were giving him."

"Oh really? Did he tell you that?" I got back to my feet, the hand of my good arm propped on my hip.

"He didn't have to," Tor said gruffly. "I could just tell."

"Torin Byrne, are you stealing my cat?" I shot at him in mock outrage. If only he knew.

"I wouldn't have to if you'd treat him right."

I shook my head. "No respect." Karma was a bitch.

Torin's eyes grew hooded as he rounded the island toward me. "That arm gets a little better, and I'll show you respect all night long, baby."

My lips quirked up in the corners. "You're trying to distract me."

He came up behind me and pulled my hair around to one side, then began to kiss the nape of my neck. "Is it working?"

"Mmm … maybe a little." A lot. It was working a lot. "I suppose … shared custody could work." I wasn't even sure what I was saying, so long as he continued what he was doing.

"It's good to have you home," he said softly, his breath warm on my skin.

I looked around the large apartment with a new perspective, pleased at what I saw. "I guess this is my home now, huh."

"Home is wherever we're together. This is just an apartment. You get me?" He coaxed me around to face him, looking at me expectantly.

I smiled and nodded. "Yeah."

"You want a new place that's just ours, all you have to do is say so."

"I'm good here," I assured him quickly.

He carried me away in his ocean eyes as his thumb stroked my cheek. "Love you, my sweet Stormy."

"Love you, too, baby."

# CHAPTER 49

*Stormy*

*Present*

I'D BEEN HOME FROM THE HOSPITAL FOR A WEEK. ONE WEEK OF blessed normalcy. Torin had unboxed my things and found a home for all of my stuff among his own. He let me provide input on placement, but that was about it, insisting I was not to overwork myself. My strength was returning with each day, and my discomfort diminishing. Now, my biggest problem was a growing case of cabin fever.

"Maybe tomorrow we can venture out? Do dinner or something," I suggested. "I could use a change of scenery."

Torin sat across the table from me, shoveling dinner into his mouth. "I suppose that's allowable." He studied me while he chewed. "You think this place is big enough? I've been thinking maybe with a baby on the way, we would be better off finding someplace new."

I did a quick sweep of the open great room and found myself yet again reluctant to consider moving, but this time, it wasn't the moving itself that bothered me. I liked being in Torin's space.

"Something about knowing I'm the only woman you've had over here makes me feel strangely attached to this place."

He raised a brow. "You like that, did you?"

"What girl wouldn't?"

"Well, you'd probably enjoy knowing you've been more than one first for me."

"Oh yeah?"

"You are the only woman I've ever kissed, aside from a couple of girls back when I was sixteen, but that hardly counts," he added dismissively.

I could hardly believe my ears. Though, it wasn't so shocking once I thought it through. The vulnerability of a kiss would have been unappealing for someone as closed off as Torin had been. I adored knowing that was something he'd only shared with me.

When I thought back to that first kiss we'd shared, warmth blossomed across my cheeks. "You must be a natural, then. I never would have suspected you weren't well-practiced." Flustered, I raised my fork to take a bite only to be hit by a wave of nausea. I set the utensil down and took a slow, deep breath.

"You okay?"

"Yeah, but I think I'm done with dinner."

Tor immediately got up and took both our plates away.

I'd been struggling with morning sickness, mostly at night, and he knew that the smell of food made it worse.

"You can finish your dinner," I urged. "I don't want you to stop eating just because I can't."

"I'll finish later." His brows furrowed as he returned to the table. "I wish we had a balcony. I'd say fresh air might help. You sure you don't want a different place? The spare bedrooms are awfully far from ours. We could find something with a balcony and nursery close to the primary bedroom."

I never could have imagined when I first met Torin that someone so incredibly sweet hid beneath that grizzly exterior of his. He'd only had a week to adjust to the idea of being a father, yet he'd embraced it wholeheartedly. I'd even go so far as to say he was excited. Big, bad, brooding Torin was looking forward to being a daddy.

My hormones went into overdrive. I wasn't sure if I wanted to cry or strip naked and beg him to screw me. I didn't get the chance to do either when the security panel buzzed, signaling that we had a guest.

Tor pressed a button, bringing up an image of Oran waiting by the elevator. He buzzed him through. They shook hands when Oran joined us in the apartment, tension thick in the air, especially when he greeted me with an awkward grimace.

It wasn't like we could hug. Aside from my gunshot wound, Oran had suffered severely bruised ribs from taking a bullet to his Kevlar vest during the showdown with Damyon. He was still moving stiffly, though I didn't think that was the reason Torin watched him warily. Oran had been plenty vocal on his suspicions about me.

"What can we do for you?" Tor finally asked.

Oran kept his gray gaze on me. "I was in the area and wanted to stop by. I think I owe Stormy an apology." He took a slow, steady breath. "I hope you understand that while I was tough on you, it was out of concern for my family."

"Of course," I assured him. "It's not easy to know who to trust." My eyes briefly drifted to Tor, hoping he cut his cousin slack. Judging by the way his blistering stare never budged from our guest, it wasn't likely.

"What you did for Torin—protecting Jolly—hasn't gone unnoticed. I wanted you to know that."

He was so stiff beneath layers of impenetrable barriers, the weight had to be unbearable. I felt bad for him. Tor had told me what Oran had gone through. I hated that he'd become so guarded and cynical. The pain of betrayal ran deep. Who knew if he'd ever find his way out of that abyss.

"It was a small price to pay for everything you all have done for me," I offered warmly.

He gave me a thin smile, then reached out and shook hands with Tor again.

"Glad you came by," Torin said, a world of meaning contained in those few words. Apology accepted.

Oran nodded. "Better get going. You two take care."

"You, too, Oran," I called to his back. He didn't turn around.

"I feel so bad for him," I murmured after the door closed behind him.

Torin led me to the living room with a hand on the small of my back. "He'll find his way. I did, and I'm pretty sure my family was close to giving up on me." He gingerly helped me onto his lap with my body crossways over his.

"I suppose we all go through struggles at some point. I

allowed myself to end up married to a Russian mobster ... in Moscow, no less."

"You never have told me how that happened."

"It was easy. He was amazing."

Torin huffed beneath me.

I smirked. "At first, that is." I added the important caveat. "He was attentive and thoughtful—charming and incredibly handsome."

"Handsome?" Tor scoffed. "He had a gruesome scar across his face."

I sucked my lips between my teeth and peered up at him through my lashes. "He didn't have that when I met him."

"Are you telling me you gave him that?"

I nodded.

Torin threw his head back and laughed from deep in his belly. I didn't think a choir of angels could sound more heavenly. "That's my girl. I'm glad you gave him hell."

"I didn't have much of a choice." Feeling the mood in the air shift, I smiled and changed tacks. "But there were plenty of wonderful moments. I was thrilled to marry him when he proposed, and the ring he gave me was spectacular. It may have been inadvertent, but it was the best thing he ever did for me because it bought me the cushion I needed to stay on the run. My engagement ring was the only thing I had on me when I escaped. I sold it to a jeweler the first chance I got. Without that sizable stash of cash, I don't know how I would have managed."

"I wondered how you'd been able to keep on the move."

"It wasn't easy, but the money helped."

He rubbed a hand across my back and kissed my cheek. "No more moving for you. Not unless you want to, but even then, you won't be alone ever again."

"That's true. I'll have the baby." I couldn't hold back my grin, knowing my teasing would rile him.

Torin grunted. "Him, too."

"Him? You know the gender already, do you?"

He shrugged. "Just a feeling. What do you think?"

"I have no idea." I paused. "Do you want to find out or be surprised?"

"You know I'm not a fan of surprises."

I shook my head with a smile. "I suppose not. Well, as long as he or she is healthy. I know it's trite, but that's all that really matters."

Torin clasped my chin between his thumb and finger, lifting my gaze to his. "Everything's going to be fine. I'll make sure of it."

I peered at him, eyes narrowed in wonderment. If it were anyone else, I would have challenged them because no one could make that sort of assertion. But with Tor, his absolute conviction was too dang persuasive. He made me believe everything truly would work out. "You're pretty incredible, you know that?" I asked softly.

"Thanks to you. I was just another surly asshole before you came along."

I grinned. "Maybe a little."

It was crazy how far we'd come in such a short time. I was beyond grateful.

With this swing of the pendulum, each day was another lottery jackpot, and I was ready to soak up every blissful minute.

# CHAPTER 50

*Torin*

*Present*

"AN AIRSTRIP? WE'RE NOT GOING SOMEWHERE, ARE WE?" STORM studied the private planes as we drove past storage hangars.

"No, we're picking something up." I'd gone out on a limb and hoped I didn't regret my actions.

In the weeks since Storm moved in with me, she'd told me all about her parents and her Southern upbringing. She'd also talked endlessly about her grandmother. A grandmother that she desperately missed but had put off contacting out of fear and embarrassment. At first, she blamed her bruises, claiming she didn't want to upset the older woman, but I could tell it was more than that. I could understand. It was a lot to have to explain.

I knew she'd reach out eventually; I was just speeding up the timeline a bit. The two had lost so much time together. I didn't want them to lose any more.

"Looks like we're right on time." I parked out front of our hangar and watched as the family jet taxied toward us.

"Is that plane what you're waiting for? It's Christmas Day. I wouldn't think anyone was working today."

"They do if you pay them enough."

The trick had been convincing the woman to come. If Stormy inherited her trusting nature, it wasn't from her grandmother. The spitfire older woman reminded me of my own nana. Why she would think I'd want to kidnap an elderly woman, I had no clue, but she'd put me through the wringer before agreeing to come.

I got out of the car when the plane stopped. When Storm didn't follow, I waved for her to join me.

"Sorry. I didn't know if you wanted me involved."

"This is for you, baby girl. Not me."

"This isn't a work errand?"

"Nope."

She gave me a curious stare as the airplane door slowly lowered and became a set of steps. The engine cut off. As the sound died away, an old woman with perfectly set silver hair and bright-pink lipstick stepped into view.

"*Honey.*" Storm's breathless exclamation was a perfect blend of astonishment and relief.

"Oh, Alina, baby. I've missed you so much." The woman put her hand over her mouth to hold back the emotions. Storm rushed up the stairs and nearly knocked the woman down with the force of her hug. Both began sobbing hysterically.

Well, shit.

The reunion had gone well. I didn't have to worry about that, but I wasn't crazy about tears either. And old woman tears? Good God, no.

"All right. You two come on down before you end up tumbling to the tarmac."

"Yes, oh my gosh. Yes." Storm spun around, making me nervous. "Do you have a bag? Can I help with anything?"

I stepped closer in case I needed to catch the damn woman. "It'll be in cargo below. All you need to do is give her a hand down."

"Right. Okay." She clasped Honey's hand and guided the two to solid ground. "I just can't believe you're here. I wanted to reach out, but there was so much to explain, and so much time had passed. I didn't know where to begin."

Once they were safely on the tarmac, I grabbed the woman's suitcase from the hold and followed them over to the car.

"I'm not goin' anywhere for the next week. You have all the time you need to tell me where on earth you've been, sweet child. I worried somethin' *fierce* for you."

The two fell into one another's arms again.

"I know, Honey. And I'm so sorry. I never would have disappeared like that if it hadn't been necessary."

Honey waved her off. "Of course, you wouldn't. I knew my Alina had her reasons. That's why I was worried. But you can tell me all about it once we're out of this wind. It's colder than a milkshake in a snowstorm out here."

I was starting to see why Storm talked about the woman

so much. She was a character—one I was already starting to like, which spoke volumes.

"Here, let me help with that." Stormy started to lift the heavy strap of her grandmother's purse from her shoulder.

"Oh no, you don't." I jumped in, draping the ridiculously heavy bag over my shoulder instead. "You aren't supposed to be lifting things, remember?"

"The doctor said not to lift *heavy* things. This is just a purse, Tor," she chided lightly.

"Don't care. No reason to chance it." I opened the back door for Honey, but the old woman didn't budge.

"No lifting? Alina, child, are you alright?" Worry creased the corners of her eyes more than they were already.

Stormy slowly grinned. "I'm more than alright. I'm pregnant, Honey. We're gonna have a baby."

The way she glowed when she spoke was the most goddamn beautiful sight I could imagine.

Honey beamed. "Oh, Alina. That's wonderful! I'm so happy for you." For the third time in so many minutes, the two hugged. Not a problem, except my weather app had listed the temperature at eleven whole degrees an hour earlier.

"Into the car, you two. We don't need either of you catching a cold."

"He's right," Honey chided, shuffling quickly inside. "You have to take extra care now."

"Great." Stormy smirked. "Now I'll have two of you hovering over me."

I cuffed the back of her neck and pulled her in for a swift kiss. "Get your ass in the car, woman."

Stormy grinned.

I tossed Honey's suitcase into the trunk. The ladies sat

together in the back seat, and I was more than happy to play chauffeur. The two had years of catching up to do.

They spent the rest of the day in conversation, with occasional bouts of laughter and tears. I gave them space. The three of us had dinner together with a light flutter of snow falling outside, then I called it an early night and retreated to the bedroom. Hours later, I was reclined in bed, scrolling on my phone, when Stormy joined me. She quietly closed the door, then prowled coyly across the room.

"Best. Christmas. Ever," she said before climbing up to straddle my lap. "Thank you, Tor. Having her here means the world to me." Her hand trailed down my bare chest, the slight movement in her hips causing her to rock along my hardening cock.

I clasped her hips and pressed myself further into her soft center. "Oh yeah?"

"Yeah." That one word on her lips felt like every holiday rolled into one.

"What would you be willing to do in return?" I asked in a gruff, deviant murmur.

I slid my hands down the soft pink silk of her pajama-clad thighs, enjoying the feel but wishing she was naked instead.

"Oh, I don't know." She rocked her hips again, arching her chest toward me. "A lot of things come to mind."

"There's only one thing I want."

"What's that?"

I hooked my finger to draw her closer. Stormy leaned down until our noses almost touched. I inhaled her delicious scent, relishing this moment. I wanted to remember it forever.

"Say you'll be my wife," I breathed, the words dancing like fireflies in the air around us.

"*What?*" she said on an exhale, her eyes widening. She hadn't been expecting it, which was the best part.

"Marry me, Stormy. I'm asking you to marry me."

"Are you serious?" She knew I wouldn't joke about a thing like that, but the shock had shaken her.

I reached over to my nightstand and took out a small blue box with the word Tiffany's on the top. Inside was another box of the same color, this one hinged and made of leather. I flipped open the lid to reveal the engagement ring I'd picked out. A round yellow diamond encircled by a ring of tiny clear diamonds.

"Does this look serious?" I lifted the ring from its cushion and took her left hand in mine. "Stormy Lawson, you are the best damn thing to ever happen to me. I don't want to go another day without knowing you're mine in every way possible. Please, end my torment and say you'll marry me." I slid the ring on her finger while she watched with glassy eyes and a quivering chin.

Finally, she nodded. "Yes, I ... of course, I'll marry you ... I don't even know..."

"Stormy?"

She reluctantly tore her gaze from the ring. "Yeah?"

"Just kiss me, baby."

"Okay."

Her body melted into mine. I'd never tasted anything more intoxicating than the kiss of my future bride—sweet, sultry, and feminine—like a euphoric dream.

I never wanted to wake up.

And I didn't have to, now that she'd agreed to be mine.

As the kiss waned, Stormy pulled away and looked back down at her hand.

"You picked this out for me?"

I guided her to lay at my side, her head on my chest. "It reminded me of you. You may have been your father's stormy girl, but you're pure sunshine to me." It sounded so damn corny, but it was true. Storm was everything bright and uplifting about this world. She warmed a person from the inside out, and I wanted her to know it.

"You can't say stuff like that, not when I'm already a bundle of hormones." Emotion choked back her words. "This has been so much to process for one day. I can barely believe it."

"That was sort of the idea. I needed to reunite you two and meet her before we could get married."

"Well, having her here wasn't exactly a prerequisite to getting engaged."

"I didn't say get engaged. I said get married."

She lowered her hand and propped herself up to look down at me. "When exactly are you expecting this wedding to happen."

"Saturday."

She stared at me deadpan for so long, I started to worry I'd broken her.

"You want to get married … on Saturday. This Saturday? Six days from now?"

"Yeah. I do."

She stared some more. "Would I need to do anything to prove I'm no longer married to Damyon?"

"If the marriage had been recorded here in the States, you might have needed a death certificate, but that's not the case. No one here is going to challenge us. And besides, that's the legal side of things. I don't give a fuck about the law. What matters to me is that you and I and the people around us know we're married—that you're mine, and I'm yours. Forever."

She slowly nodded, her eyes lifting from the ring to me and back again. "Saturday. With Honey there?"

"With whoever you want there."

"I don't even know where there is."

"Does it matter, if you and I are together?" I asked gently.

Her entire body softened, relaxing into me. "No, I guess it doesn't."

"So Saturday?"

A hesitant yet excited smile teased at her lips. "Saturday."

"Thank *fuck*." I rolled us in one swift motion, Stormy giggling with delight. "I love you, Stormy soon-to-be Byrne. To the depths of my fucking soul."

"Love you more," she whispered.

This time, our kiss transitioned into more. We moved with leisurely intent, relishing the feel of one another. Each touch was reverent. Every taste savored. I made love to the woman who'd brought meaning to my life.

She'd been in danger when we met, but I'd been the one in need of saving. I owed her everything. I'd been too full of anger and pain to even realize what I'd been missing. Storm changed all that. Her radiant sunshine made it impossible to hide in the dark. And once I'd had a taste of her warmth, there was no going back. She was it for me, and I'd happily spend every day of the rest of my life loving her the way she deserved to be loved.

# EPILOGUE
*Stormy*

"YOU JUST MADE THE BIGGEST MISTAKE OF YOUR LIFE, TORIN Byrne." I grinned wickedly at my new husband as he guided us on the dance floor to Frankie Valli's "Can't Take My Eyes off You." As far as first dance songs went, it was a popular choice, but the lyrics took on a whole other meaning for us. I loved a good inside joke.

"Well, I'm locked in now. We said I do, and the whole damn family was here to see it."

"The mistake wasn't marrying me, goober."

"Damn straight," he murmured, pulling me in tighter.

"Your mistake was showing me how well you can dance."

Torin made an amused rumble deep in his chest. "The two things I do best in this life are fighting and fucking—

354

both involve knowing how to move. What made you think I couldn't dance?"

"You run a strip club, and not once have I ever seen you sway to the beat or even tap a foot."

"Makes my job easier. People see a surly asshole watching them, they don't try shit."

"I suppose that's true, but now that *I* know..." My lips curved into a devious, delighted smile. "We may have to explore this new hidden talent."

His eyes narrowed but not enough to fully hide the mirth in those Caribbean depths. "Oh yeah? In what way?"

"Dance lessons," I blurted excitedly.

"What for? You said yourself I already know how to move."

"This would be to learn real dances like the tango and salsa dancing."

"Sounds more like appetizers than dancing," he teased.

I shot him a wry look before dropping my gaze shyly. "It may seem a little silly, but it's something I've always thought would be so fun to do. You don't have to, though."

"Hey," he urged in a gentle demand for my attention. "I'm only playing. You want dance lessons, you got it. I'm happy to give my baby anything she wants."

"Really? You'd do that for me?"

"Anything, Storm. All you ever have to do is ask." He said it with such ardent conviction that my heart did a little backflip in my chest.

"Love you, Torin Byrne."

"Love you more, Stormy Byrne."

I felt utterly euphoric after the most perfect wedding day a girl could ask for. It also had to have set some sort of record for the largest wedding thrown together in the shortest amount of time. Torin would have been good with eloping, but every time I thought of who I wanted with me on our big day, the list just kept growing. The last time I got married, I'd been alone, and the entire marriage ended up being the biggest mistake of my life. This time, I wanted to be surrounded by the people I loved.

We never could have made it happen if it wasn't for the amazing ladies who volunteered to help. Noemi and Pippa handled flowers and the overall aesthetic elements. Micky was responsible for my hair and makeup, while Rowan handled invitations. Tor secured the hotel ballroom venue —I didn't want to know how. And over a *dozen* of us stormed the bridal salon to pick out my dress. I thought the poor attendant would have a heart attack, but I was delighted to have every one of them with me. Even Torin's mother and grandmother were present. They adored Honey. I felt like we were on a Brady Bunch reality TV show, except it was unscripted and genuine and totally perfect.

The ceremony was short but elegant, transitioning seamlessly into the reception on the other side of the divided room. I wanted the celebration to be fun rather than formal, so we had finger foods instead of a sit-down dinner. That made room for a dance floor, and thus, the opportunity to have a first official dance as husband and wife.

"You sure you don't want to do a mother and son dance?" I asked as we swayed to the music. "It won't bother me, I promise."

"I can dance with her later. We don't need a special audience." He'd refused to have a mother-son dance if I couldn't do a father-daughter dance. I hated to deny his mother the memory, but Torin was adamant. "But since you bring up the topic of parents," he continued, "I've been wondering something."

"Yeah?"

"Do you still think about finding your birth mother?"

We'd spent hours talking over the past week about everything under the sun, including my year in Russia. He'd been more reluctant to discuss his ordeal in the detention facility, but I couldn't blame him. I wasn't crazy about reliving some of my memories either. One of the things I had passed on, however, was the excitement I'd felt when Damyon would come to me with progress on the search for my mother. Finding my roots had seemed almost essential during that time, but as I danced in my husband's arms, surrounded by a world of people who supported us, I didn't feel the same urgency.

"No, actually. I have all the family I need right here." My voice grew thin with the strain of emotion—joyful, gratitude-filled emotion—as I met Torin's penetrating stare.

"That's it. I need to fuck my wife." He pulled away, sweeping one arm out to encourage others onto the dance floor.

"Tor," I whisper-yelled. "It's the middle of the wedding!"

He smiled at some guests. "Don't care, beautiful," he said out of the corner of his mouth. "I've waited long enough already." He led me off the dance floor as though we were merely headed for refreshments rather than our much more salacious intent. My poker face was atrocious. Anyone paying attention would have seen my giddy grin and known exactly what we were up to.

Not that it mattered. This was our day, and we'd spend it how we wanted.

That ended up being in a room used for storing folding

tables and chairs. Torin propped a chair under the door handle, then grabbed a table, extended the legs, and had it set up all in a matter of seconds.

The stare he pierced me with stirred up a cataclysmic landslide of desire throughout my body. Even my fingertips tingled with the need to touch him. The corner of his mouth quirked upward as he summoned me with a hooked finger. He leaned in and teased me with the warmth of his lips ghosting across my own.

"Hike up your gown."

I did as he instructed. I was so drunk on his spell, I would have done just about anything to see his eyes light with approval.

Torin tucked his hands under my armpits and lifted me onto the table like I'd been no more than a child. He pressed his body between my legs. Anticipation bubbled like champagne in my veins as he placed a serenade of kisses along my neck and shoulder, lowering himself to his knees.

"Sweet Jesus, tell me you weren't bare this entire time." His guttural words had me grinning with delight.

"I couldn't have panty lines showing through my gown, could I?"

His strong hands spread my thighs wide before he devoured me with ravenous energy. Minute after minute, he had my body building to a dizzying crescendo.

"I can't tell if not wearing panties is the best or worst idea ever. I have a hard enough time keeping my hands off you as it is." He licked and sucked and nipped at my flesh with such a voracious appetite that my body responded in equal measure. In hardly any time at all, the consuming bliss of a full-body release lit a fire deep in my belly, branching out into every molecule of my being.

"Mmm, I like to hear my wife when she comes." He trailed one more long lick up my slit. "I'd dance to that music any day."

Without allowing me time to recover, he lifted me in his arms and braced my back against the wall.

"What's my name?" he asked, eyes growing sharp as a knife's edge.

"Torin Byrne," I breathed readily.

"And yours?"

"Stormy Byrne."

"Goddamn right it is." He surged inside me and lay claim to my body. "You're mine. My wife. My *everything*."

"*Yes.*" It was all I could say as he fucked me with mindless abandon until both of us were breathless and spent.

When we finally left that storage room, I did so on legs more wobbly than a newborn fawn.

"So much for dancing," I murmured.

Tor didn't respond aside from the smug grin creeping across his face.

"That make you happy?" I teased.

"Can't say I'm disappointed. You don't need to dance with anyone but me."

"There you two are!" Rowan and Pippa swept toward us. "Did you want to go ahead and do the garter and bouquet tosses?"

"Sure!" It would give me time to recover. Despite Tor's joking, I was definitely going to do more dancing at my wedding. *Lots* more dancing.

Ten minutes later, the girls had everything set up. A cluster of young and some not-so-young women, including Honey, to my utter delight, emerged when we announced the bouquet toss. I would have tossed it to her had I been able to aim backward, but as it turned out, I didn't have to. The young woman who caught it gave the bundle of flowers to my grandmother, who was tickled pink. Everyone cheered riotously, sending my heart soaring.

Next came the garter removal.

As I sat in the chair watching Torin's predatory approach, the room and all its occupants disappeared. My awareness narrowed to my husband and myself, both of us aware of what he'd find when he went in search of the garter. His turquoise eyes had never looked so vibrant as he approached. So inspired and alive.

To the crowd's delight, he moved preternaturally slowly, a panther stalking its prey. His crooked smirk blossomed to a Cheshire grin when he squatted down before me.

I had to bite my lip to keep my composure.

He eased my dress up, positioning himself so I was never fully exposed. When he lowered his face to remove the garter with his teeth, I heard his robust inhale as though savoring an expensive cigar. He relished the evidence of our earlier encounter in a way only I could appreciate.

A scalding flush danced across my cheeks.

The crowd went insane with delight as Torin slid the garter down my leg with his teeth. I wasn't sure I'd ever seen anything sexier in my life. My head swam with an overflow of joy.

So much for recovering.

I stayed seated as Torin launched the garter into a somewhat reluctant crowd of men. I wasn't sure if it was intentional, but the silky fabric shot straight over the group and slammed into Oran's chest as he approached from the opposite end of the room. He'd missed the ceremony—a fact that had been noticed by all—but that wasn't the biggest shock of the night. That came in the form of the gorgeous woman at his side.

Oran reflexively caught the garter, waving it good-naturedly in the air as everyone cheered. The atmosphere dipped and swerved from giddy to awkward in a flash. His divorce hadn't been final for long, and we all knew how jaded he'd become, especially where women were concerned.

The crowd dispersed relatively quickly, likely sensing the uncomfortable shift. We took the opportunity to greet our newly arrived guests. And it seemed we weren't the only ones interested in knowing what was happening. Keir and Rowan also converged on the newcomers.

"Congratulations, you two," Oran hugged Tor, then placed a gracious kiss on my cheek. "I'm so sorry I was late, but it couldn't be helped. You see, we have some news of our own to celebrate. Everyone, I'd like to introduce Lina Schultze, my fiancée."

I knew Oran, but not as well as the others, which helped me shake off my surprise and congratulate the two. The others all stood, eyes wide and mouths gaping.

"Oran, what a wonderful surprise." I gave him a hug, then shook hands with the stunning blonde at his side. "Lina, I'm Stormy. It's lovely to meet you."

"Thank you, Stormy. I'm so sorry to hijack your day. I told Oran he needed to wait." The derisive tension in her tone was unmistakable.

"This calls for a toast," Keir rallied next and signaled over a server circulating nearby with a tray of champagne flutes. Torin stood stock-still at my side until I could catch his stare as I handed him a glass. A pointed look from me was all he needed to at least pretend to be civil.

Lina reached for a glass when the server approached and

accidentally knocked a glass down the front of Oran's immaculate suit. "Oh, baby! How *clumsy* of me."

Oran peered down at the dripping liquid, seemingly unbothered. "It's no problem, sweetheart." He took a napkin from the server and said the next part under his breath. "You can lick it off me later."

I'd been closest, and after a quick glance around, I was certain I'd been the only one to hear him. I also noticed that Rowan had gone as white as a sheet. I had no idea what had happened, but I knew something was up.

"I'm so glad you two could make it, and congratulations again." I placed a hand on Lina's arm to convey my sincerity, then turned to my friend. "Ro, can you help me with my dress? I need to run to the restroom."

She nodded distractedly. I took her hand and led her away, anxious to know what had upset her.

"What on earth is wrong? You look like you've seen a ghost."

"Not a ghost." She shook her head. "I know that woman. I've been keeping tabs on my ex-boyfriend's father, Lawrence Wellington. He's a horrible, terrifying person. That's the woman he's been dating for months. The first woman in years he's dated with any sort of regularity."

And now, Oran was engaged to her?

Why would such a beautiful young woman date someone like Wellington? Rowan swore he was an awful human being. And why would Oran want a woman like that? Though, it sounded like he wanted to punish her more than marry her.

What in the holy heck was going on?

I had no clue, but it sounded like trouble.

Thank you so much for reading *Ruthless Salvation!* *The Byrne Brothers* is a series of interconnected standalone novels, and the next book in the lineup is Vicious Seduction, which you can read more about below.

**Bonus Epilogue**
Before you do anything else, however, make sure you grab your FREE bonus epilogue for *Ruthless Salvation.*
Will Stormy have a boy or a girl?! Find out in this fun-filled installment a year down the road!

Scan the QR code or head to my website listed below for your free download.
www.jillramsower.com/bonus-content/

**Bonus Epilogue**

**Vicious Seduction (The Byrne Brothers #4)**
Oran's heart is broken and his trust shattered, but when he

decides to steal his enemy's lover by forcing her into a fake engagement, he ends up taking on more than he bargained for.

**Vicious Seduction**

♦

**Missed the first *Byrne Brothers* novel?**
In Silent Vows, Conner chose his arranged marriage bride because she was mute, thinking he wouldn't ever have to talk to her. But when he learns Noemi was silent to protect herself from an abusive father, he becomes obsessed with his new wife and vengeance on her behalf.

**Silent Vows**

**Stay in touch!!!**

Make sure to join my newsletter and be the first to hear about new releases, sales, and other exciting book news! Head to www.jillramsower.com or scan the code below.

# HELP FOR VICTIMS OF DOMESTIC ABUSE

While the characters I write about are not real, the issue of domestic violence is a reality for many. If you want out of a dangerous relationship but are scared to make the move, there are people who will help. Don't wait until it's too late. Call the National Domestic Violence Hotline at 1-800-799-7233.

# ACKNOWLEDGMENTS

The writing process for Ruthless Salvation ended up somewhat segmented, in part because of the dual timelines, but also because I was fortunate enough to go on a trip with my family to Japan smack in the middle of the writing process. That made the editing process *especially* important. Continuity and consistency can be hard enough over the course of several months of writing, but adding in a two-week break in the middle, and I was lucky to remember character names when I got back, let alone who said what and when.

Enter my partner in crime and sister from another mister.

Sarah, as always, was invaluable. Her nearly 100 item-long action list for alpha edits was crucial—from things like telling me when dialogue is too formal to pointing out that a badass doesn't kick a pebble, he kicks a rock. She helps me mold my books into something magical, and I'm truly grateful.

At this stage of the game, I'm usually SO over edits. My wandering mind has already latched onto shiny new ideas and is ready to move on, but I'm so glad I force myself to keep at it because my dream team of beta readers are incredible at helping me smooth out any remaining imperfections.

To Megan, Colleen, Melissa, and Patricia, thank you so very much for your quick reading and thoughtful feedback!

There is no better feeling than sending a manuscript off to the editor, and I can always count on Jenny to give my books the perfect polish. (She just cringed at the start of that sentence, which is why I intentionally left it that way. 😉) Thank you, Jenny, for making my words intelligible!

For the first time in my writing career, my husband didn't participate directly in the writing process as an alpha reader. However, he still played an important role. Aside from his endless patience and support, he's always ready to help me with questions like … what's the best way to burn down a yacht? Thank you, baby!

And last but certainly not least, I want to thank all my devoted readers. I cherish every page read and review posted. When a reader reaches out to say they enjoyed my story, I practically levitate with joy. Thank you all from the very depths of my heart.

# ABOUT THE AUTHOR

Jill Ramsower is a life-long Texan—born in Houston, raised in Austin, and currently residing in West Texas. She attended Baylor University and subsequently Baylor Law School to obtain her BA and JD degrees. She spent the next fourteen years practicing law and raising her three children until one fateful day, she strayed from the well-trod path she had been walking and sat down to write a book. An addict with a pen, she set to writing like a woman possessed and discovered that telling stories is her passion in life.

# Social Media & Website

**Release Day Alerts, Sneak Peak, and Newsletter**
To be the first to know about upcoming releases, please join
Jill's Newsletter. (No spam or frequent pointless emails.)

Official Website: www.jillramsower.com
Jill's Facebook Page: www.facebook.com/jillramsowerauthor
Reader Group: Jill's Ravenous Readers
Follow Jill on Instagram: @jillramsowerauthor
Follow Jill on TikTok: @JillRamsowerauthor